A Girl
With
A Monkey

Leonard Michaels

Mercury House   San Francisco

A Girl
With
A Monkey

new and
selected stories

Published in the United States by Mercury House, San Francisco, California, a nonprofit publishing company devoted to the free exchange of ideas and guided by a dedication to literary values. Mercury House and colophon are registered trademarks of Mercury House, Incorporated. Visit us at www.wenet.net/~mercury.

United States Constitution, First Amendment: Congress shall make no law respecting an establishment of religion, or prohibiting the free exercise thereof; or abridging the freedom of speech, or of the press; or the right of the people peaceably to assemble, and to petition the Government for a redress of grievances.

Cover art: *"Frau bie der Toilette mit roten und weissen Lilien"* (Woman at her Toilette, with Red and White Lilies), 1938, by Max Beckmann. Oil on canvas, 43½" x 25¾" (110.5 x 65.4 cm). San Francisco Museum of Modern Art, bequest of Marian W. Sinton. Copyright © 2000 Artists Rights Society (ARS), New York / VG Bild-Kunst, Bonn.

Some of the stories included here appeared in *Going Places* (1969) and *I Would Have Saved Them If I Could* (1975), published by Farrar, Straus & Giroux. An earlier version of "Viva La Tropicana" appeared in *Best American Short Stories*, 1991, having been first published by *Zyzzyva*. "Tell Me Everything" debuted in *The Threepenny Review* before it was compiled in *Pushcart Prize XVIII: Best of the Small Presses*. "A Girl With a Monkey," first published by *Partisan Review*, later appeared in *Best American Short Stories*, 1997.

This book is made possible thanks to generous support from the National Endowment of the Arts.

Printed on acid-free paper and manufactured in the United States of America.

Library of Congress Cataloging-in-Publication Data:

Michaels, Leonard, 1933–
    A girl with a monkey : new and selected stories / Leonard Michaels.
    p. cm.
    ISBN 1-56279-120-6 (alk. paper)
    I. United States—Social life and customs—20th century—Fiction. I. Title.

PS3563.I273 G57 2000
813'.54—dc21

99-086600

To Michael di Capua

Contents

Introduction; Life in Stories

A PRINCESS is playing with a golden ball, which is already excellent storytelling because you can easily imagine it rolling away into a pond where a disgusting frog will retrieve it. This happens, as everyone knows, in the fairy tale called "The Frog Prince." You're sorry the princess lost her golden ball, and sad that she was playing alone. A ball is a child's basic toy, and suggests innocence. Gold suggests noble birth, privilege, and desire. In sum, the golden ball is appropriate to the desirable, precious, childlike, lonely princess, who, in her innocence, is a bit too attached to material objects.

Naturally, the disgusting frog is lust. He says he will retrieve the ball if she agrees to marry him. She agrees. The frog retrieves it. The princess takes the ball and says forget about marriage. The frog complains to the princess's father, and he, a wise king, says she must keep her promise. So she does. Upon marrying the princess, the frog is transformed into a handsome prince. Thus, from the pond of animal imagination, ugly lust pops up, captures a princess, and is magically transformed into a figure of love.

The princess surrenders her lust for objects when she surrenders her body. In exchange she gets an improved character and delightful company. But can anyone simply forget that the prince is an ex-frog? or that the princess was deceitful? The dark side of things gives the fairy tale strange seriousness.

Most stories have a sequence of events and a transformation. You understand the transformation somewhat the way you understand, or "get," a joke, as if, suddenly, it were your possession. The French critic Roland Barthes compares the pleasure of such getting to erotic experience. Others have noticed the connection, too. In a story called "The Adventure of a Reader," Italo Calvino focuses sharply on sex and reading.

A man takes a novel to the beach. While reading, his attention wanders to an attractive woman nearby. She invites him to lie beside her. He does and he attempts to continue reading, though she is offering sex. He isn't averse, but he wants to finish the novel. She continues offering. He continues being not averse. She becomes exasperated, and takes off her bathing suit. He puts his novel aside, after noting the page he was reading, and they have sex abruptly. They please each other, but the solicitations of the inner life, and the allure of the outer world, are never reconciled. Afterward, the woman calls him to join her in the ocean, but he yearns for the erotic world of the novel.

There are equally compelling pleasures in the non-erotic, or rational, world. And there are people who live in both, like Leonardo da Vinci, who applied his gift for drawing to engineering problems and scientific studies of nature, or Chekhov, a doctor, who wrote plays and stories. Chekhov said he could write a story about an ashtray, as if he were indifferent to the erotic value of a subject, and could make anything into a literary form. He might also have meant form was easy, no more consequential than an ashtray. Isaac Babel, also among the great short story writers, didn't think it was easy. I was glad to learn that because it was never easy for me. I was always more concerned with form than anything else.

The stories in this book were written during times of political and cultural change, and changes in my personal life, from the early sixties through the nineties. But I don't often use or make reference to these changes, at least not in a journalistic, realistic, or confessional manner. I joined protest marches against the war in Vietnam, and I tried to deal with problems at work and at home, but when I shut the door to my room, I started worrying mainly about the shape and rhythm of sentences.

Of course I had to write about subjects, and there is love, marriage, work, class relations, materialistic lust, urban violence, politics, and other such matters in my stories, but I sometimes wondered if my interest in form wasn't self-indulgent or, worse yet, bourgeois. Jean-Paul Sartre, who detested everything bourgeois, liked to walk around with a big wad of money in his pocket. It amused him, presumably, to think he wasn't drawing interest on surplus capital, which is among the chief crimes of a money economy, or the bourgeois mentality. I never had a big wad of money, but I once found seventy-five dollars in the pocket of a jacket I hadn't worn for years. In such forgetfulness, I felt my heart was pure and my concern with form might be serious.

While I was scribbling in my room, some of my students at the University of California committed themselves to revolution and went underground. One student whom I didn't know well was killed in a gunfight with the police. It was beyond depressing to remember that, when she went into hiding, her boyfriend came to my house to deliver her term paper, and it was difficult to continue to think, as I do, in spite of all that makes such thinking questionable, that artistic form speaks of the time.

It's hard for most people to write a story, but many can tell one as easily as they carry a tune. Some of us, however, can't do either, just as some can't tell a joke. What fails is a sense of the form, or transformation. Though the form often changed in my stories, I was frequently concerned with the same general subject: the way men and women seem unable to live with or without each other. I'd read about this subject in the Brontës, Tolstoy, Stendhal, and many contemporary writers, but my sense of the sadomasochistic dynamic at the erotic core didn't come from books or adult experience. It came from impersonal or archetypal regions, the same place fairy tales and dreams come from. Magnified by the imagination of childhood, it survives as dark energy in some of my stories. "The Frog Prince" contains elements of the erotic core, such as submission and domination, and a moralistic father who, like the Freudian superego, is ferocious. But think of this little story purely as a form, and a princess and a frog, A Beauty and a Beast, exist in countless versions.

I fancied that I was doing, in forms, not subjects, a little of what others were doing in music, especially jazz musicians. But my stories were made of words, not notes, and were therefore traditionally intelligible. Nevertheless, when I was asked what does this or that story mean, I'd think it doesn't mean anything. It describes some reality, like friendship, sex, life in the city, or, speaking very generally, as if about a prevailing mood, what it's like to be alive in the late twentieth century.

In another of his brilliant stories, "The Adventure of a Photographer," Calvino takes up the theme of subjects and forms. A man who wants to photograph his wife thinks he must photograph her every minute of the day, or some aspect of her presence will remain unphotographed, and make his whole effort meaningless. In his increasing desperation, when his wife isn't home, he photographs her absence. What begins as a rich possibility in regard to a subject ends in rich futility. The camera clicks and clicks at the void.

This obsession with a subject is particularly evident in movies, most famously in Antonioni's *Blow Up*. In one scene a model, or subject, submits her body, with gorgeous writhing, to her camera-wielding master, who clicks at her compulsively as if to get her essence. The model is the mystery of the world, the eternal subject with its inexhaustible allure, always changing.

I once asked a friend to show me his hands. He held them forward, palm up and palm down, as if to say it can't be done. I'd asked for a subject, he presented a form. In either case, something must remain unseen, even if part of oneself, or there would be no call for imagination, in either its aesthetic or moral aspect.

Note

Several years after I published "Honeymoon," I returned to the story and wrote "Second Honeymoon." I wasn't dissatisfied with the first version, but felt a lingering interest in the form. Both versions are here. Like the hands of my friend, one is very different from the other and yet much the same.

—Rome, 1999

A Girl
With
A Monkey

A Girl With a Monkey

IN THE SPRING of the year following his divorce, while traveling alone in Germany, Beard fell in love with a young prostitute named Inger and canceled his plans for further travel. They spent two days together, mainly in Beard's room. He took her to restaurants for lunch and dinner. The third day Inger told Beard she needed a break. She had a life before Beard arrived. Now she had only Beard. She reminded him that the city was famous for its cathedral and zoo. "You should go look. There is more to see than Inger Stutz." Besides, she'd neglected her chores, and missed a dental appointment as well as classes in paper restoration at the local museum.

When she mentioned the classes, Beard thought to express interest, ask questions about paper restoration, but he wasn't interested. He said, "You could miss a few more." His tone was glum. He regretted it, but felt justified because she'd hurt his feelings. He'd spent a lot of money on Inger. He deserved better. He wasn't her life, but he'd canceled his plans, and he wouldn't be staying forever. She didn't have to remind him of the cathedral and zoo. Such things had been noted in his travel itinerary by the agent in San Francisco. He also had a travel guide.

Beard had in fact planned to do a lot of sightseeing, but moments after he checked into his hotel there was a knock at the door and he supposed it was a bellhop or chambermaid, and he saw the girl. She was very apologetic and apparently distressed. She'd come to the wrong room. Beard was charmed, not deceived. He invited her in.

Now, the evening of the third day, Beard said, "I don't want to hear about your chores or classes." He would double her fee.

Beard wasn't rich, but he'd inherited money and the court excluded his inheritance from the divorce settlement. It was enough money to let him be expansive, if not extravagant.

5

He'd quit his job in television production in San Francisco and gone to the travel agent. The trip cost plenty, but having met Inger and fallen in love, he was certainly getting value for his money until she said, "Please don't tell me what I could do or could not do. And it isn't a question of money."

The remark was inconsistent with her profession, even if Inger was still young, only a semi-pro, but it was the way she said "could," exactly as Beard had said it, that bothered him. He detected hostility in her imitation, and he was afraid that he'd underestimated Inger, maybe provoked a distaste for his character that was irredeemable.

He'd merely expressed his feelings, merely been sincere, yet somehow offended her. Her reaction was unfair. He did not even know what he'd said that was offensive. Worse yet, he was afraid that he'd established with Inger the same relations he'd had with his ex-wife. In twenty-five years of marriage, she'd had many fits of irrational hostility over his most trivial remarks. Beard could never guess what he might say to make her angry. Now in another country, in love with another woman—a prostitute, no less—Beard was caught up in miseries he'd divorced.

The more things change, he thought, they don't.

Inger knew nothing about Beard's marriage, but she'd heard that one's clients sometimes become attached, and it was hard to get free of them. Beard was only her fifth client. What troubled her particularly was that she'd upset Beard more than she might have expected. He sounded deranged, shouting in the crowded restaurant, "I'll pay double," and slapping the table. How embarrassing. What had the waiter thought? She felt slightly fearful. "You are a sweet man," she said. "Very generous. Many women in Germany would be yours for nothing."

"I prefer to pay for you. Can't you understand?"

She understood but shook her head no, astonished and re-

6

proachful at once. "I understand that you are self-indulgent. If I were like you, I would soon become dissolute. My life would be irregular. I would feed my monkey table scraps instead of monkey food, because it gives me pleasure. She would then beg every time I sit down at the dinner table. It would be no good for her or for me."

"I'm not your monkey."

"You think you're more complicated."

Beard was about to smile, but he realized Inger wasn't making a joke. Her statement was flat and profoundly simple. Beard wasn't sure what she intended. Maybe she was asking a question. But it seemed she really saw in Beard what she saw in her monkey, as if all sentient beings were equivalent. She put him in mind of Saint Francis of Assisi.

As had happened several times during his acquaintance with Inger, he was overcome by a sort of mawkish adoration. His eyes glistened. He'd never felt this way about a woman. Spiritual love. At the same time, he had a powerful desire to ravish her. Of course he'd done that repeatedly in the hotel room, in the bed and on the floor, and each time his desire had been satisfied, yet it remained undiminished, unsatisfied.

"Well, what are you, then?" she asked softly.

Beard, surprising himself, said, "I'm a Jew." With a rush of strong and important feeling, it struck him that he was indeed a Jew.

Inger shrugged. "I might have Jewish blood. Who knows about such things?"

Beard had anticipated a more meaningful, more sensitive response. He saw instead, once again, the essential Inger. She was, in her peculiar way, as innocent as a monkey. She had no particular, cultivated sensibility. No idea of history. She was what she was, as if she'd dropped into the world yesterday. A purely objective angelic being. He had her number, he thought. Having her number didn't make him detached. His feelings were no less intense, no less wonderful, and—no other word for it—unsatisfied. She got to him like certain kinds of music. He thought of unaccompanied cello suites.

"Inger," he whispered, "have pity. I'm in love with you."

"Nonsense. I'm not very pretty."

"Yes, you are."

"If that's how you feel ..."

"It is."

"You feel this now. Later, who knows?"

"Could you feel something for me?"

"I'm not indifferent."

"That's all?"

"You may love me."

"Thanks."

"You're welcome. But I think ..."

"I'm self-indulgent."

"It's a burden for me."

"I'll learn to be good."

"I applaud this decision."

"When can I see you again?"

"You will pay me what you promised?"

"Of course."

She studied his face, as if to absorb a new understanding, and then, with no reservations in her voice, said, "I will go home tonight. You may come for me tomorrow night. You may come upstairs and meet my roommate."

"Must you go home?"

"I dislike washing my underwear in a bathroom sink."

"I'll wash your underwear."

"I have chores, things I have to do at home. You are frightening me."

"I'll call a taxi."

"No. My bicycle is still at the hotel."

The next morning Beard went to a barber shop and then shopped for a new jacket. So much time remained before he

8

could see Inger. In the afternoon he decided to visit the cathedral, a Gothic structure of dark stone. It thrust up suddenly, much taller than the surrounding houses, on a curved, narrow medieval street. Beard walked around the cathedral, looking at saintly figures carved into the stone. Among them he was surprised by a monkey, the small stone face hideously twisted, shrieking. He couldn't imagine what it was doing there, but the whole cathedral was strange, so solemn and alien amid the ordinary houses along the street.

Men in business suits, students in their school uniforms, and housewives carrying sacks of groceries walked by without glancing at the cathedral. None seemed to have any relation to it, but surely they felt otherwise. They lived in this city. The cathedral was an abiding feature of their landscape, stark and austere, yet complicated in its carvings. Beard walked inside. As he entered the nave, he felt reduced, awed by the space. Most of all, he felt lonely. He felt a good deal, but it struck him that he could never understand the power and meaning of the Christian religion. With a jealous and angry God, Jews didn't need such space for worship. A plain room would do. It would even be preferable to a cathedral, more appropriate to their intimate, domestic connection to the deity, someone they had been known to defy and even to fight until, like Jonah, they collapsed into personal innerness, in agonies and joys of sacred delirium.

Walking back to the hotel, he remembered that Inger had talked about her monkey. The memory stirred him, as he had been stirred in the restaurant, with sexual desire. Nothing could be more plain, more real. It thrust against the front of his trousers. He went into a café to sit for a while and pretend to read a newspaper.

That evening in the hotel room, with his fresh haircut and new jacket, he presented himself to the bathroom mirror. He had once been handsome. Qualities of handsomeness remained in his solid, leonine head, but there were dark sacks

under his eyes that seemed to carry years of pain and philosophy. They made his expression vaguely lachrymose. "You
are growing the face of a hound," he said to his reflection, but
he was brave and didn't look away, and he decided he must
compensate for his losses. He must buy Inger a present, something new and beautiful, a manifestation of his heart.

In a jewelry store window in the hotel lobby, he noticed a
pair of gold earrings set with rubies like tiny globules of
blood. Obviously expensive. Much too expensive for his travel
budget, but he entered the store and asked what they cost,
though he knew it was a mistake to ask. He was right. The
price was even higher than he had guessed. It was nearly half
of his inheritance. Those earrings plus the cost of the trip
would leave him barely enough money to pay his rent in San
Francisco, and he didn't have a job waiting for him when he
returned.

He left the store and walked about the streets looking in
other store windows. Every item that caught his attention
was soon diminished by his memory of the swirl of gold and
the impassioned red glob within.

Those earrings were too expensive. An infuriating price. It
had been determined by a marketing demon, thought Beard,
because the earrings now haunted him. He grew increasingly
anxious as minutes passed and he continued walking the
streets, pointlessly looking into shop windows, unable to forget the earrings.

He was determined not to return to the jewelry store, but
then he let himself think: if he returned to the store only to
look at the earrings—not to buy them—they would be gone.
So it was too late to buy the earrings, he thought, as he hurried back to the store. To his relief, they were still there and
more beautiful than he remembered.

The salesperson was a heavily made-up woman in her
fifties who wore a black, finely pleated silk dress and gold-
rimmed eyeglasses. She approached and stood opposite Beard

at the glass counter. He looked down strictly at a necklace, not the earrings, though only a little while ago he'd asked her the price of the earrings. She wasn't fooled. She knew what he wanted. Without being asked, she withdrew the earrings from their case and put them on the counter. Beard considered this highly impertinent, but he didn't object. As if making a casual observation, she said, "I've never seen earrings like these before. I'm sure I'll never see any like these again."

"They're much too expensive."

"Do you think so?" She looked away toward the street, apparently uninterested in his opinion. It was late afternoon, nearly closing time. Her indifference to Beard's remark annoyed him.

"Too expensive," he said, as if he didn't really want the earrings but was inviting her to haggle.

"Should I put them away?" she asked.

Beard didn't answer.

"They are expensive, I suppose," she said. "But prices fluctuate. If you like, I'll keep your business card and phone you if the earrings aren't sold in a few weeks."

Beard heard contempt in her voice, as if she were saying the point of jewelry is to be expensive, even too expensive. He drew his wallet slowly from his jacket pocket, and then, with a thrill of suicidal exultation, he slapped his credit card, not his business card, on the glass beside the earrings. She plucked it up, stepped away, and ran the card through a machine. He signed the receipt quickly to disguise the tremor in his hand.

When he arrived at Inger's apartment house, his heart was beating powerfully. He felt liberated, exceedingly happy, and slightly sick. He planned to take Inger to a fine restaurant. He'd done so before. She'd seemed not the least impressed, but tonight, after dinner, he would give her the earrings. The quality of the light in the restaurant, the delicious food, the wine, the subtle ministrations of the staff—such things matter. The earrings would intensify the occasion. She would be impressed, even if she didn't think precisely like a whore. Besides, it would matter to Beard.

A woman in a short skirt opened the door. She was older than Inger, and had cold violet eyes. Her black hair was cut level with her ears and across into severe, straight bangs, emphasizing her hard thin-lipped expression. She looked somehow damaged and petrified by her beauty. Beard introduced himself. The woman said she was Greta Matti, Inger's roommate, then said, "Inger is gone."

"Impossible."

"It is possible," said Greta, her lips briefly, unpleasantly curled. Beard understood that Greta disliked being contradicted, but he didn't believe her. The woman was malicious.

"She took her monkey," she said. "Please go look for yourself. No clothes in her closet, no suitcase, no bicycle."

Greta turned back into the apartment. Beard entered behind her and looked where she gestured toward a room, and then followed her into it. Closets and drawers were empty. There was nothing, no sign of human presence. Stunned by the emptiness, Beard felt he himself had been emptied.

"You never know a person," said Greta. "She seemed so shy and studious, but she must have done something criminal. I was an idiot to let her move in, a girl with a monkey. Half the time it was I who fed the beast. The telephone never stopped ringing."

Beard followed Greta to the kitchen. A teapot had been set on a small table with a cup and saucer.

"Where did she go?" he said. He didn't expect a positive, useful answer. Who would disappear like that and leave an address? But what else could he say?

"You are not the first to ask. I don't know where she comes from or where she went. Would you like a cup of tea?"

Greta sat at the table and turned slightly toward Beard. She crossed her legs. It was clear that she didn't plan to stand

up again to get another cup and saucer, and she seemed merely to assume Beard would stay. Her legs, he couldn't not notice, were long, naked, and strikingly attractive in high heels.
He glanced at the white flesh of her inner thigh and felt hum-
bled and uncomfortable.

Greta poured tea for herself without waiting for his an-
swer, and took a sip. Did she think her legs gave him enough?
He wanted to ask questions, perhaps learn something about
Inger. He knew hardly anything about her.

"I'm sorry," said Greta, softening a little. "Her disappearance is very inconvenient for me. Perhaps it is worse for you."

Beard nodded. "Does Inger owe you money?"

"Technically, I owe her money. She paid a month in ad-
vance. I can make another cup of tea."

Beard was inclined to say yes. He needed company, but the
whiteness of Greta's legs had become unbearable; repulsively
carnal. He couldn't not look at them.

"Thank you," he said. "I must go."

Beard found a phone directory in a bar, looked up the address of the museum, and then hailed a taxi. He'd remembered
that Inger took classes in paper restoration. They were given in
the evening. At the museum, an administrator told him that
Inger had quit the program. Beard next went to the restaurants where they had gone together. He didn't expect to find
her in any of them. To his painful disappointment, it was just
as he expected. He returned to the hotel. Inger's bicycle was no
longer in the lobby where it had been propped against a wall
for two days. Its absence made him feel the bleakness of the
marble floor, the sterility of the potted plants beside the desk,
the loneliness of hotel lobbies.

In his room, Beard unwrapped the earrings and set them
under the lamp on the night table. He studied the earrings
with grim fascination, as if to penetrate their allure, the mystery of value. It came to him that, after creating the universe,

God saw it was good. "So what is good about it?" Beard asked himself. He smoked cigarette after cigarette, and felt tired and miserable, a condition long associated with thought.

The earrings, shining on the night table, told him nothing. They looked worthless. But it was value—the value of anything aside from life itself—that Beard thought about. As for life itself, he assumed its value was unquestionable because he hadn't ever wanted to kill himself. Not even this minute when he felt so bad. Before he went to sleep, Beard read a train schedule and set the alarm on his travel clock.

At noon he checked out of his hotel, wearing his new jacket, and went to a restaurant where he ordered a grand lunch. He refused to suffer. He ate the lunch assiduously, though without pleasure, and then he took a taxi to the train station. The ticket he bought was first class, another luxurious expense, but he wanted—angrily—to pamper himself, or, as Inger would say, to be "self-indulgent."

As the train pulled out of the station, Beard slid the compartment door shut and settled beside the window with a collection of colorful, expensive magazines that he'd bought in the station. The magazines were full of advertisements for expensive things. Almost every page flared with brilliant color, and they crackled sensuously. They smelled good, too. He stared at pictures of nearly naked models and tried to feel desire. Exactly for what he couldn't say. It wasn't their bodies. Maybe it was for the future, more experience, more life. Then he reached into his jacket pocket to get his cigarettes and the earrings, intending to look at them again and resume his engagement with deep thought. He felt his cigarettes, but the earrings weren't in his pocket. Nor were they in any other pocket.

Beard knew instantly that he needn't bother to search his pockets, which he did repeatedly, because he remembered putting the earrings on the night table and he had no memory of picking them up. Because he hadn't picked them up. He knew. He knew.

As the train left the city and gained speed, he quit search-ing his pockets. Oh God, why had he bought the earrings? How could he have been so stupid? In an instant of emotional lunacy, he'd slapped his credit card down in the jewelry store and undone himself. The earrings were a curse, in some way even responsible for Inger's disappearance. He had to get hold of himself, think realistically, practically. He had to figure out what to do about retrieving them.

It was urgent that he communicate with the hotel. Perhaps he could send a telegram from the train, or from the next sta-tion. He would find a conductor. But really, as he thought fur-ther about it, he decided it wasn't urgent to communicate with the hotel. It was a good hotel. This was Germany, not America. Nobody would steal his earrings. They would soon follow him to his destination, another good hotel. They were not gone forever. He had nothing to worry about. This effort to reassure himself brought him almost to tears. He wanted desperately to retrieve the earrings. He stood up and went to the door. About to slide it open and look for a conductor, he heard a knock. He slid the door open with a delirious expec-tation. The conductor would be there, grinning, the earrings held forth in his open hand. Beard stared into the face of Inger.

"Hello," he said, in a gentle, reproachful voice.

She said, looking at his eyes, her expression bewildered and yet on the verge of recognition, "I'm so sorry. I must have the wrong—" and then she let go of her suitcase and said, "*Gott behüte!*" The suitcase hit the floor with a thud and bumped the side of her leg.

Beard said, "Inger," and he didn't think so much as feel, with an odd little sense of gratification, that she wasn't very pretty. There was a timeless, silent moment in which they stared at each other and his feelings collected. The moment gave Beard a chance to see Inger exactly as she was: a slender, pale girl with pensive gray eyes whose posture was exceptionally straight. She made an impression of neatness, correctness, and youth. In this access of plain reality, he felt no anger and no concern for the earrings. As he could now see, they would look absurd on the colorless Inger. He felt only that his heart was breaking, and there was nothing he could do about it.

With a slow, uncertain smile, Inger said, "How are you?"

Beard picked up her suitcase. "You always travel first class?"

"Not always."

"It depends on the gentleman who answers the door."

"I'm very pretty," she said, her tone sweet and tentative and faintly self-mocking.

"Also lucky."

"I don't think so."

"I'm sure of it."

He put her suitcase onto the seat strewn with magazines. Then he took her hand, drew her toward him, and slid the door shut behind her. She said, "Please. Do give me a moment," but she didn't resist when he pressed her to the floor, his knee between her thighs. Her gray eyes were noncommittal and vast as the world. Beard raised up on his knees to undo his trousers and then he removed Inger's sandals. He kissed her feet and proceeded to lick her legs and slide her skirt to her hips. Then he hooked the crotch of her underpants with an index finger and drew them to the side and he licked her until she seized his hair with her fists and pulled him up, needing him inside as much as he needed her. He whispered, "I love you," his mouth against her neck, and he shut his eyes in a trance of pleasure and thrust into her, in her clothes, as the train pressed steadily into a mute and darkening countryside.

—1996

16

Murderers

WHEN MY UNCLE Moe dropped dead of a heart attack I became expert in the subway system. With a nickel I'd get to Queens, twist and zoom to Coney Island, twist again toward the George Washington Bridge—beyond which was darkness. I wanted proximity to darkness, strangeness. Who doesn't? The poor in spirit, the ignorant and frightened. My family came from Poland, then never went any place until they had heart attacks. The consummation of years in one neighborhood: a black Cadillac, corpse inside. We should have buried Uncle Moe where he shuffled away his life, in the kitchen or toilet, under the linoleum, near the coffee pot. Anyhow, they were dropping on Henry Street and Cherry Street. Blue lips. The previous winter it was Cousin Charlie, forty-five years old. Moe, Charlie, Sam, Adele—family meant a punch in the chest, fire in the arm. I didn't want to wait for it. I went to Harlem, the Polo Grounds, Far Rockaway, thousands of miles on nickels, mainly underground. Tenements watched me go, day after day, fingering nickels. One afternoon I stopped to grind my heel against the curb. Melvin and Arnold Bloom appeared, then Harold Cohen. Melvin said, "You step in dog shit?" Grinding was my answer. Harold Cohen said, "The rabbi is home. I saw him on Market Street. He was walking fast." Oily Arnold, eleven years old, began to urge: "Let's go up to our roof." The decision waited for me. I considered the roof, the view of industrial Brooklyn, the Battery, ships in the river, bridges, towers, and the rabbi's apartment. "All right," I said. We didn't giggle or look to one another for moral signals. We were running.

The blinds were up and curtains pulled, giving sunlight, wind, birds to the rabbi's apartment—a magnificent metropolitan view. The rabbi and his wife never took it, but in the light and air of summer afternoons, in the eye of gull and pigeon, they were joyous. A bearded young man, and his young pink wife, sacramentally bald. Beard and Baldy, with everything to see, looked at each other. From a water tank on the opposite roof, higher than their windows, we looked at them. In psychoanalysis this is "The Primal Scene." To achieve the primal scene we crossed a ledge six inches wide. A half-inch indentation in the brick gave us fingerholds. We dragged bellies and groins against the brick face to a steel ladder. It went up the side of the building, bolted into brick, and up the side of the water tank to a slanted tin roof that caught the afternoon sun. We sat on that roof like angels, shot through with light, derealized in brilliance. Our sneakers sucked hot slanted metal. Palms and fingers pressed to bone on nailheads.

The Brooklyn Navy Yard with destroyers and aircraft carriers, the Statue of Liberty putting the sky to the torch, the dull remote skyscrapers of Wall Street, and the Empire State Building were among the wonders we dominated. Our view of the holy man and his wife, on their living-room couch and floor, on the bed in their bedroom, could not be improved. Unless we got closer. But fifty feet across the air was right. We heard their phonograph and watched them dancing. We couldn't hear the gratifications or see pimples. We smelled nothing. We didn't want to touch.

For a while I watched them. Then I gazed beyond into shimmering nullity, gray, blue, and green murmuring over rooftops and towers. I had watched them before. I could tantalize myself with this brief ocular perversion, the general cleansing nihil of a view. This was the beginning of philosophy. I indulged in ambience, in space like eons. So what if my uncle Moe was dead? I was philosophical and luxurious. I didn't even have to look at the rabbi and his wife. After all, how many times had we dissolved stickball games when the rabbi came home? How many times had we risked shameful

discovery, scrambling up the ladder, exposed to their windows—if they looked. We risked life itself to achieve this em-
inence. I looked at the rabbi and his wife.

Today she was a blonde. Bald didn't mean no wigs. She had
ten wigs, ten colors, fifty styles. She looked different, the
same, and very good. A human theme in which nothing begat
anything and was gorgeous. To me she was the world's lesson.
Aryan yellow slipped through pins about her ears. An olive
complexion mediated yellow hair and Arabic black eyes.
Could one care what she really looked like? What was really?
The minute you wondered, she looked like something else, in
another wig, another style. Without the wigs she was a baldy-
bean lady. Today she was a blonde. Not blond. A blonde. The
phonograph blared and her deep loops flowed Tommy Dorsey,
Benny Goodman, and then the thing itself, Choo-Choo Lopez.
Rumba! One, two-three. One, two-three. The rabbi stepped
away to delight in blond imagination. Twirling and individual,
he stepped away snapping fingers, going high and light on his
toes. A short bearded man, balls afling, cock shuddering like a
springboard. Rumba! One, two-three. Olé! *Vaya*, Choo-Choo!

> *I was on my way to spend some time in Cuba.*
> *Stopped off at Miami Beach, la-la.*
> *Oh, what a rumba they teach, la-la.*
> *Way down in Miami Beach,*
> *Oh, what a chroombah they teach, la-la.*
> *Way-down-in-Miami-Beach.*

She, on the other hand, was somewhat reserved. A shift in
one lush hip was total rumba. He was Mr. Life. She was dancing. He was a naked man. She was what she was in the garment of her soft, essential self. He was snapping, clapping,
hopping to the beat. The beat lived in her visible music, her
lovely self. Except for the wig. Also a watchband that dese-

crated her wrist. But it gave her a bit of the whorish. She never took it off.

Harold Cohen began a cocktail-mixer motion, masturbating with two fists. Seeing him at such hard futile work, braced only by sneakers, was terrifying. But I grinned. Out of terror, I twisted an encouraging face. Melvin Bloom kept one hand on the tin. The other knuckled the rumba numbers into the back of my head. Nodding like a defective, little Arnold Bloom chewed his lip and squealed as the rabbi and his wife smacked together. The rabbi clapped her buttocks, fingers buried in the cleft. They stood only on his legs. His back arched, knees bent, thighs thick with thrust, up, up, up. Her legs wrapped his hips, ankles crossed, hooked for constriction. "Oi, oi, oi," she cried, wig flashing left, right, tossing the Brooklyn Navy Yard, the Statue of Liberty, and the Empire State Building to hell. Arnold squealed oi, squealing rubber. His sneaker heels stabbed tin to stop his slide. Melvin said, "Idiot." Arnold's ring hooked a nailhead and the ring and ring finger remained. The hand, the arm, the rest of him, were gone.

We rumbled down the ladder. "Oi, oi, oi," she yelled. In a freak of ecstasy her eyes had rolled and caught us. The rabbi drilled to her quick and she had us. "OI, OI," she yelled above congas going clop, doom-doom, clop, doom-doom on the way to Cuba. The rabbi flew to the window, a red mouth opening in his beard: "Murderers." He couldn't know what he said. Melvin Bloom was crying. My fingers were tearing, bleeding into brick. Harold Cohen, like an adding machine, gibbered the name of God. We moved down the ledge quickly as we dared. Bongos went tocka-ti-tocka, tocka-ti-tocka. The rabbi screamed, "MELVIN BLOOM, PHILLIP LIEBOWITZ, HAROLD COHEN, MELVIN BLOOM," as if our names, screamed this way, naming us where we hung, smashed us into brick.

Nothing was discussed.

The rabbi used his connections, arrangements were made. We were sent to a camp in New Jersey. We hiked and played volleyball. One day, apropos of nothing, Melvin came to me and said little Arnold had been made of gold and he, Melvin, of shit. I appreciated the sentiment, but to my mind they were both made of shit. Harold Cohen never again spoke to either of us. The counselors in the camp were World War II veterans, introspective men. Some carried shrapnel in their bodies. One had a metal plate in his head. Whatever you said to them they seemed to be thinking of something else, even when they answered. But step out of line and a plastic lanyard whistled burning notice across your ass.

At night, lying in the bunkhouse, I listened to owls. I'd never before heard that sound, the sound of darkness, blooming, opening inside you like a mouth.

—1975

Second Honeymoon

At NELLY'S CLUB, a honeymoon hotel in the Catskill Mountains, which was known in the fifties as the "borscht belt," I saw a young woman fall in love with her waiter. He bent close to her ear and asked if she wanted steak or chicken. She looked at him, his face so close to hers, and the strength went out of her, as if more ravishing words were never spoken. She slumped and sat gazing with big brown lovesick eyes. Her mouth was open to answer his question, but she didn't. Smitten.

The waiter was good looking, but a few hours earlier in the city she'd have passed him without a glance. She seemed elegant and very ladylike, wearing a pink silk blouse, pink cashmere sweater, and pearls. In fact, too elegant looking for this huge and clamorous dining room with its limited menu, offering only a choice between steak or chicken for a main dish, and no wine. I knew she'd eaten in finer places, not that I knew about such places. They existed in Manhattan, where I went only on my way to Yankee Stadium, and in the great cities of Europe, where I'd never been.

But Nelly's, I believed, was very good by Catskill standards, which weren't contemptible. If you didn't want steak or chicken, and you made a fuss, the waiter could get you boiled beef, which had a grayish hue, lank stringy texture, and insipid taste. The only alternative, but there were a few guests who preferred such nothingness, as if eating were an indulgence they experienced only to the degree that was necessary. I used to marvel at their restraint at Nelly's, of all places, a honeymoon hotel where the body was king and queen.

At Nelly's, almost everyone accepted what was offered, and it was served in big quantities on big plates. Our guests didn't walk away hungry. They could get doubles, even triples, of any dish, and the kitchen never ran out of anything. The four chefs were quick and efficient even when the dining room was full, which meant eight hundred people. Between courses there was never a long wait. The chefs were usually good natured, but they could suddenly lose their minds and become violent and frightening. They worked all day between a long steam table and great black iron stoves where constant fires heated pots and cauldrons. The fires cooked the food along with the chefs' faces and hands, making them look bloated, as if about to burst, and shiny, and red. Meat is meat. The head chef, Igor, was better paid than the headwaiter, and was the most feared of anyone who managed the hotel, including the owners. He planned the meals, bought all the food, did most of the work at the steam table, and was boss of the other three chefs.

Igor was a big powerful Ukrainian with a piglike face. He had a gigantic torso and head, but short legs and arms. He could lift huge cauldrons of hot soup and handle the hottest plates with bare hands. In the middle of July, with a full house to feed, his wife shot him dead with his Luger. I imagined Igor's immense bulk, bloated by cooking fires, its fearsomeness gone, on the floor. Another chef, a Japanese Hawaiian, took over and proved as good as the Ukrainian. The headwaiter replaced the Hawaiian until another chef was hired. We didn't miss a meal. The ambulance and the police came in the middle of night. Hotel guests saw nothing. It impressed me that, as the hotel owners were talking to the police, they were thinking of tomorrow's breakfast, lunch, and dinner. Nobody mourned the loss of the gigantic being, Igor, except me, though only because nobody else did.

THERE was an antique gold marriage ring on the young woman's finger. She also wore a thin gold bracelet and thin gold watch, neither of which was perfectly consistent with her pearls, but the effect was pretty. Her curly light brown hair was parted over her right ear, and fell lightly away to the level of her chin. It looked a bit too fashioned, but much alive with shampoo sparkle. When she was smitten, she looked dopey. Otherwise her face was pert and intelligent. Marriage had made her hypersusceptible to love, I figured, because I heard that such disasters had happened before at Nelly's. Not often, but sometimes a honeymoon was over soon after the couple checked in. The evil destroyer could be a bellhop, a dance instructor, or the tummler, the hotel's resident comic spirit, who mingled with the guests and made a hilarious tumult day and night, all summer long.

It could happen to a husband, too. The war between the Guelphs and the Ghibellines began when a man fell in love on his way to be married. Sudden and subversive love was familiar in Hollywood's romantic comedies of the era, some of them classics. They were based on this deadly triangle. A woman who is about to marry the wrong man is carried away by love for the right man. The wrong man dresses better, and has better manners, but he is almost always rich, and therefore the product of money marrying money for generations, breeding defectives in body and soul—a weakling, a drunk, a sadist, or he speaks too well, uses too many words, and has a vaguely British accent that meant his blood is thin. America loved Churchill and knew that his people suffered total war, in horrifying air raids, while we slept nights. Nevertheless, the accent alone could suggest a pansy.

The young woman's poor husband, who looked to me like a regular guy, tried to make light of the drama in the dining room. He said, "Our waiter has frightened Sheila."

Three other couples at the table, also newlyweds, smiled with embarrassment at the young woman, and grimaced benevolently at Morris, her brave young husband. The moment was unnerving and unpleasant. It seemed to last forever. Nobody was laughing. They were frightened, maybe. If it could happen to Sheila Kahn, it could happen to anyone.

I felt sorry for her. She must have been frightened, too, and I felt more sorry for her husband. He had a likable face with plump cheeks, a heavy mouth, and hazel eyes quick with sensations, questions, and amusement. He liked to eat and talk. Maybe his hands flapped too much in his happiness, but he'd been having a great time, and didn't deserve such a painful shock. It was easier to look at Sheila than him. An actor makes us cry, but a poor chump with real pain makes us run away, which is what I did. I was the busboy. There were dishes to carry off. Afterward I would serve coffee and dessert.

THE WAITER, Larry Starker, had long been a hit with women. Six feet tall, broad shouldered, a flat belly, and, because he carried himself gracefully, he seemed taller than he was. He had regular features with small cold gray lights set high in his face, like minerals. Unnerving eyes; slightly tipped and faintly menacing. They took you in as if from a great distance. He had a straight well-shaped nose, sensuous long lips, and a cleft chin. He was dark, with an olive and coppery coloring that carried, as a cloud carries sunlight, a fine gray or silvery sheen. Leonardo or Caravaggio would have been challenged to do his color. His hair was purest black. All in all, like Sheila, he looked superior to this dining room, since he could have been a movie star.

Insofar as a man can love another for his beauty, I loved— not him exactly, not the person, but I confess that, when Larry spent evenings with other guys on the dining-room staff, I felt jealousy. He was too aloof to give anyone more than he gave anyone else, and he couldn't have been aware of my feelings. Probably took them for granted. Everybody was, at a distance, in love with him.

He didn't always treat me nicely, though we talked a lot. I was his busboy and roommate. There were a few times when he threatened to become my friend, but he always drew back, as if he felt more closeness stirring in himself than he liked. I wanted the friendship, but I could be cool, too. We came from the same streets, the same Brooklyn neighborhood.

MY HEART went out to Sheila. I thought Larry had hurt her, though he'd only been trying to find out what she wanted to eat. Maybe he didn't have to bend so close. He wasn't unaware of his effect. I saw how he looked at himself in the mirror at night, as he combed his hair before going out, and, besides, he told me that he modeled for the covers of sleazy paperbacks, and showed me one where he appeared as a Teutonic barbarian in furs, about to molest a semi-naked woman. She lay sprawled at his feet, manacled, writhing in terror-pleasure. He wasn't proud of the picture, but also not ashamed. He was bemused, and even curious, as if he expected me to explain it. I'd have preferred not to have seen it. I was moral by nature, and there was resistance in me to hanky-panky, though I was an average horny eighteen-year-old, several years younger than Larry. Not a baby, but without sexual experience. I'd never seen things from the other side.

In the winter, when he went back to the city, aside from modeling, Larry worked for a Manhattan escort service, accompanying wealthy, middle-aged women to dinner in fine restaurants or to the theater. He could have been their son. The job required only his company and good manners. Wearing a rented tux, he'd slept through operas and Broadway shows, too bored to be good company. The women forgave him. He'd once been employed by a woman in Philadelphia. According to his story, they were going out to dinner and she brought along a woman friend. At the end of the evening, the friend wanted Larry to drive her home to New York. His employer said, "I paid for him," and the friend said, "I'm drunk. Do you want me to get killed?" The employer said, "Sleep it off on a bench." Larry looked at me, as if I might laugh with him. I shrugged, not knowing what to make of the story, and the incipient laughter died in Larry's face, as if I'd let him down. I would see this failure again, my failure, when he tried to talk to me about personal matters.

He said, as if I needed an explanation, that he hadn't applied for the escort or the modeling jobs. He'd been approached in the street by Philly Burns, a famous neighborhood guy, who became the tummler at Nelly's. It was his idea. He talked Larry into letting him be his agent. Larry sometimes went out with the girl models, though he was less interested in sex than most guys his age. He said, "I don't like how it looks."

"You have to look?"

"Yeah, I have to look."

"Do it in the dark."

"I said I have to look. Are you deaf?"

LARRY'S great passions were sports and marijuana. He asked me to smoke with him. We had conversations when stoned, but I don't remember any. He once asked if marijuana was politically acceptable. The question was intended to needle me. He had a cruel streak that appeared when he felt criticized. I hadn't criticized, but he knew my politics were leftist and he suspected I was against marijuana, though I smoked with him whenever he asked. It disturbed me that he liked to smoke naked, as if to leave no doubt that his proportions were exceptional, if not obscene.

As his busboy I cleared Larry's three tables after each course—eight settings to a table, twenty-four places—and I poured coffee and tea, and served desserts. After the meal, Larry and I set up for the next night's meal, spreading fresh white cloths, two per table, and laying out silver, crockery, and glasses. Then we hurried out of the dining room and went to the bunkhouse to shower and change. When the guys finished dressing for the evening, they left for a neighboring hotel. Larry would usually go with them. I'd usually stay in the bunkhouse and read.

On Sunday afternoons, just before the guests checked out, they tipped us. Larry kept sixty percent, which was customary. He was a good waiter, but he didn't make more than average tips. His icy eyes weren't ingratiating. I disapproved of working for tips, which was degrading, and for this reason I worked extremely hard, as if my job were a personal dedication. But I needed the tips, and when the amount I made was less than I'd expected, I'd feel worse than disappointed, since I'd compromised my political values by working so hard, and then been rewarded with less than that was worth. Our salary was nominal, nearly nothing. Room and board came with the job.

My parents were communists, and so was I. They'd worked for the party, at the risk of their lives, in Russia, Berlin, and Paris, and finally in the United States, in New York City, where they risked less, but both of them had been arrested, and my mother had once been beaten up while distributing leaflets near the westside docks in Manhattan. My father, Yussel Kukov, who had known Parvus, Markov, and Lenin, was partners with a junk merchant, Masha Kagan, a distant relative from Kiev, and also a communist, albeit the soft kind, a populist. He adored my father, who was mainly a theoretician, neither soft nor hard. Like Trotsky, he could write, but he lacked the great man's ability to stir a crowd with oratory. When my father tried to negotiate a buy or make a sale, Masha begged him to do something else. Whatever it was, do something else. In any deal, my father could figure out how to lose money.

They dealt in scrap metal taken sometimes from a train wreck, or cars smashed up on the highway. The business thrived upon destruction, injuries, and death, which put bread on our table. My father once came home with a piece of steel. "A school bus," he said, holding up the steel. "This could be a vacation for us in Miami. A couple of kids and a teacher were killed."

"We must not cease to do our duty," I said, nine years old at the time. I didn't speak for the impersonal cause of communism, but to head off his depression, a black silence that might last a week and leave me feeling helpless and lost. There were tears in his eyes because of the kids and their teacher, whom he'd not even known, and he was also smiling at me. It was the smile of two feelings, as in the face of a clown, which I find difficult to resist or reject. It exploits the human face, which is sufficiently ironic to begin with, since the mouth that kisses also bites. He made me cry, too, and then embraced me, as if a grown man and a child could be one in their feelings.

Technically a junkman; actually a scholar, though he'd never been formally associated with an institution. Masha thought of him as a rabbi, but my father believed in man, not in a deity, and would hear no talk about divine creation. His ontological views, like those of Marx, derived from Spinoza, a believer who was the source of disbelief in subsequent thinkers. My father said, "Don't ask me about the beginning of the universe. Being here, how can you ask from the point of view of what isn't? You must think in terms consistent with material reality. What's here, not what isn't, is basic."

Through friends, he was occasionally invited to lecture at a school that was founded by the party. He prepared sometimes all night, and then rehearsed, setting up a mirror on the table of our kitchen in the Brooklyn apartment. From the window, which looked out upon backyards, I saw clotheslines with every sort of garment pinned to them swaying in the breeze. I looked at dangling shirts and underwear not to look at him. He embarrassed me with his histrionics.

To his reflection in the mirror, my father said, "For the purpose of this lecture, I am Karl Marx. I want you to attack me. I will defend every paragraph, sentence, and word in the master's books. Begin. What? Ah, I see. You think my views on alienation are unclear, even contradictory. You didn't do your homework, comrade. I will explain in detail, from the earliest appearance of the word to where I reject it. First I must say a few words about alienation in Hegel." A few words could take an hour as he wandered backward in time, from Hegel to the Middle Ages and feudalism, occasionally checking the texts.

My mother made speeches standing in a flatbed truck outside of factories in New York and Pennsylvania, and sometimes, when she held forth in Union Square, she took me with her. She talked about wages, health conditions, and unions. Against icy winds she screamed, rather than talked, against racism, and the oppression of women. She talked also in the sun. Pigeons collected at the edge of the crowd. Derelicts snoozed on the benches. Even when I was little I noticed the general indifference, a quality of the world that lingered in memory for years. Moving through the crowd, my father distributed literature written, typed, and mimeographed by himself.

My mother talked about benefits for workers, and my father's literature talked about real needs, which meant, ultimately, the high must be brought low. One encouraged action, the other raised consciousness—during lunch hour. The crowd gathered to listen while munching cheese and tomato sandwiches wrapped in wax paper, drawn from greasy brown grocery bags. They chewed roasted chestnuts and gripped yellow, heavily salted pretzels in oily fingers. Always smoking cigarettes. Always wearing hats. The era was more proper than today. A man wore a hat, carefully molded and dented, tipped slightly to the left or right. Even gangsters wore hats. The news photographer, Weegee, photographing a gangster's corpse in the street, would throw down a hat. You'd see a man truly reduced, no longer among the behatted millions.

As mother spoke, her demeanor became impassioned with

visions of paradise as if it could be had before one o'clock,
when the workers returned to their jobs. I was different from
her, not being a public person, but like my father, a reader,
and often sick with a chest problem. My mother never read
anything. She'd never gone further than elementary school
in Russia. She learned mainly in meeting rooms and coffee-
houses of Europe and New York, and from lovers. She'd smile
when she finished a speech, and extend her hand. "Would
you like to say a word to the people, Joseph?"

I never said a word to the people. You need a gift to be
speaker. You must have presence, know you have it, and like
its effect. My mother was fast on her feet, and could deal
with hecklers. The crowd admired and adored her, even the
hecklers, more for her brains than her politics, and more for
her looks than her brains. She wasn't a beauty—there was a
twist near the top of her nose, and she lacked a tooth near the
incisor, both of which resulted from the beating, and she had
a fine scar at the corner of her left eye—but she had the thing,
anyway, whatever it is, in her voice and eyes. When she
touched the top of her nose and looked unhappy, my father
said, "Without it, Yetta, I wouldn't love you so much. Nobody
else would either. You are beautiful." So she would touch the
scar.

Even my father's good friends were drawn to her romanti-
cally. Whom she slept with never became an issue. It was his
excruciating boast, accompanied by a philosophical sigh, that
she'd had intense relations with the great Torko Blotnik. He
wrote her letters from his exile in South America. While she
pretended to look for her glasses, I'd read her Blotnik's letters. A hero, also a thinker, but he played games with a woman who couldn't read. It was incomprehensible.

There were also young Reds from City College. She met
them in bars in Greenwich Village, big talkers, drinkers, smokers, and lovers. My father was sanguine about her romances.
He had the invincible idea that women aren't property, which

explained his refusal to feel jealousy, but I think he didn't really care. Her romances were trivial, a waste of time. Maybe, because he loved her, he didn't care. When she committed suicide, his being changed, his looks, his voice, his mind. He had his first heart attack at the funeral. A year later he was dead. I didn't forgive her, and that's all I can say. The rest is in my thoughts and feelings, which are in my words whether or not I talk about her. I'd always been a reader, but I became a compulsive reader after he died, and I started smoking.

I lived with my uncle Sol in Brighton Beach, and went to a private Hebrew school in the basement of a run-down building on Kings Highway, next door to a pool hall. Sol wasn't a communist, and he hadn't spoken to my father for years, but he showed up at the funeral and took me home immediately. At the school, when a book fell on the floor, you had to pick it up and kiss it. I was in awe of such profound respect for books, but I learned Hebrew too slowly, and couldn't force myself to study. I preferred to read easily and quickly in English, flying along the lines from left to right. Sometimes I felt, because of my father's death, probably, I was competing against time and mortality. I could never read enough. But there were no books in which I didn't find pleasure, however minimal, so I read a stupendous amount of what comrades might consider tomes of staggering stupidity, especially bourgeois novels, but I loved them as well as the acceptable novels.

Then Sol was caught smuggling diamonds from Brazil. He was heavily fined, and police investigators came to his store on Canal Street, at the edge of Chinatown, to look at the inventory and the books. The affair was reported in the trade magazines and soon known to people in the business, everywhere from Tokyo to Pretoria. He was humiliated. His business failed. Sol got caught because he'd force-fed the diamonds to a monkey, in tiny sacks, and then claimed to be importing the animal from the Amazon jungles as a pet. Lying dead in its cage, it was a suspicious pet. Custom officers cut open its belly. The diamonds were brilliantly evident. Stomach acids had eaten the sacks.

Sol hustled from thing to thing, but couldn't make himself whole. He was reluctant to turn to those who could help him, swindlers and fences. Soon he could no longer afford the pittance for tuition, so I left the Hebrew school. I was living on my own, with help from Masha, about the time others were entering their senior year in high school.

No public school ever made a difference. I taught myself everything, albeit chaotically. Sometimes I failed the easiest classes. If I'd been unable to read, it would have made a difference. I'd have preferred not to live. This had to do with my father, I suppose. Death is materially conclusive, but it isn't the end.

I had a few friends, all of them like me, readers, and heavy smokers. It was less an addiction than a compensatory style for a childhood that resembled old age. We were rarely seen playing city games on concrete and asphalt. Not because we didn't want to. It is grimly painful to stand waiting, praying to be chosen, when neighborhood guys choose up sides, and they are one player short, but they don't even look at you. I never showed the grief of being left out. At least I wasn't driven away, as might be a wounded beast from the herd. The playground had benches. The streets had stoops. I could sit and watch with the others like me.

It wasn't until I was sixteen that I discovered my nervous system was related to my muscles. I got my first job in the Catskills, through Masha's political connections, as a counselor. He used to do such things for my father, and now for me. The job was in a communist camp for little Red children. Later I moved on to hotels. The physical labor was good for me. I could soon swim and, eventually, dribble a basketball. I was included in games. But harm had been done. I played with unnatural intensity, not so much to win as to pass for normal.

THE ACTUAL Larry Starker, as opposed to the semi-naked barbarian on book covers, was from my neighborhood in Brooklyn, but we'd never talked. We passed in the street, him with his healthy friends, me with kids who had yellow fingers, and knew about books, an interest that never took an appropriate shape in the future. My friend Serge Kantor, for example, taught himself ancient Persian, and could trace his ancestors back through great-grandparents and beyond. They had dealt in spices and drugs along the trade route from Persia to China. He eventually became an inspector for the New York City Department of Health, and spent many years looking for rat droppings in restaurants.

Outside my smoky circle of the unchosen, nobody knew Serge could read ancient Persian. Had the word gotten out, nobody would have given a damn. But he also knew baseball statistics, and was frequently consulted to resolve arguments among the better coordinated. There were others like Serge, nervous intellectual boys, who ran and threw a ball like girls, but, if the subject happened to come up in the playground, there was one boy who could tell you what there was to know about the pre-Socratic philosophers as easily as he could name every stop on the Brighton Beach express. The subject never came up.

LARRY had completed a year and a half of medical school in Canada, then dropped out. He could do the work, but couldn't bear the face of a corpse, and hated the rigorous hierarchy of professors and students. There was also anti-Semitism. He didn't look Jewish, so he wore a star of David to make classmates watch their mouths, and he was ready with his fists, which you could see in the long arms, the thickness of his neck, and how his shoulders sloped. His back had the deep fissure with the vertical columns of muscle that speak of strength. The prospect of working with sickness, and giving people the worst news, was not for him. "Around forty, you begin to die," he said. "No exceptions. If you want to know, I'll tell you what goes first, and what next." He made it sound personal.

Larry returned to the States and hung around Brighton Beach. When he wasn't modeling or escorting, he was shooting pool and playing handball. Challengers came to Brighton Beach looking for a game with Larry Starker. They were like the gunfighters in a western movie. They came from as far away as the Bronx, men with terrific reflexes and rock-hard palms, who could hit killers with either hand. They showed up in the playground Saturday mornings with a cohort of admirers. The challenger began slamming the ball against the backboard. His admirers stood along the sidelines, taking bets. Half the neighborhood gathered to watch, and I often stood with the others, and felt the blood lust for battle and victory, as well as the sickening fear that our hero, Starker, might lose a game. At some point, he removed his wristwatch. Then he would begin slamming, too, until they stopped and tossed a coin to decide who serves first.

Some challengers were older than Larry, some younger. They were Jews or Italians. Once there was a Chinese guy who had a blinding serve, though he didn't look strong. He went seventeen to nothing before Larry recovered the serve. But it began to rain hard and the game was called. The Chinese guy said, "I could beat you." Larry said, "I'm shitting in my pants." When I heard this I was thrilled to near delirium, as if I'd overheard a nasty exchange between Stalin and Trotsky. Thus, I began to worship Larry long before I met him in the Catskills. The Chinese guy didn't show up again, and Larry's record stayed perfect. Nobody had ever beaten Larry Starker. He walked away with dollars, and never risked his own money. Local guys bankrolled him. Like a lot of naturals, Larry was left-handed, and he never had to practice. He was always at the top of his form, having come like that from the womb.

LARRY had worked four summers at Nelly's Club before I was hired and appointed his busboy. He didn't recognize me as being from the neighborhood. I wasn't surprised. I was in fact relieved, but my feelings were hurt anyway. When I told him where I was from, he stared at me for a few seconds, but nothing reminded him.

We worked side by side, serving hundreds of newlyweds three meals a day, from June to Labor Day. They stayed a week, then checked out, and a new group checked in. Coming and going all summer long, hundreds upon hundreds doing this one thing. They arrived late for meals, then ate plenty. Day and night, there was joy at either end of their torsos. The dining-room staff was exhilarated by the happy parade until the middle of the week, when you would as soon strangle them as serve them yet another herring breakfast, dairy lunch, and meat dinner.

I shared their happiness mostly with my eyes. I saw how to feel and wished the couples well, but in my heart I believed the majority were enslaved by ideological radiations, in which subjects become objects, as the state requires. Some of the couples weren't young, although recently married, or else they were renewing their vows and enjoying a second honeymoon.

I believed I would never get married, despite the exemplary parade of the happy couples, or the examples of Lenin and Marx. Kierkegaard says a man marries or thinks. It came to me, looking at the couples, that if everyone married everyone else, the world would have a collective being without revolution. "The new man," or "The Communist," as envisioned by Marx, would arrive. I was a little cynical, but it wasn't gratuitous. I thought marriage, which gave me life, had killed my parents.

The dining-room staff was free for a few hours every day. I could read then. Sometimes Larry asked about what I was reading. Once, after I talked about Spinoza's conception of substance, Larry said, "You talk the way I talk about Hank

Greenberg." My heart became knotted with frustration. He'd been thinking only about me, not what I said. I'd been sincere, not theatrical.

"Well, I don't know how I talk. Anyway, I was trying to tell you how a person thinks. Even if he is wrong or deluded or crazy. It's as real as his nose. That's why people suffer."

"Yeah, yeah, I know what you mean. What do you mean?"

"The dialectics. It happens in nature, and in your head."

"It doesn't happen in my head."

"You aren't aware of it."

"I don't know what goes on in my own head?"

"No, you don't. I'll give you the books."

"We have a little time before dinner. Talk fast."

"It's too complicated, and you aren't really interested."

"If you know what you're talking about, you can make it simple for people. So I'll be interested. If you can't, you don't know."

"It would take too long. Leave me alone."

"Come on, come on, I'm waiting. Make me interested."

"All right. Take the beauty business. When you work as a model you increase the suffering of people who don't look like you, and increase their false need to look like you. Okay? I put this simply."

"It's good of you, and I appreciate it. There are days when I have trouble with my shoelaces, you know what I mean? I make the little knot, and one day I can do it, and the next day it baffles me."

"I'm not surprised. As I was saying, instead of helping people to understand they are part of nature, and nature is part of themselves, you alienate them from nature and from themselves. This is what makes progress impossible. Progress means transforming the world objectively and subjectively."

"Give me a break. When I work as a model, it isn't to alienate anybody from anything, or to stop progress, whatever the hell that is. It's to make a couple of bucks. If you're bald or

38

have a hooked nose, it's what you have. Meaningless. Who cares?"

"You care, but I'll not mention personal considerations. Let's admit everybody cares, and let's not pretend it isn't true. They shouldn't, but they care, and it's your fault. Not to get personal. People think a certain way and suffer. It isn't necessary. Change the way people think, and everything will change. Suffering will end."

"That's in Spinoza?"

"No. Spinoza says the opposite, that people need illusions. What you give them when you model is illusions. Marx says you have to get rid of illusions in everybody. He is correct."

"It's an illusion that you have to give anybody illusions. And it's an illusion that you can get rid of illusions. In the lab, I saw people on tables with no more illusions."

I SHOULDN'T have been moved by his looks, but I had eyes, and they had opinions. With him around, I knew I wasn't beautiful. I wanted the friendship, but when he talked to me about his personal business, it was less than intimate. Maybe he needed something from me, but it wasn't me, only another proof of his greatness. He would draw me out until he heard what he could jump on. As with the illusions. He was vain in his mind and body, and ceaselessly competitive, and I don't even know why I loved whatever it was. We sat up late, smoking his marijuana, and I would listen to his stories always with the feeling that he had more to offer. From good-looking people, you expect what they don't often have. They can't be held entirely responsible, and you can't stop making allowances.

His looks confused me. Maybe I was gay, but I thought I would have known. My problem was that I didn't know how to talk to girls, though I felt incoherent yearnings for this one and that one in school and the neighborhood. I lacked the courage, and I had no hope that they wanted to talk to me. I wasn't physically repulsive, and I knew guys on the staff less attractive than I was, funny-looking guys who "scored," as they put it. I heard plenty of sex stories. I even suspected girls wanted it worse than the guys, and I made myself available sometimes, as if ready to score, standing at the bar of a neighboring hotel, or at the edge of the dance floor. A little after midnight, I was in the bunkhouse—while others didn't come back until dawn. Larry went dancing, and, as far as I knew, never put sex moves on the available girls, though little was required of him. But he didn't tell me everything. I admired his reserve. Even if he wasn't nice to me, I felt he had character, and was too principled to abuse his advantages. His principles were aesthetic, rather than moral, but at least he had them. He was waiting for the right girl, I supposed.

WHEN LARRY and I talked it was usually in our room, which was in a reconstructed chicken coop, the staff bunkhouse, down a steep grassy hill, far from the main house and the kitchen and dining room. Couples stayed in rooms in the main house, or, for a little more money, in cottages where they could cook for themselves, if they liked.

Our room was narrow and held two cots, about two feet apart. Our clothes hung in a closet that had no door. Suitcases were under the cots. At the end of a long hall, a large bathroom, with showers, sinks, and toilet bowls, served the bunkhouse, twelve rooms. There was no privacy. There were no doors and no windows, only tall rectangular openings with screens to keep out insects. I fell asleep listening to crickets, owls, and bats. They seemed close, almost in bed with me, and I liked going to sleep with them.

Every room had a bare light bulb where moths went swirling. You snapped a beaded chain to light the bulb and to turn it off. Nights were cool, but most of us slept naked, under a sheet and thin wool blanket. There was no modesty. Once one of the guys fell asleep on his back and had a sex dream. His dick stood straight up, like a mast, the sheet drooping from it like sails. His roommate called the rest of us. We crowded at the door to look. Somebody got a camera and photographed him. Even asleep, dreams were on display. You could say there was less than no privacy.

The men stomped gleaming and naked from the shower. They sang and joked constantly. They sang in Spanish because the hotel's Latin band never did anything in English, and the songs were haunting and infectious. A guy from Far Rockaway, who didn't know a word of Spanish, would sing, with tears in his voice, *"Dondey, dondeystabatoo,"* the lyric of a cha-cha-cha. You can hear the beat and the caesura, how it breaks like a line in poetry. It means "Where are you?" The "sta" is the same as "stay" in English, or stand, station, stop, or understand. It broke my heart to stand at the edge of the dance floor and think these things instead of dancing.

The men played cards during the afternoon free hours, or went up to the basketball court, or the swimming pool. At night they took off to go dancing at other hotels. It was a great life despite being a form of capitalist degradation and the lowest kind of enslavement. Tips. I liked the hard work more than I didn't, and I wasn't without susceptibilities to the sensuous beauty of the music and dancing, or the sheer happiness in the physical presence of these guys. They were loud and wild in the evenings, and made reading difficult. It drove me crazy sometimes, but I didn't hate them, and at the end of the summer I regretted collecting my books and saying goodbye.

THERE WERE no women on the dining-room staff. The head-waiter, a Hungarian named Nadar, with a militaristic idea of how to run a dining room, had objections to women that he put gently, delicately. "A woman, you know, requires much time to prepare herself for the public. Then there is the problem of a woman's hair. It raises questions of cleanliness. You must remember that we are dealing here with food."

You couldn't argue with such a personality. It wasn't just

his objections, but his entire being, that spoke. Besides, he had concentration camp numbers on his forearm, an awesome sight, and a reminder that he had ideas about life unavailable to you. I never saw Nadar on the hotel grounds or at any of the facilities, never even saw him walking the paths or the grassy areas, but once I happened to see him emerge from his cottage wearing only shorts. He had unnaturally white skin that seemed incapable of being burned, let alone tanned. As a headwaiter, formally dressed in a jacket and tie, moving about the dining room during meals, chatting with guests, snapping commands at the waiters, he looked excellent.

Since all the guests were couples, we had no choice but to go to neighboring hotels to meet women. At last, by some miracle, I met one. She was sixteen, from Holland, an au pair, who was incredibly blond and creamy. I managed, despite extreme terror, to attach myself to her by asking a thousand questions. When she answered the first, I had the next question ready, and before she finished answering, the next was ready. I didn't hear much that she said. The most stupid question was whether they spoke Dutch in Holland. She looked startled, and said, "What do you think, we speak Italian?" I'd never seen anyone who looked so clean. A white and yellow being with pale blue eyes, like robin's eggs. I was reluctant to touch her, except when dancing. I couldn't even do a foxtrot, but I went out on the floor with her and, like a robot, imitated the movements, shuffling after the beat. She'd made a mistake about me, I thought, and at any moment, any evening, would send me back to the bunkhouse. But she seemed to like me, and she waited for me to arrive at her hotel every night, and then danced only with me, though I was a miserable klutz, and she was quite good. Her English was also good, only slightly accented. Anything she said seemed feelingful and charming. I was in love.

At last, one night I asked her to go for a walk. We could see the road only intermittently when clouds passed across the moon, illuminating the gravel. On either side and up ahead it was utterly black, but we continued walking ever more deeply into it, and then without saying a word, I took her hand and drew her off the road. We sat under an oak tree, both of us now silent, thinking our separate thoughts, and as distant from each other as we were from the moon. Then I lay back. A moment later she imitated me, so that we were side by side. I kissed her and she kissed me, and then I touched her breasts. It was what I was supposed to do, I thought, even though I liked her.

She didn't stop me, perhaps because she thought she wasn't supposed to stop me, but lay utterly still beneath my hand as if she were dead or exceedingly alert and waiting to feel something. She didn't tell me with word or movement what to do or not do, and when she responded a little I was soon wild. I'd never known such freedom and it—the free-dom—took me with a shock of pleasure everywhere through my body. I didn't want to continue or to stop. I was frightened of what was becoming of myself, another person whose exis-tence I could never have anticipated. This may have been Helga's experience, too. She seemed not only receptive but grateful that this person had arrived, and saved her from being a virgin. There was a lot of kissing.

The memory returned frequently. I thought this is what Hegel means by "the cunning of reason," or the determining force of history, since the sexual act is, after all, literally a di-alectic, and leads to material production, or reproduction, of the race. I'd compare it now, more than thirty years later, to what one feels, with much less intensity, when suffused with the ambient feminine spirit of a beautiful city. The sex itself, the doing of it, I realized, was almost irrelevant. Mere plea-sure. The greater and important pleasure had little relation to touching, which is, after all, only a sufficient, not a necessary, cause. I had seen this when we photographed my unfortunate sleeping colleague in the bunkhouse. He was fully engaged in a sexual act, and yet without a woman and without touching himself, and I don't believe he was dreaming of a city. I didn't wait to see his dream consummated, as did the others, who made a racket of approval with shouts and applause.

After I had touched Helga's breasts, and at first nothing more, I felt I had damaged her, though she said no word of reproach, but when I withdrew my hand she responded. She took my hand and replaced it on her breast. Then one thing led to another.

Afterward, we walked back to the hotel with our arms about each other's waist. She was exceptionally nice to me the following night, but somehow her eyes never met mine. Something had changed in the intervening hours. She danced with others and, the few times we spoke, she didn't look at me once. A chemical reaction had occurred, with strong exclusionary force. I'd been a fool, I thought. I should not have done it. She hated me.

LARRY SAID, "What's with the Dutch girl? I saw her dancing with Howie, the sleeping sex fiend."

"You wouldn't understand."

"Tell me slowly, one word at a time. Little words."

"I don't want to take advantage of her."

"She could give you odds."

"I'm not talking about handball."

"Life is handball."

"You're wrong, as usual. Life is the dining room. Morris Kahn won't tip, I bet, and it's your fault. Anyhow, I don't care about Helga. There are a lot of girls."

"Tell me something. I tried to read one of your books, *The Phenomenology of the Spirit*. How the fuck can you understand it?"

"You read it twice."

"What if I can't understand it twice."

"You read it a third time. The way you learn a language. Repetition is everything."

"I already learned a language."

I was glad when it was time to go to work in the dining room. From the beginning to the end of a meal, I didn't have to think. I was running, deranged by my desire to be the greatest busboy and not think about anything.

THE YOUNGEST of us on the dining-room staff were my age. The oldest were about twenty-five. From June to Labor Day, we worked ten hours a day, seven days a week, and wore black shoes and pants, a white short-sleeved shirt of thin cloth or nylon, and a black clip-on bow tie. At the beginning of a meal we looked quite spiffy, standing at our stations, welcoming the guests. Minutes later, we looked hectic, flushed, disheveled, sweaty, and desperately harassed. Nadar would watch us with his hands clasped behind his back, and you could see the disapproval in his expression. What could we do? It was a hot summer, and we were running with dishes and food, wearing bow ties.

By the end of the summer I could load my busboy tray, which was a large wide aluminum oval, called a "master tray," with more than a hundred dishes, arranging them in concentric circles in an overlapping pattern called a "rose bud." I then carried the load at a quick pace twenty yards to the kitchen, then through the long kitchen to the dishwashers. The kitchen floor was bare wood. When wet the wood became black, and soft, and slick, and you had to be careful or your tray would tip and send dishes streaming to the floor. You would land hard amid broken china. I saw that happen several times, and I rushed to the disaster to help clean up the mess, and felt pity for the busboy.

The dishwashers were men who came and went; haggard

bloodless faces and tattooed arms. None lasted long, and we almost never talked to them. They worked at a machine that blasted the dishes with hot water and detergent. First they swept the dishes clean of food, then stacked them on end, on a conveyer belt. When a dish or glass broke and a man got cut, blood was everywhere, but nothing stopped. There was no time. Thousands of dishes were continuously arriving, carried by busboys who dumped them on a counter to the side of the machine. Literally dumped, tipping their tray so as to let the dishes slide into the counter. The clatter was deafening, magnified by the smallness of the room, which was dense and hot with steam. A man at the machine would be screaming curses in the cloud of steam as he worked against the deluge of dishes, splattered with his blood, and the busboys continued rushing into the room with more dishes, more tremendous clatter. Back in the kitchen, there was also screaming. The chefs were monsters of impatience, slapping meat and vegetables on plates, or ladling soup into bowls, and screaming, "Pick it up, pick it up. Next." And the waiters who stood in line screamed back, "I'm next and I said two boiled beefs, not three chickens, asshole."

AFTER the incident in the dining room, Sheila and Morris Kahn had meals delivered to their cottage by a bellhop. I thought Morris wouldn't tip unless he and Sheila returned to the dining room. I regretted losing the few dollars, but figured Sheila was more unlucky. Poor Morris loved her more than she deserved, I thought, until I overheard a couple arguing, the man severely critical of Sheila, but the woman kept saying, "She can't help it."

I couldn't understand what she meant, though I'd touched Helga's breasts and been taken by the powerful surge, my body like a piece of flotsam in a flood. It didn't strike me as the male version of being unable to help it. I could think only that, because I had done it, or "gone all the way," I had been cast into the misery of infinite bleakness and regret. Some kinds of understanding are more helpful than what is offered by thinking. I lacked the necessary understanding. Thinking did me no good. Helga had rejected me. I felt the most terrible regret, and guilt, and love, and anger. I wanted to demand an explanation, but feared she might tell me what I couldn't survive hearing.

SHEILA'S curly hair fell about a witty face, which had lips both pointy and luscious. She was average height and had a "nice figure," what we now call a "body." She was shy, I believed, and therefore helplessly revealing, but I could see in her angelic demeanor a touch of mischievousness. I knew nothing about her beyond what I could see, and what I had seen happen, but she was, after all, unquestionably cute. I imagined that let her get away with things another woman wouldn't try. I learned this from actresses in movies, and I assumed Sheila believed she could take liberties, and go pretty far. I found out it was farther than I'd have thought, not that I thought anything specific.

On the evening of the third day, Morris and Sheila returned to the dining room for the evening meal. Wearing a new blue dress and high heels, Sheila looked collected, cool, and invulnerable, but she didn't make it past the matzo ball soup. She stood abruptly, hurrying from the table. Morris gazed after her, his ears inflamed, as if they had been pinched. A smile, feeling for a shape in Morris's lips, perished as the blue dress went away, fleeing among the tables.

Larry, setting up for the next meal, said, "I didn't do anything."

But in his gray eyes he was guilty of being Larry Starker. I think he thought that, too. It made no difference whether or not he had done anything. Nobody gets through life without causing pain in other people. Not even Saint Francis. How his father must have felt when Saint Francis stood with no clothes

47

and announced his conversion from the high life to the higher life. Loveable, surely, but I think of his poor father. Political revolutionaries often left a trail of broken people, some of them family and friends. Larry didn't do anything, but I saw how he primped in the evening before going off to dance at a neighboring hotel. As we were setting up for the next meal, I said, "A guy like you doesn't need this job. You don't even have to work because people would pay for you."

"I could sit in the library like Marx."

"You're not smart enough. I don't need to remind you that Marx is the greatest mind of the modern world."

"So I'm not Karl Marx. You don't know anything about me or my mind. Nothing."

"What should I know?"

"Like my father is upstate, and presently residing in a penitential institution, you know what I mean?"

"He is?"

"My brother Herky is a junkie. I'd beat his brains out, if he had any left and showed up again. My mother is a hypochondriac. I'm talking about pathology, not a neurosis. For her, hypochondria is the same as a medical degree. She diagnoses herself fifty times a day. Everything she comes up with is fatal, and it's my fault. I pay the rent."

"You pay the rent?"

"Leave it like that, Joseph."

"If you want to talk some more, I'll listen."

"Finish up. Machito is playing down the road. I've got to be there when the congas start rolling, and the guiro is hissing like ten snakes."

He began dancing around the tables as he laid out the silver, and singing, "Annabacoa, coa, coa/Annabacoa co," the name of a town in Cuba. It was always a little odd hearing this at a kosher hotel. In the Catskills, thousands of Jews were doing the mambo. When I went to Helga's hotel, I saw her doing it, too, a girl so blond dancing to rhythm so black, and she could do it with the best. I watched her until the number ended, and then withdrew before she noticed I was there.

MORRIS lingered to the end of the meal talking about politics with the men at the table, his voice loud and officious. "According to my sources," he said pompously, then lectured the newlyweds, letting nobody else say anything. He didn't look at the wives. He felt particularly shamed in front of them, I think, because they knew what he felt better than another man could know, or wanted to know. As a matter of brotherly sensitivity, I believe, men choose not to know certain things, and not to feel what another man feels. It's partly to preserve his dignity, and partly to save themselves from contamination when it is a question of crippling hurt. Even if they feel it and know it, they can make their hearts into stone, and this is the same as making nothing of something, and getting on with the business of being a man. I'm aware that times have changed, and the present era is not manly in spirit, but lasciviously inquisitive. That's what I thought, dying inside for Morris. I'd have done anything to help him. But I believed he was beyond help, except perhaps from another woman.

The next morning, halfway through breakfast, Morris arrived without Sheila. He carried the *Times*, maybe to suggest he was an intelligent person who had interests beyond domestic life. Larry approached. Not glancing up, Morris opened the *Times* and said, "Scrambled eggs." Larry hustled away and returned with scrambled eggs. Morris said, "The eggs are cold." Larry started away with the eggs. Morris said, "Fuck eggs. I want pancakes." Larry hurried across the twenty yards from the table to the kitchen, and returned with pancakes. Morris ate nothing. He read the *Times*, and was still at the table after all the other guests had left the dining room. Larry had to stay, serving Morris more toast, more coffee, the two of them and me in the echoing vacancy and desolation of the dining room. Larry glanced at me, giving his head a little toss to indicate that I should go. But I stayed. He had to stay, I would stay, though there was nothing for me to do. Larry's white rayon shirt was stained with large gray pools of sweat. The material clung to his back and chest. Chest hair, pressing up beneath rayon, made a scribble of dark lines.

Morris demanded syrup for his now cold pancakes, then didn't use it, then decided he wanted scrambled eggs after all. Larry brought him another order of scrambled eggs. Morris didn't eat them. He ordered more toast and coffee, then more, then more. The other couples, after chatting quietly, had left the table almost furtively, still chatting as if nothing unusual were happening. Nobody tried to make conversation with Morris.

Morris was about thirty, but had a younger looking face. It seemed not intended to know unhappiness, or any complexity of feeling. He'd wanted to make a scene, give Larry trouble, make him blow up, maybe get fired. But Morris didn't know how to make his anger a provocation. He was being very problematic and irritating, but not taken with the seriousness he didn't really want. If it came to blows, Larry could have beaten him senseless, but I'm sure he would have done nothing. He'd already done enough. After breakfast, Morris checked out of Nelly's Club with Sheila. At the desk, in an envelope with Larry's name scrawled across the front, Morris left a fifty-dollar tip, far more than if he'd stayed a week and never missed a meal. The tip exceeded the requirements of an apology. Larry gave me half.

I said, "In the old days, when gangsters came to the Catskills, it would have been bad for you. I mean if Morris was a gangster, you would have ended in a mountain lake. Bodies were dumped in lakes."

"Morris isn't a gangster, and I didn't do anything."

"He could have gangster connections. I know guys in Brooklyn who could do you with a phone call. A word on the street, man, and you would be gone."

"Why are you talking about gangsters?"

"There are gangsters. They're here. Do you know Johnny Miraggio? He runs Brighton Beach. You wouldn't screw around with his girlfriend, believe me."

"You're right. I wouldn't look in Gloria Romano's general direction. Not in her sister Angelina's direction either. I don't know Johnny Miraggio's mother, so I walk looking at my shoes since I might look—by accident—at her. Then I'd be fucking gone."

"I was trying to tell you something in your best interest. I don't exactly mean gangsters, but they're here. I'm not totally ridiculous."

"All right, Joseph, gangsters are here. But I don't know what you're telling me. Don't get too excited. Morris isn't a gangster. He doesn't have connections. He's a podiatrist, which is a line of work different from a torpedo. I read an article about him in the sports section of the *Mirror*. He works with baseball players, fits them with special shoes if they have feet trouble."

"Oh, man, I don't believe it."

"Believe what?"

"You read a fascist hyena rag like the *Mirror?*"

A FEW days after Morris and Sheila checked out of Nelly's, Larry began to receive phone calls from the city, sometimes in the middle of the night. It was no secret who was calling him. I said, "You didn't do anything. So don't do anything."

"Yeah, yeah."

"I'll answer the phone and say you're out. I don't mind."

"Thanks for the offer, but I'll answer the phone."

"Why?"

"Why? What do you mean—why?"

"Do you like her or something?"

"Most beautiful clothes you ever saw. She's crazy about cats, brings strays into the room. I hate cats. They're filthy. But I don't say anything. I can't stand it when she cries."

"What room?"

"The room, that's all."

"You mean like in *Anna Karenina*? I've been wondering ever since I read the book, where did they go? Now I get it. Anna and the son of a bitch who ruined her life used to go to a room. Sheila cries a lot?"

"I don't even know what I said, and I can't make her tell me. She cries, cries. I feel like hitting her."

"You hit her?"

"You think I'd hit a woman?"

"If you ever hit her, Larry, you'll have to deal with me. I don't give a shit if you're bigger. I'll tear your head off with my bare hands. I mean it."

He was laughing, actually laughing.

"What about the room?" I said. "Where is this room? A lot of people like you must want to go to the room. You have to make a reservation? You've seen her alone, then?"

"Once."

"Where?"

"In the room. I told you. But never again. I don't want you to get upset and worry. You're also scaring me."

"Good."

DURING the break between lunch and dinner, a few weeks later, as we lay on our cots in the bunkhouse, Larry said, "I have to talk to you."

I was groggy with heat and fatigue, and lying with my weepy face hidden in the pillow. I'd had a meeting with Helga moments earlier, and was profoundly unhappy, but I heard what Larry said. Something in his voice that resembled a real feeling, or anyhow a new feeling. I put aside my unhappiness and I sat up and wiped my eyes, as if to get the sleep out of them. He said, "Put on your sneakers."

I put on my sneakers and followed him out of the bunkhouse. We strolled to the handball courts. I had to squint against the afternoon sun, which seemed to sear my brain. Larry had brought a ball and gloves. "You lefty or righty?" he asked. I said, "Righty." He gave me the right-hand glove. I didn't ask what he wanted to talk to me about. I merely walked beside him with expectation, ready to listen, and maybe I hoped a little it would be bad news.

He said, "Do you want to serve?"

"No. You serve."

He served, whacking the hard, black, rubber ball low to the ground. It struck the wooden backboard, making the sound of a gun shot, and came at me and hit my hand like a ball peen hammer. We played one game. Larry won by eighteen points. He let me have three points, but it didn't feel friendly. It felt unfriendly. He'd hit the ball hard on every play. It stung worse and worse, and left my palm burning. My whole hand became numb, except for a pain deep in the bones that wouldn't go away. Then my hand became swollen and hot, the throbbing pain in the center of my palm, in the bones. We walked slowly back to the bunkhouse. He said, "You ever hear of Bluestone Manufacturing?"

"No."

I'd forgiven him for the three pity points.

He said, "You don't know shit."

My expectation, my readiness to listen, were instantly gone.

"Fuck you. Do you want to talk to me or what?"

"Sheila's father owns Bluestone and McCorkle Manufacturing."

"Wow. An exploiter of the wage slaves. How interesting."

"Don't give me your communist bullshit. The firm makes armaments. It's big, big."

"That's best. Armaments for our boys. Better than throwing rocks, and basic to monopoly capitalism, and the perpetuation of a war economy. I never heard of Bluestone and McCorkle Manufacturing."

"Are you out of your mind or what?"

"Because I never heard of Bullshit Manufacturing I'm out of my mind? Did you ever hear of Lev Davidovitch Bronstein? My mother probably slept with him."

"He's your dad? What does he do?"

"He isn't my dad, and my dad isn't alive."

"Oh. You have any idea how rich she is?"

"How rich is she? How do you know all this, anyway?"

"She told me."

"Where, in your dreams?"

"At the Flamingo. It's a dump motel. Nobody we know would go there."

"You're banging Sheila? Is that what you're telling me? I mean you're banging her?"

"Dig me, Joseph. She never heard of *The Phenomenology of the Spirit* or the Fongoola of the Patootee. We go dancing at Corey's, which is a place miles from here. Everybody on the floor is doing this. Watch me."

Larry snapped his fingers, one and two, one and two, and he started dancing. It looked all right to me, but there was contempt in his expression. Then he said, "Sheila is going like this." He snapped his fingers again, one and two, and said, "Can you dig it, Joseph? One and two." He danced again, slightly differently.

"Don't make fun of me."

WHEN YOU know something awful is going to happen maybe, and then you find out there is no maybe, it can be upsetting. I knew. Then I knew. It was different, totally different, but it had only to do with Larry. What I found out about Helga was nothing I knew.

The summer was nearly over. Helga appeared at Nelly's in the afternoon, and waited outside the dining room until the lunch meal was over. When the staff came out and started toward the bunkhouse, I saw her standing alone, far away in a grassy area of hillside. She didn't call my name, but I had to notice her because there was nothing else blond in the Catskills. I separated from the other guys and went to her. She looked at my eyes and said, "I'm pregnant." Her voice was soft and plain. It held only the fact, no recrimination, no expectation of anything from me. I took in the information, and said nothing. She looked steadily at me, and then frowned, and then, as if she'd read my heart, she recognized that my fate, if it mattered to her, was whatever she wanted. She took my hand. "Don't worry. I'm going home tomorrow."

"I'll go with you."

"Why?"

"Because I can buy a plane ticket. No other reason."

"You'll spend everything you made this summer. What will you do in Amsterdam? I'll write to you. I came here to get your address."

"I love you."

"Yes?"

I moved to embrace her, but she put her hands on my chest and said, "Please. I'll write to you, and then we'll see. Where should I write?"

When I went back to the bunkhouse and put my face in the pillow, I was unhappy for the worst reason. It couldn't have been more selfish, and had little to do with Helga's condition, not even its practical implications for me. But only because I didn't want her to go away.

LARRY had been disappointed in me, as if he'd done his best

and I'd failed to be worthy. He'd asked for something, and I'd let him down. I should have said "Congratulations," but I was thinking not about him and Sheila, only that I'd go to the courts and practice. Before the end of the summer, I'd humiliate him. I was trying not to think of Sheila's expression when she fell in love with Larry. It was bad. It stank up the world. Whatever I felt was mixed up with my own feelings about Helga, about which I intended to say nothing.

"You wanted to talk to me." I said. "You drag me out in the heat, burn me in a handball game, tell me I don't know shit, and I'm out of my mind."

"I can't talk to you."

"Try."

"I tried."

"You were talking to yourself, not me."

"You don't want to hear, anyway. I can tell. You're not really listening. So forget it."

LARRY STARKER didn't return to Nelly's after that first summer, and I never saw him in the neighborhood again.

I returned to Nelly's twice more, and was promoted to waiter in my third summer. One Friday night in August, near the end of my third summer, Larry appeared in the casino, at the bar, drinking alone. He was wearing a dark blue suit, black loafers with tassels, a silvery silk tie, and a white-on-white shirt. It was Friday night, so I figured he was a weekend guest. But he looked sharper than any of the guests. Then, with a blaze of insane joyousness, I realized I was looking at Larry Starker. My heart swelled and pumped as I walked right up to him, grinning like some kind of half-wit, and I held out my hand.

I was more than bursting with eagerness to talk. I wanted to tell him about Helga, how we had been going steady for three years, but I wasn't going to tell him about the baby I'd never seen, a girl, in Amsterdam, being cared for by Helga's family. I wanted to tell him that Nadar, the Hungarian, was no longer headwaiter, and there was talk of hiring women next summer. I wanted to tell him I'd taken over his station, and that Helga was going to school in New York, and we were planning a trip to Europe this fall so I could see the baby who was already speaking Dutch, and meet Helga's family. Meanwhile, this fall, I would register for night classes at N.Y.U., and take aptitude exams for law school, and that I'd been reading Kojeve and Lukacs, and I could hit killers in handball, and do the mambo.

A mob of words, a churning multitude, which would tell him these things was pressing forward, though I was saying nothing, and just smiling. The words were like bees swarming in my head, which is how ten thousand pages can look in retrospect, the tiny individual blacknesses of their being, massed.

Larry stared, then shook my hand, with no recognition in the gray eyes, but I didn't feel hurt so much as faintly diminished. I remembered that his eyes could sometimes look dull, like turtle eyes, and fixed. He simply didn't recognize me. He'd reached forward mechanically and we were shaking hands, mechanically. It would come to him in an instant, I knew, as I said, "Larry Starker, Larry Starker." Before I could concede to his slight difficulty and say my own name, the hotel tummler, Philly Burns, Larry's former agent, shoved between us, slapping Larry on the shoulder, saying to me, "Excuse me, kid," and then to Larry, "Let's go, Larry. You're onstage. I appreciate your agreeing to do it. Could be good for you, too. You don't need work, I know, but it's good to have leverage. You hear what I'm saying? Who can tell what's down the road, baby. You signed prenuptials, no? Ha, ha, I'm making a joke, did you notice?"

Larry glanced at me as he turned away and shrugged, saying, "We'll talk later, man. Hang around, okay? I paid for a bourbon. You take it. We'll talk later."

"Okay."

He hadn't remembered my name, and not with perfect cer-
tainty who I was, but I could tell he was sure I was somebody
he knew. I would hang around and talk to him later. I was fantastically happy, though my happiness had acquired an edge,
or a skin like a fine spread of imperceptible scar tissue. It had
been three years. I'd forgotten a lot of things myself. Anyway,
there was the great feeling. Here he was. Here I was. We'd
talk. I was so pleased, I was spinning.

Philly Burns disappeared backstage with Larry, then reappeared alone, and called for everyone's attention. People
drifted toward tables and chairs that were arranged in front
of the stage, which was wide and deep. I remained where I
was, standing at the bar. My hand was shaking, and some of
Larry's bourbon dribbled down my chin. The Latin band as-
sembled onstage, leaving the front of the apron clear.

"You dancers in the audience are in for a treat," said Philly
Burns. "We have a couple with us tonight who won last year's
All-City Latin Dance contest. Mambo Larry, king of handball, and his gorgeous gorgeous gorgeous wife Sheila. Give
these kids a hand."

It was as if no time had passed. There had always been
Sheila. There had always been this moment, hidden, gathering itself for revelation, like a flower in a seed, or what Hegel
calls "the notion," wherein one idea lives inside another until
it blooms and fills all the space. I applauded with the crowd,
and the quality of my excitement seemed to darken and rise
inside me like a wave of rich and savage appreciation, and I remembered the Saturday mornings in Brighton Beach, at the
handball courts, when the challengers would show up and the
neighborhood collected along the sidelines to watch Larry do
battle.

The band played a fast mambo as Larry and Sheila walked
out, hand in hand, onto the stage. Then they turned to face
each other, smiling beautifully as they assumed the formal em-

brace of ballroom dancers, and held still for a short count, and
then began moving as one to the music. I'd never seen anything more beautiful, and the emotion was looming bigger and
bigger. I ordered another drink, and lit a cigarette. At one
point, Sheila whirled free of Larry's embrace, and her dress
whirled high up her legs. Her underpants flashed into sight.
Two men standing beside me, hotel guests, slightly drunk,
started laughing. I turned with lethal fury in my expression,
and set down my drink and cigarette. They took one look at
me and shut up, which left me with a good murderous feeling.

The dance number lasted only a few minutes. Larry was
very dignified as he led Sheila through turns, sometimes re-
leasing her to dance alone before drawing her back to him. He
did nothing flamboyant to show how good he was. A dancer
has only to walk and you see it in the way his feet caress the
floor. The audience applauded with enthusiasm, and then the
band played a cha-cha-cha. Larry and Sheila danced its ritual
chase, and there was fine erotic tension in their style. They
stayed exquisitely close, then separated, then drew close
again, but didn't touch once. When the dance ended, Larry
and Sheila, holding hands, faced the audience and bowed.
The applause had the volume and depth of true appreciation.
Philly Burns appeared onstage, encouraging more applause.
"Didn't I tell you? These kids are fantastic. Let's hear it."

I went backstage, and found them in a dressing room. I
reminded Larry immediately that I'd been his busboy three
years ago. He grabbed my shoulders and pulled me to him and
hugged me. "Joseph. Forgive me, man. Too much has happened. Man, I'm living a whole other life, in a whole other
world. You wouldn't believe it."

He didn't ask anything about me. I couldn't blame him.
He'd just been onstage in front of a couple of hundred people,
and naturally was full of himself.

"You two looked pretty great," I said.

"You liked our routine?"

"I've seen a lot of dancers in the mountains. You two are the best."

I smiled and nodded at Sheila, who had taken a chair, and now sat with her legs crossed. She smiled back shyly, and said nothing. We hadn't been introduced. I could have introduced myself, but it would call attention to the lapse.

"Sheila is four months pregnant. We won't be dancing much longer."

Sheila rolled her eyes, as if it were something she'd heard too often, and it had ironic significance only she could appreciate. She was less cute than I remembered, and more womanly, more reserved than shy, and I glimpsed depth in her brown eyes, and realized that she made serious judgments. Could even be bored by Larry. I remembered the telephone calls, and their meetings in the motel, and it came to me that I didn't know anything about her, and it came to me that I didn't know anything about Larry, either. He didn't think to ask about me.

Larry said there was no money in exhibition dancing, but it's a lot of fun. They'd spent a year traveling in the Caribbean and Europe. Sheila's father had given him a position with the company. Larry used the vacation to visit company offices in London, Munich, and Milan. The food in London wasn't bad, but you had to know where to eat. Sheila's father had a membership in an eating club, which they visited. He also knew Harley Street doctors. Sheila had had a little trouble. Larry talked about their dance routine. They'd picked up new steps in Havana, where Sheila's father had a piece of ownership in two hotels, and they took advantage of his membership in an exclusive yacht club.

"Let's show Joseph mambo Cubana," he said to Sheila. She raised her eyebrows and blew out a little sigh.

Larry ignored her response, and clapped out the measure and did his steps alone, carrying himself proudly. Sheila continued to sit, watching him, motionless, a little weary, not in the mood to dance anymore. Then he smiled at her, barbarian pleasure flashed in his eyes and teeth, and then, as if in a trance of desire, Sheila rose slowly from her chair, drawn by a power not within herself, slowly, as if against failing resistance, toward Larry. I remembered how the woman had said, "She can't help it."

That was how she looked, but I wasn't convinced she couldn't help it, only that she knew how she looked as she stepped toward him, as if subjected helplessly to an illusion of a commanding presence. It might have been how she wanted to look. It was appealing, I thought, and even if it wasn't real, it was real, and what she wanted more than she didn't. If Larry had told her to fly, she could have done that, too, and not able to help it. If he told her to seize a white-hot iron, she could have done that, too, without burning her hands. I thought this is how everything is done, and nothing would happen otherwise, so the least thing is miraculous. Great enemies of illusion, like Marx and Gandhi, could see into it, but it hardly makes any difference if you choose to dismiss it after years in a library, or by eating a pinch of salt, or taking off your clothes like Saint Francis, or if you choose to surrender to it, as Sheila was doing. What's here is here, and it's an illusion, and it's real, which is what Larry would say, probably, and Sheila would assent, if she thought about it. I suspected that she did. This was insidious thinking and against my nature, but I couldn't alienate myself from what transpired of its own within.

They held each other and moved together, and there was no sound except for their shoes sliding to a beat. I could hear it and see it in how they moved, and felt it quickening in my body as if Machito had given the count and his band were blasting music. Except for shoes scraping the floor, Larry and Sheila danced in silence and invoked soundless music from the earth. Watching them, I felt more left out than I'd ever felt in the playground when the guys were choosing up sides, but

I didn't feel grief. Gooseflesh swept along my arms like a breeze across the surface of a Catskill lake, and, at the bottom of the lake I saw Larry Starker, his ankles chained to cinder blocks, his hair streaming upward, and his arms flailing slowly. It was a nutty and awful hallucination, not an illusion. I couldn't shake free of its ungenerous source in my feelings. Fish had eaten his eyes. The hallucination had nothing to do with real life, but I supposed it was telling me that Morris had connections, even if he was a podiatrist, and, even if he was wrong for Sheila, he had a say in things. I was looking at a gangster hit. Larry hadn't done anything, but there was a bullet hole in his forehead.

—1999

In the Fifties

IN THE FIFTIES I learned to drive a car. I was frequently in love. I had more friends than now.

When Khrushchev denounced Stalin my roommate shit blood, turned yellow, and lost most of his hair.

I attended the lectures of the excellent E. B. Burgum until Senator McCarthy ended his tenure. I imagined N.Y.U. would burn. Miserable students, drifting in the halls, looked at one another.

In less than a month, working day and night, I wrote a bad novel.

I went to school—N.Y.U., Michigan, Berkeley—much of the time.

I had witty, giddy conversation, four or five nights a week, in a homosexual bar in Ann Arbor.

I read literary reviews the way people suck candy.

Personal relationships were more important to me than anything else.

I had a fight with a powerful fat man who fell on my face and was immovable.

I had personal relationships with football players, jazz musicians, ass-bandits, nymphomaniacs, non-specialized degenerates, and numerous Jewish premedical students.

I had personal relationships with thirty-five rhesus monkeys in an experiment on monkey addiction to morphine. They knew me as one who shot reeking crap out of cages with a hose.

With four other students I lived in the home of a chiropractor named Leo.

I met a man in Detroit who owned a submachine gun; he claimed to have hit Dutch Schultz. I saw a gangster movie that disproved his claim.

I knew card sharks and con men. I liked marginal types because they seemed original and aristocratic, living for an ideal or obliged to live it. Ordinary types seemed fundamentally unserious. These distinctions belong to a romantic fop. I didn't think that way too much.

I knew two girls who had brains, talent, health, good looks, plenty to eat, and hanged themselves.

I heard of parties in Ann Arbor where everyone made it with everyone else, including the cat.

I worked for an evil vanity publisher in Manhattan.

I worked in a fish-packing plant in Massachusetts, on the line with a sincere Jewish poet from Harvard and three lesbians; one was beautiful, one was grim; both loved the other, who was intelligent. I loved her too. I dreamed of violating her purity. They talked among themselves, in creepy whispers, always about Jung. In a dark corner, away from our line, old Portuguese men slit fish into open flaps, flicking out the bones. I could see only their eyes and knives. I'd arrive early every morning to dash in and out until the stench became bearable. After work I'd go to bed and pluck fish scales out of my skin.

I was a teaching assistant in two English departments. I graded thousands of freshman themes. One began like this: "Karl Marx, for that was his name ..." Another began like this: "In Jonathan Swift's famous letter to the Pope ..." I wrote edifying comments in the margins. Later I began to scribble "Awkward" beside everything, even spelling errors.

I got A's and F's as a graduate student. A professor of English said my attitude wasn't professional. He said that he always read a "good book" after dinner.

A girl from Indiana said this of me on a teacher-evaluation form: "It is bad enough to go to an English class at eight in the morning, but to be instructed by a shabby man is horrible."

I made enemies on the East Coast, the West Coast, and in the Middle West. All now dead, sick, or out of luck.

I was arrested, photographed, and fingerprinted. In a soundproof room two detectives lectured me on the American way of life, and I was charged with the crime of nothing. A New York cop told me that detectives were called "defectives."

I had an automobile accident. I did the mambo. I had urethritis and mononucleosis.

In Ann Arbor, a few years before the advent of Malcolm X, a lot of my friends were black. After Malcolm X, almost all my friends were white. They admired John F. Kennedy.

In the fifties I smoked marijuana, hash, and opium. Once I drank absinthe. Once I swallowed twenty glycerine caps of peyote. The social effects of "drugs," unless sexual, always seemed tedious. But I liked people who inclined the drug way. Especially if they didn't proselytize. I listened to long conversations about the phenomenological weirdness of familiar reality and the great spiritual questions this entailed—for example, "Do you think Wallace Stevens is a head?"

I witnessed an abortion.

I was godless, but I thought the fashion of intellectual religiosity more despicable. I wished that I could live in a culture rather than study life among the cultured.

I drove eighty-five miles per hour on a two-lane blacktop. It was nighttime. Intermittent thick white fog made the headlights feeble and diffuse. Four others in the car sat with the strict silent rectitude of catatonics. If one of them didn't admit to being frightened, we were dead. A Cadillac, doing a hundred miles per hour, passed us and was obliterated in the fog. I slowed down.

I drank old-fashioneds in the apartment of my friend Julian. We talked about Worringer and Spengler. We gossiped about friends. Then we left to meet our dates. There was more drinking. We all climbed trees, crawled in the street, and went to a church. Julian walked into an elm, smashed his glasses, vomited on a lawn, and returned home to memorize Anglo-Saxon grammatical forms. I ended on my knees, vomiting into a toilet bowl, repeatedly flushing the water to hide my noises. Later I phoned New York so that I could listen to the voices of my parents, their Yiddish, their English, their logics.

I knew a professor of English who wrote impassioned sonnets in honor of Henry Ford.

I played freshman varsity basketball at N.Y.U. and received a dollar an hour for practice sessions and double that for games. It was called "meal money." I played badly—too psychological, too worried about not studying, too short. If pushed or elbowed during a practice game, I was ready to kill. The coach liked my attitude. In his day, he said, practice ended when there was blood on the boards. I ran back and forth, in urgent sneakers, through my freshman year. Near the end I came down with pleurisy, quit basketball, started smoking more.

I took classes in comparative anatomy and chemistry. I took classes in Old English, Middle English, and modern literature. I took classes and classes.

I fired a twelve-gauge shotgun down the hallway of a railroad flat into a couch pillow.

My roommate bought the shotgun because of his gambling debts. He expected murderous thugs to come for him. I'd wake in the middle of the night listening for a knock, a cough, a footstep, wondering how to identify myself as not him when they broke through our door.

My roommate was an expensively dressed kid from a Chicago suburb. Though very intelligent, he suffered in school. He suffered with girls though he was handsome and witty. He suffered with boys though he was heterosexual. He slept on three mattresses and used a sun lamp all winter. He bathed, oiled, and perfumed his body daily. He wanted soft, sweet joys in every part, but when some whore asked if he'd like to be beaten with a garrison belt he said yes. He suffered with food, eating from morning to night, loading his pockets with fried pumpkin seeds when he left for class, smearing caviar paste on his filet mignons, eating himself into a monumental face of eating because he was eating. Then he killed himself.

A lot of young, gifted people I knew in the fifties killed themselves. Only a few of them continue walking around.

I wrote literary essays in the turgid, tumescent manner of darkest Blackmur.

I used to think that someday I would write a fictional version of my stupid life in the fifties.

I was a waiter in a Catskill hotel. The captain of the waiters ordered us to dance with the female guests who appeared in the casino without escorts and, as much as possible, fuck them. A professional tummler walked the grounds. Wherever he saw a group of people merely chatting, he thrust in quickly and created a tumult.

I heard the Budapest String Quartet, Dylan Thomas, Lester Young, and Billie Holiday together, and I saw Pearl Primus dance, in a Village nightclub, in a space two yards square, accompanied by an African drummer about seventy years old. His hands moved in spasms of mathematical complexity at invisible speed. People left their tables to press close to Primus and see the expression in her face, the sweat, the muscles, the way her naked feet seized and released the floor.

Eventually I had friends in New York, Ann Arbor, Chicago, Berkeley, and Los Angeles.

I did the cha-cha, wearing a tux, at a New Year's party in Hollywood, and sat at a table with Steve McQueen. He'd become famous in a TV series about a cowboy with a rifle. He said he didn't know which he liked best, acting or driving a racing car. I thought he was a silly person and then realized he thought I was. I met a few other famous people who said something. One night, in a yellow Porsche, I circled Manhattan with Jack Kerouac. He recited passages, perfectly remembered from his book reviews, to the sky. His manner was ironical, sweet, and depressing.

I had a friend named Chicky who drove his chopped, blocked, stripped, dual-exhaust Ford convertible, while vomiting out the fly window, into a telephone pole. He survived, lit a match to see if the engine was all right, and it blew up in his face. I saw him in the hospital. Through his bandages he said that ever since high school he'd been trying to kill himself. Because his girlfriend wasn't good looking enough. He was crying and laughing while he pleaded with me to believe that he really had been trying to kill himself because his girlfriend wasn't good looking enough. I told him that I was going out with a certain girl and he told me that he had fucked her once but it didn't matter because I could take her away and live somewhere else. He was a Sicilian kid with a face like Caravaggio's angels of debauch. He'd been educated by priests and nuns. When his hair grew back and his face healed, his mind healed. He broke up with his girlfriend. He wasn't nearly as narcissistic as other men I knew in the fifties.

I knew one who, before picking up his dates, ironed his dollar bills and powdered his testicles. Many women thought he was extremely attractive and became his sexual slaves. Men didn't like him.

I had a friend who was dragged down a courthouse stairway, in San Francisco, by her hair. She'd wanted to attend the House Un-American hearings. The next morning I crossed the Bay Bridge to join my first protest demonstration. I felt frightened and embarrassed. I was bitter about what had happened to her and the others she'd been with. I expected to see thirty or forty people like me, carrying hysterical placards around the courthouse until the cops bludgeoned us into the pavement. About two thousand people were there. I marched beside a little kid who had a bag of marbles to throw under the hoofs of the horse cops. His mother kept saying, "Not yet, not yet." We marched all day. That was the end of the fifties.

—1975

City Boy

"PHILLIP," she said, "this is crazy."

I didn't agree or disagree. She wanted some answer. I bit her neck. She kissed my ear. It was nearly three in the morning. We had just returned. The apartment was dark and quiet. We were on the living room floor and she repeated, "Phillip, this is crazy." Her crinoline broke under us like cinders. Furniture loomed all around—settee, chairs, a table with a lamp. Pictures were cloudy blotches drifting above. But no lights, no things to look at, no eyes in her head. She was underneath me and warm. The rug was warm, soft as mud, deep. Her crinoline cracked like sticks. Our naked bellies clapped together. Air fired out like farts. I took it as applause. The chandelier clicked. The clock ticked as if to split its glass. "Phillip," she said, "this is crazy." A little voice against the grain and power. Not enough to stop me. Yet once I had been a man of feeling. We went to concerts, walked in the park, trembled in the maid's room. Now in the foyer, a flash of hair and claws. We stumbled to the living room floor. She said, "Phillip, this is crazy." Then silence, except in my head where a conference table was set up, ashtrays scattered about. Priests, ministers, and rabbis were rushing to take seats. I wanted their opinion, but came. They vanished. A voice lingered, faintly crying, "You could mess up the rug, Phillip, break something . . ." Her fingers pinched my back like ants. I expected a remark to kill good death. She said nothing. The breath in her nostrils whipped mucus. It cracked in my ears like flags. I dreamed we were in her mother's Cadillac, trailing flags. I heard her voice before I heard the words. "Phillip, this is crazy. My parents are in the next room." Her cheek jerked against mine, her breasts were knuckles in my nipples. I burned. Good death was killed. I burned with hate. A rabbi shook his finger, "You shouldn't hate." I lifted on my elbows, sneering in pain. She wrenched her hips, tightened muscles in belly and neck. She said, "Move." It was imperative to move. Her parents were thirty feet away. Down the hall between Utrillos and Vlamincks, through the door, flick the light and I'd see them. Maybe like us, Mr. Cohen adrift on the missus. Hair sifted down my cheek. "Let's go to the maid's room," she whispered. I was reassured. She tried to move. I kissed her mouth. Her crinoline smashed like sugar. Pig that I was, I couldn't move. The clock ticked hysterically. Ticks piled up like insects. Muscles lapsed in her thighs. Her fingers scratched on my neck as if looking for buttons. She slept. I sprawled like a bludgeoned pig, eyes open, loose lips. I flopped into sleep, in her, in the rug, in our scattered clothes.

Dawn hadn't shown between the slats in the blinds. Her breathing sissed in my ear. I wanted to sleep more, but needed a cigarette. I thought of the cold avenue, the lonely subway ride. Where could I buy a newspaper, a cup of coffee? This was crazy, dangerous, a waste of time. The maid might arrive, her parents might wake. I had to get started. My hand pushed along the rug to find my shirt, touched a brass lion's paw, then a lamp cord.

A naked heel bumped wood.

She woke, her nails in my neck. "Phillip, did you hear?" I whispered, "Quiet." My eyes rolled like Milton's. Furniture loomed, whirled. "Dear God," I prayed, "save my ass." The steps ceased. Neither of us breathed. The clock ticked. She trembled. I pressed my cheek against her mouth to keep her from talking. We heard pajamas rustle, phlegmy breathing, fingernails scratching hair. A voice, "Veronica, don't you think it's time you sent Phillip home?"

A murmur of assent started in her throat, swept to my cheek, fell back drowned like a child in a well. Mr. Cohen had spoken. He stood ten inches from our legs. Maybe less. It was impossible to tell. His fingernails grated through hair. His voice hung in the dark with the quintessential question. Mr. Cohen, scratching his crotch, stood now as never in the light. Considerable. No tool of his wife, whose energy in business kept him eating, sleeping, overlooking the park. Pinochle change in his pocket four nights a week. But were they his words? Or was he the oracle of Mrs. Cohen, lying sleepless, irritated, waiting for him to get me out? I didn't breathe. I didn't move. If he had come on his own he would leave without an answer. His eyes weren't adjusted to the dark. He couldn't see. We lay at his feet like worms. He scratched, made smacking noises with his mouth.

The question of authority is always with us. Who is responsible for the triggers pulled, buttons pressed, the gas, the fire? Doubt banged my brain. My heart lay in the fist of intellect, which squeezed out feeling like piss out of kidneys. Mrs. Cohen's voice demolished doubt, feeling, intellect. It ripped from the bedroom.

"For God's sake, Morris, don't be banal. Tell the schmuck to go home and keep his own parents awake all night, if he has any."

Veronica's tears slipped down my cheeks. Mr. Cohen sighed, shuffled, made a strong voice. "Veronica, tell Phillip ..." His foot came down on my ass. He drove me into his daughter. I drove her into his rug.

"I don't believe it," he said.

He walked like an antelope, lifting hoof from knee, but stepped down hard. Sensitive to the danger of movement, yet finally impulsive, flinging his pot at the earth in order to cross it. His foot brought me his weight and character, a hundred fifty-five pounds of stomping schlemiel, in a mode of apprehension so primal we must share it with bugs. Let armies stomp me to insensate pulp—I'll yell "Cohen" when he arrives.

Veronica squealed, had a contraction, fluttered, gagged a shriek, squeezed, and up like a frog out of the hand of a child I stood spread-legged, bolt naked, great with eyes. Mr.

Cohen's face was eyes in my eyes. A secret sharer. We faced each other like men accidentally met in hell. He retreated flapping, moaning, "I will not believe it one bit."

Veronica said, "Daddy?"

"Who else you no good bum?"

The rug raced. I smacked against blinds, glass broke and I whirled. Veronica said, "Phillip," and I went off in streaks, a sparrow in the room, here, there, early American, baroque and rococo. Veronica wailed, "Phillip." Mr. Cohen screamed, "I'll kill him." I stopped at the door, seized the knob. Mrs. Cohen yelled from the bedroom, "Morris, did something break? Answer me."

"I'll kill that bastid."

"Morris, if something broke you'll rot for a month."

"Mother, stop it," said Veronica. "Phillip, come back."

The door slammed. I was outside, naked as a wolf.

I needed poise. Without poise the street was impossible. Blood shot to my brain, thought blossomed. I'd walk on my hands. Beards were fashionable. I kicked up my feet, kicked the elevator button, faced the door, and waited. I bent one elbow like a knee. The posture of a clothes model, easy, poised. Blood coiled down to my brain, weeds burgeoned. I had made a bad impression. There was no other way to see it. But all right. We needed a new beginning. Everyone does. Yet how few of us know when it arrives. Mr. Cohen had never spoken to me before; this was a breakthrough. There had been a false element in our relationship. It was wiped out. I wouldn't kid myself with the idea that he had nothing to say. I'd had enough of his silent treatment. It was worth being naked to see how mercilessly I could think. I had his number. Mrs. Cohen's, too. I was learning every second. I was a city boy. No innocent shitkicker from Jersey. I was the A train, the Fifth Avenue bus. I could be a cop. My name was Phillip, my style New York City. I poked the elevator button with my toe. It rang in the lobby, waking Ludwig. He'd come for me, rotten with sleep. Not the first time. He always took me down, walked me through the lobby, and let me out on the avenue. Wires began tugging him up the shaft. I moved back, conscious of my genitals hanging upside down. Absurd consideration; we were both men one way or another. There were social distinctions enforced by his uniform, but they would vanish at the sight of me. "The unaccommodated thing itself." "Off ye lendings!" The greatest play is about a naked man. A picture of Lear came to me, naked, racing through the wheat. I could be cool. I thought of Ludwig's uniform, hat, whipcord collar. It signified his authority. Perhaps he would be annoyed, in his authority, by the sight of me naked. Few people woke him at such hours. Worse, I never tipped him. Could I have been so indifferent month after month? In a crisis you discover everything. Then it's too late. Know yourself, indeed. You need a crisis every day. I refused to think about it. I sent my mind after objects. It returned with the chairs, settee, table and chandelier. Where were my clothes? I sent it along the rug. It found buttons, eagles stamped in brass. I recognized them as the buttons on Ludwig's coat. Eagles, beaks like knives, shrieking for tips. Fuck'm, I thought. Who's Ludwig? A big coat, a whistle, white gloves, and a General MacArthur hat. I could understand him completely. He couldn't begin to understand me. A naked man is mysterious. But aside from that, what did he know? I dated Veronica Cohen and went home late. Did he know I was out of work? That I lived in a slum downtown? Of course not.

Possibly under his hat was a filthy mind. He imagined Veronica and I might be having sexual intercourse. He resented it. Not that he hoped for the privilege himself, in his coat and soldier hat, but he had a proprietary interest in the building and its residents. I came from another world. The other world against which Ludwig defended the residents. Wasn't I like a burglar sneaking out late, making him my accomplice? I undermined his authority, his dedication. He despised me. It was obvious. But no one thinks such thoughts. It made me laugh to think them. My genitals jumped. The elevator door slid open. He didn't say a word. I padded inside like a seal. The door slid shut. Instantly, I was ashamed of myself, thinking as I had about him. I had no right. A better man than I. His profile was an etching by Dürer. Good peasant stock. How had he fallen to such work? Existence precedes essence. At the controls, silent, enduring, he gave me strength for the street. Perhaps the sun would be up, birds in the air. The door slid open. Ludwig walked ahead of me through the lobby. He needed new heels. The door of the lobby was half a ton of glass, encased in iron vines and leaves. Not too much for Ludwig. He turned, looked down into my eyes. I watched his lips move.

"I vun say sumding. Yur bisniss vot you do. Bud vy you mek her miserable? Nod led her slip. She has beks unter her eyes."

Ludwig had feelings. They spoke to mine. Beneath the uniform, a man. Essence precedes existence. Even rotten with sleep, thick, dry bags under his eyes, he saw, he sympathized. The discretion demanded by his job forbade anything tangible, a sweater, a hat. "Ludwig," I whispered, "you're all right." It didn't matter if he heard me. He knew I said something. He knew it was something nice. He grinned, tugged the door open with both hands. I slapped out onto the avenue. I saw no one, dropped to my feet, and glanced back through the door. Perhaps for the last time. I lingered, indulged a little melancholy. Ludwig walked to a couch in the rear of the lobby. He took off his coat, rolled it into a pillow, and lay down. I had never stayed to see him do that before, but always rushed off to the subway. As if I were indifferent to the life of the building. Indeed, like a burglar. I seized the valuables and fled to the subway. I stayed another moment, watching good Ludwig, so I could hate myself. He assumed the modest, saintly posture of sleep. One leg here, the other there. His good head on his coat. A big arm across his stomach, the hand be-tween his hips. He made a fist and punched up and down.

I went down the avenue, staying close to the buildings. Later I would work up a philosophy. Now I wanted to sleep, forget. I hadn't the energy for moral complexities: Ludwig cross-eyed, thumping his pelvis in such a nice lobby. Mirrors, glazed pots, rubber plants ten feet high. As if he were gener-ating all of it. As if it were part of his job. I hurried. The buildings were on my left, the park on my right. There were doormen in all the buildings; God knows what was in the park. No cars were moving. No people in sight. Streetlights glowed in a receding sweep down to Fifty-ninth Street and beyond. A wind pressed my face like Mr. Cohen's breath. Such hatred. Imponderable under any circumstances, a father cursing his daughter. Why? A fright in the dark? Freud said things about fathers and daughters. It was too obvious, too hideous. I shuddered and went more quickly. I began to run. In a few minutes I was at the spit-mottled steps of the subway. I had hoped for vomit. Spit is no challenge for bare feet. Still, I wouldn't complain. It was sufficiently disgusting to make me live in spirit. I went down the steps flat-footed, stamping, elevated by each declension. I was a city boy, no mincing creep from the sticks.

A Negro man sat in the change booth. He wore glasses, a white shirt, black knit tie and a silver tie clip. I saw a mole on his right cheek. His hair had spots of gray, as if strewn with ashes. He was reading a newspaper. He didn't hear me ap-proach, didn't see my eyes take him in, figure him out. Shirt, glasses, tie—I knew how to address him. I coughed. He looked up.

"Sir, I don't have any money. Please let me through the turnstile. I come this way every week and will certainly pay you the next time."

He merely looked at me. Then his eyes flashed like fangs.

Instinctively, I guessed what he felt. He didn't owe favors to a white man. He didn't have to bring his allegiance to the Transit Authority into question for my sake.

"Hey, man, you naked?"

"Yes."

"Step back a little."

I stepped back.

"You're naked."

I nodded.

"Get your naked ass the hell out of here."

"Sir," I said, "I know these are difficult times, but can't we be reasonable? I know that ..."

"Scat, mother, go home."

I crouched as if to dash through the turnstile. He crouched, too. It proved he would come after me. I shrugged, turned back toward the steps. The city was infinite. There were many other subways. But why had he become so angry? Did he think I was a bigot? Maybe I was running around naked to get him upset. His anger was incomprehensible otherwise. It made me feel like a bigot. First a burglar, then a bigot. I needed a cigarette. I could hardly breathe. Air was too good for me. At the top of the steps, staring down, stood Veronica. She had my clothes.

"Poor, poor," she said.

I said nothing. I snatched my underpants and put them on. She had my cigarettes ready. I tried to light one, but the match failed. I threw down the cigarette and the matchbook. She retrieved them as I dressed. She lit the cigarette for me and held my elbow to help me keep my balance. I finished dressing, took the cigarette. We walked back toward her building. The words "thank you" sat in my brain like driven spikes. She nibbled her lip.

"How are things at home?" My voice was casual and morose, as if no answer could matter.

"All right," she said, her voice the same as mine. She took her tone from me. I liked that sometimes, sometimes not. Now I didn't like it. I discovered I was angry. Until she said that, I had no idea I was angry. I flicked the cigarette into the gutter and suddenly I knew why. I didn't love her. The cigarette sizzled in the gutter. Like truth. I didn't love her. Black hair, green eyes, I didn't love her. Slender legs. I didn't. Last night I had looked at her and said to myself, "I hate communism." Now I wanted to step on her head. Nothing less than that would do. If it was a perverted thought, then it was a perverted thought. I wasn't afraid to admit it to myself.

"All right? Really? Is that true?"

Blah, blah, blah. Who asked those questions? A zombie; not Phillip of the foyer and rug. He died in flight. I was sorry, sincerely sorry, but with clothes on my back I knew certain feelings would not survive humiliation. It was so clear it was thrilling. Perhaps she felt it, too. In any case she would have to accept it. The nature of the times. We are historical creatures. Veronica and I were finished. Before we reached her door I would say deadly words. They'd come in a natural way, kill her a little. Veronica, let me step on your head or we're through. Maybe we're through, anyway. It would deepen her looks, give philosophy to what was only charming in her face. The dawn was here. A new day. Cruel, but change is cruel. I could bear it. Love is infinite and one. Women are not. Neither are men. The human condition. Nearly unbearable.

"No, it's not true," she said.

"What's not?"

"Things aren't all right at home."

I nodded intelligently, sighed, "Of course not. Tell me the truth, please. I don't want to hear anything else."

"Daddy had a heart attack."

"Oh God," I yelled. "Oh God, no."

I seized her hand, dropped it. She let it fall. I seized it

again. No use. I let it fall. She let it drift between us. We stared at one another. She said, "What were you going to say? I can tell you were going to say something."

I stared, said nothing.

"Don't feel guilty, Phillip. Let's just go back to the apartment and have some coffee."

"What can I say?"

"Don't say anything. He's in the hospital and my mother is there. Let's just go upstairs and not say anything."

"Not say anything. Like moral imbeciles go slurp coffee and not say anything? What are we, nihilists or something? Assassins? Monsters?"

"Phillip, there's no one in the apartment. I'll make us coffee and eggs ..."

"How about a roast beef? Got a roast beef in the freezer?"

"Phillip, he's my father."

We were at the door. I rattled. I was in a trance. This was life. Death!

"Indeed, your father. I'll accept that. I can do no less."

"Phillip, shut up. Ludwig."

The door opened. I nodded to Ludwig. What did he know about life and death? Give him a uniform and a quiet lobby— that's life and death. In the elevator he took the controls. "Always got a hand on the controls, eh Ludwig?"

Veronica smiled in a feeble, grateful way. She liked to see me get along with the help. Ludwig said, "Dots right."

"Ludwig has been our doorman for years, Phillip. Ever since I was a little girl."

"Wow," I said.

"Dots right."

The door slid open. Veronica said, "Thank you, Ludwig." I said, "Thank you, Ludwig."

"Vulcum."

"Vulcum? You mean, 'welcome'? Hey, Ludwig, how long you been in this country?"

78

Veronica was driving her key into the door.

"How come you never learned to talk American, baby?"

"Phillip, come here."

"I'm saying something to Ludwig."

"Come here right now."

"I have to go, Ludwig."

"Vulcum."

She went directly to the bathroom. I waited in the hallway between Vlamincks and Utrillos. The Utrillos were pale and flat. The Vlamincks were thick, twisted, and red. Raw meat on one wall, dry stone on the other. Mrs. Cohen had an eye for contrasts. I heard Veronica sob. She ran water in the sink, sobbed, sat down, peed. She saw me looking and kicked the door shut.

"At a time like this ..."

"I don't like you looking."

"Then why did you leave the door open? You obviously don't know your own mind."

"Go away, Phillip. Wait in the living room."

"Just tell me why you left the door open."

"Phillip, you're going to drive me nuts. Go away. I can't do a damn thing if I know you're standing there."

The living room made me feel better. The settee, the chandelier full of teeth, and the rug were company. Mr. Cohen was everywhere, a simple, diffuse presence. He jingled change in his pocket, looked out the window, and was happy he could see the park. He took a little antelope step and tears came into my eyes. I sat among his mourners. A rabbi droned platitudes: Mr. Cohen was generous, kind, beloved by his wife and daughter. "How much did he weigh?" I shouted. The phone rang.

Veronica came running down the hall. I went and stood at her side when she picked up the phone. I stood dumb, stiff as a hat rack. She was whimpering, "Yes, yes ..." I nodded my head yes, yes, thinking it was better than no, no. She put the phone down.

"It was my mother. Daddy's all right. Mother is staying with him in his room at the hospital and they'll come home together tomorrow."

Her eyes looked at mine. At them as if they were as flat and opaque as hers. I said in a slow, stupid voice, "You're allowed to do that? Stay overnight in a hospital with a patient? Sleep in his room?" She continued looking at my eyes. I shrugged, looked down. She took my shirt front in a fist like a bite. She whispered. I said, "What?" She whispered again, "Fuck me." The clock ticked like crickets. The Vlamincks spilled blood. We sank into the rug as if it were quicksand.

—1969

Crossbones

AT THE END of the summer, or the year, or when he could do more with his talent than play guitar in a Village strip joint ... and after considering his talent for commitment and reluctance she found reluctance in her own heart and marriage talk became desultory, specifics dim, ghostly, lost in bed with Myron doing wrong things, "working on" her, discovering epileptic dysrhythmia in her hips and he asked about it and she said it hurt her someplace but not, she insisted, in her head, and they fought the next morning and the next as if ravenous for intimacy and disgraced themselves yelling, becoming intimate with neighbors, and the superintendent brought them complaints that would have meant nothing if they had not exhausted all desire for loud, broad strokes, but now, conscious of complaints, they thrust along the vital horizontal with silent, stiletto words, and later in the narrowed range of their imaginations could find no adequate mode of retraction, so wounds festered, burgeoning lurid weeds, poisoning thought, dialogue, and the simple air of their two-room apartment (which had seemed with its view of the Jersey cliffs so much larger than now) now seemed too thick to breathe, or to see through to one another, but they didn't say a word about breaking up, even experimentally, for whatever their doubts about one another, their doubts about other others and the city—themselves adrift in it among messy one-night stands —were too frightening and at least they had, in one another, what they had: Sarah had Myron Bronsky, gloomy brown eyes, a guitar in his hands as mystical and tearing as, say, Lorca, though Myron's particular hands derived from dancing, clapping Hasidim; and he had Sarah Nilsin, Minnesota blonde, long bones, arctic schizophrenia in the gray infinities of her eyes, and a turn for lyric poems derived from piratical

saga masters. Rare, but opposites cleave in the divisive angu-
larities of Manhattan and, as the dialectics of embattled in-
dividuation became more intense, these two cleaved more
tightly: if Sarah, out for groceries, hadn't returned in twenty
minutes, Myron punched a wall, pulverizing the music in his
knuckles, but punched, punched until she flung through the
door shrieking stop; and he, twenty minutes late from work,
found Sarah in kerchief, coat, and gloves, the knotted cloth
beneath her chin a little stone proclaiming wild indifference
to what the nighttime street could hold, since it held most for
him if she were raped and murdered in it. After work he ran
home. Buying a quart of milk and a pack of cigarettes, she suffered stomach cramps.

Then a letter came from St. Cloud, Minnesota. Sarah's father was going to visit them next week.

She sewed curtains, squinting down into the night, pluck-
ing thread with pricked, exquisite fingertips. He painted
walls lately punched. She bought plants for the windowsills,
framed and hung three Japanese prints, and painted the hall
toilet opaque, flat yellow. On his knees until sunrise four days
in a row, he sanded, then varnished floor boards until the oak
bubbled up its blackest grain, turbulent and petrified, and
Monday dawned on Sarah ironing dresses—more than enough
to last her father's visit—and Myron already twice shaved,
shining all his shoes, urging her to hurry.

In its mute perfection their apartment now had the air of a
well-beaten slave, simultaneously alive and dead, and reflected, like an emanation of their nerves, a severe, hectic harmo-
ny; but it wouldn't have mattered if the new curtains, pictures, and boiling floors yelled reeking spiritual shambles
because Sarah's father wasn't that kind of minister. His ser-
mons alluded more to Heidegger and Sartre than Christ, he
lifted weights, smoked two packs of cigarettes a day, drove a
green Jaguar and, since the death of Sarah's mother a year ago

in a state insane asylum, had seen species of love in all human relations. And probably at this very moment, taking the banked curves of the Pennsylvania Turnpike, knuckles pale on the walnut wheel, came man and machine leaning as one toward Jersey, and beyond that toward love.

Their sense of all this drove them, wrenched them out of themselves, onto their apartment until nothing more could make it coincident with what he would discover in it anyway, and they had now only their own absolute physical being still to work on, at nine o'clock, when Myron dashed out to the cleaners for shirts, trousers, and jackets, then dressed in fresh clothing while Sarah slammed and smeared the iron down the board as if increasingly sealed in the momentum of brute work, and then, standing behind her, lighting a cigarette, Myron was whispering as if to himself that she must hurry and she was turning from the board and in the same motion hurled the iron, lunging after it with nails and teeth before it exploded against the wall and Myron, instantly, hideously understood that the iron, had it struck him, had to burn his flesh and break his bones, flew to meet her with a scream and fists banging her mouth as they locked, winding, fusing to one convulsive beast reeling off walls, tables, and chairs, with ashtrays, books, lamps shooting away with pieces of themselves, and he punched out three of her teeth and strangled her until she dissolved in his hands and scratched his left eye blind—but there was hope in corneal transplantation that he would see through it again—and they were strapped in bandages, twisted and stiff with pain a week after Sarah's father didn't arrive and they helped one another walk slowly up the steps of the municipal building to buy a marriage license.

—1969

Eating Out

Basketball Player

I WAS the most dedicated basketball player. I don't say the best. In my mind I was terrifically good. In fact I was simply the most dedicated basketball player in the world. I say this because I played continuously, from the time I discovered the meaning of the game at the age of ten until my mid-twenties. I played outdoors on cement, indoors on wood. I played in heat, wind, and rain. I played in chilly gymnasiums. Walking home I played some more. I played during dinner, in my sleep, in movies, in automobiles and buses, and at stool. I played for more than a decade, taking every conceivable shot, with either hand, from every direction. Masses cheered my performance. No intermission, no food, no other human concern, year after year they cheered me on. In living rooms, subways, movies, and schoolyards I heard them. During actual basketball games I also played basketball. I played games within games. When I lost my virginity I eluded my opponent and sank a running hook. Masses saw it happen. I lost my virginity and my girl lost hers. The game had been won. I pulled up my trousers. She snapped her garter belt. I took a jump shot from the corner and another game was underway. I scored in a blind drive from the foul line. We kissed good night. The effect was epileptic. Masses thrashed in their seats, loud holes in their faces. I acknowledged with an automatic nod and hurried down the street, dribbling. A fall-away jumper from the top of the key. It hung in the air. Then, as if sucked down suddenly, it zipped through the hoop. Despite the speed and angle of my shots, I never missed.

Pleasure

MY MOTHER was taking me to the movies. We were walking

85

fast. I didn't know what movie it would be. Neither did my mother. She couldn't read. We were defenseless people. I was ten years old. My mother was five foot nothing. We walked with fast little steps, hands in our pockets, faces down. The school week had ended. I was five days closer to the M.D. My reward for good grades was a movie—black, brilliant pleasure. Encouragement to persist. We walked in a filthy, freezing, blazing wind for half a mile. The pleasure I'll never forget. A girl is struck by a speeding car. A beautiful girl who speaks first-class English—but she is struck down. Blinded, broken, paralyzed. The driver of the car is a handsome doctor. My mother whispers, *"Na,"* the Polish word that stimulates free-associational capacities in children. Mind-spring, this to that. The doctor operates on the girl in a theater of lights, masks, and knives. She has no choice in this matter. Blind and broken. Paralyzed. Lucky for her, she recovers. Her feeling of recovery is thrilling love for the doctor. He has this feeling, too. It spreads from them to everywhere, like the hot, vibrant, glowing moo of a tremendous cow, liquefying distinctions. The world is feeling. Feeling is the deadly car, the broken girl and blinding doctor, the masks, knives, and kisses. Finally there is a sunset. It returns me with smeared and glistening cheeks to the blazing wind. I glance at my mother. She whispers, *"Na?"* Intelligence springs through my mind like a monkey, seizing the bars, shaking them. We walk fast, with little steps, our hands in our pockets; but my face is lifted to the wind. It shrieks, "Emmmmmdeee." My call.

Something Evil

I SAID, "Ikstein stands outside the door for a long time before he knocks. Did you suspect that? Did you suspect that he stands there listening to what we say before he knocks?" She said, "Did you know you're crazy?" I said, "I'm not crazy. The expression on his face, when I open the door, is giddy and squirmy. As if he'd been doing something evil, like listening

outside our door before he knocked." She said, "That's Ikstein's expression. Why do you invite him here? Leave the
door open. He won't be able to listen to us. You won't make
yourself crazy imagining it." I said, "Brilliant, but he isn't
due for an hour and I won't sit here with the door open." She
said, "I hate to listen to you talk this way. I won't be involved
in your lunatic friendships." She opened the door. Ikstein
stood there, giddy and squirmy.

Answers

I BEGAN two hundred hours of continuous reading in the
twelve hours that remained before examinations. Melvin
Bloom, my roommate, flipped the pages of his textbook in a
sweet continuous trance. Reviewing the term's work was his
pleasure. He went to sleep early. While he slept I bent into the
night, reading, eating Benzedrine, smoking cigarettes. Shrieking dwarfs charged across my notes. Crabs asked me questions. Melvin flipped a page, blinked, flipped another. He
effected the same flipping and blinking, with no textbook,
during examinations. For every question, answers marched
down his optical nerve, neck, arm, and out onto his paper
where they stopped in impeccable parade. I'd look at my
paper, oily, scratched by ratlike misery, and I'd think of
Melvin Bloom. I would think, Oh God, what is going to happen to me.

Mackerel

SHE DIDN'T want to move in because there had been a rape on
the third floor. I said, "The guy was a wounded veteran,
under observation at Bellevue. We'll live on the fifth floor." It
was a Victorian office building, converted to apartments.
Seven stories, skinny, gray, filigreed face. No elevators. We
climbed an iron stairway. "Wounded veteran," I said. "Predictable." My voice echoed in dingy halls. Linoleum cracked
as we walked. Beneath the linoleum was older, drier linoleum.

The apartments had wooden office doors with smoked-glass windows. The hall toilets were padlocked; through gaps we could see the bowl, overhead tank, bare bulb dangling. "That stairway is good for the heart and legs," I said. She said, "Disgusting, dangerous building." I said, "You do smell piss in the halls and there has been a rape. The janitor admitted it. But people live here, couples, singles, every sex and race. Irish, Italian, Puerto Rican families. Kids run up and down the stairway. A mackerel-crowded iron stream. Radios, TVs, whining day and night. Not only a piss smell, but pasta, peppers, incense, marijuana. The building is full of life. It's life. Close to the subways, restaurants, movies." She said, "Rapes." I said, "One rape. A wounded man with a steel plate in his head, embittered, driven by undifferentiated needs. The rent is forty dollars a month. To find this place, you understand, I appealed to strangers. From aluminum phone booths, I dialed with ice-blue fingers. It's January in Manhattan. Howling winds come from the rivers." "The rape," she said. I said, "A special and extremely peculiar case. Be logical." Before we finished unpacking, the janitor was stabbed in the head. I said, "A junkie did it. A natural force, a hurricane." She said, "Something is wrong with you. I always felt it instinctively." I said, "I believe I'm not perfect. What do you think is wrong with me?" She said, "It makes me miserable." I said, "No matter how miserable it makes you, say it." She said, "It embarrasses me." I said, "Even if it embarrasses you, say it, be frank. This is America. I'll write it down. Maybe we can sell it and move to a better place." She said, "There's too much." I said, "I'll make a list. Go ahead, leave out nothing. I have a pencil." She said, "Then what?" I said, "Then I'll go to a psychiatrist." She said, "You'll give a distorted account." I said, "I'll make an exact, complete list. See this pencil. It's for making lists. Tell me what to write." She said, "No use." I said, "A junkie did it. Listen to me, bitch, a junkie did it."

Eating Out

FOUR MEN were at the table next to mine. Their collars were open, their ties loose, and their jackets hung on the wall. One man poured dressing on the salad, another tossed the leaves. Another filled the plates and served. One tore bread, another poured wine, another ladled soup. The table was small and square. The men were cramped, but efficient nonetheless, apparently practiced at eating here, this way, hunched over food, heads striking to suck at spoons, tear at forks, then pulling back into studious, invincible mastication. Their lower faces slid and chopped; they didn't talk once. All their eyes, like birds on a wire, perched on a horizontal line above the action. Swallowing muscles flickered in jaws and necks. Had I touched a shoulder and asked for the time, there would have been snarling, a flash of teeth.

What's New

MY MOTHER said, "So? What's new?" I said, "Something happened." She said, "I knew it. I had a feeling. I could tell. Why did I ask? Sure, something happened. Why couldn't I sit still? Did I have to ask? I had a feeling. I knew, I knew. What happened?"

The Burglar

I DIALED. The burglar answered and said Ikstein wasn't home. I said tell him I called. The burglar laughed. I said, "What's funny?" The burglar said, "This is a coincidence. When you called I was reading a passage in Ikstein's diary which is about you." I said, "Tell me what it says." The burglar snorted, "Your request is compromising. Just hearing it is compromising." I said, "I'm in the apartment below Ikstein's. We can easily meet and have a little talk about my request. I'll bring something to drink. Do you like marijuana? I know where Ikstein hides his marijuana. I have money with me, also a TV set and a Japanese camera. It's no trouble for me to

carry everything up there. One trip." He said if I came upstairs he would kill me.

Like Irony

HE PRIED me open and disappeared inside, made me urinate,
defecate, and screech, then slapped my dossier shut, stuck it
in his cabinet, slammed drawer, swallowed key. "Well," he
said, "how have you been?" I said, "Actually, that's what I'm
here to find out." He said, "People have feelings. They do
their best. Some of us say things to people—such as you—in a
way that is like irony, but it isn't irony. It's good breeding,
manners, tact—we have delicate intentions." I apologized.
"So," he said, "tell me your plans." I said, "Now that I know?"
"That's right," he said, "I'm delighted that you aren't very
stupid."

One Thing

IKSTEIN played harpsichord music on the phonograph and
opened a bottle of wine. I said, "Let's be frank, Ikstein.
There's too much crap in this world." He said, "Sure." The
harpischord was raving ravished Bach. Windows were open.
The breeze smelled of reasons to live. I told him I didn't care
for love. Only women, only their bodies. Talk, dance, conversation—I could do it—but I cared about one thing only. When
it was finished, I had to go. Anyhow, I said, generally speaking, women can't stand themselves. Generally speaking, I
thought they were right. "How about you, Ikstein?" He made
a pleased mouth and said, "I love women, the way they look,
talk, dress, and think. I love their hips, necks, breasts, and ankles. But I hate cunts." He stamped the floor. I raised my
glass. He raised his. "To life," I said.

Male

SHE was asleep. I wondered if I ought to read a newspaper.
Nobody phoned. I wanted to run around the block until I

dropped dead, but I was afraid of the muggers. I picked up the phone, dialed Ikstein, decided to hang up, but he answered: "This is Ikstein." I said, "Can I come up?" He said nothing. I said, "Ikstein, it's very late, but I can hear your TV." He said, "When I turn it off, I'll throw you out." I grabbed my ciga- rettes. His door was open. He didn't say hello. We watched a movie, drank beer, smoked. Side by side, hissing gases, insular and simpatico. It was male. I farted. He scratched his scalp, belched, tipped back in his chair with his legs forked out. His bathrobe fell apart, showing the vascular stump. It became a shivering mushroom, then a moon tree waving in the milky flicker. He said, "Well, look who wants to watch the movie." I said, "Hang a shoe on it." He refolded his robe and flicked off the TV. "If you decide to come out," he said, "let me be the first to know. Now go away." I went downstairs, sat on the bed, and put my hand on her belly. She whimpered, belly falling under my palm. She was asleep. I felt like a crazy man.

Dixie

RICHARD IKSTEIN was printed on his mailbox. His nighttime visitors called him "Dixie." In every accent, American and foreign, sometimes laughing, sometimes grim. When he fell our ceiling shuddered. Flakes of paint drifted down onto our bed. She hugged me and tried to make conversation: "They're the last romantics." He was pleading for help. "If you like ro- mance so much," I said, "why don't you become a whore." I twisted away, snapped on the radio, found a voice, and made it loud enough to interfere with his pleading. We couldn't hear his words, only sobs and whimpers. By the time he stopped falling, our bed was gritty with paint and plaster dust. We were too tired to get up and slap the sheets clean. In the morning I saw blood on our pillows. "It's on your face too," she said. "You slept on your back." I was for liberation of every kind, but I dressed in silent, tight-ass fury and ran up- stairs. "Look at my face, Ikstein," I shouted, banging at his door. It opened. The police were dragging him to a stretcher. I showed them my stained ceiling and bloody pillows. Obvious, but I had to explain. I told them about Ikstein's visitors, how he pleaded and sobbed. The police took notes. She cried when they left. She cried all morning. "The state is the greatest human achievement," I said. "Hegel is right. The state is the only human achievement." She said, "If you like the state so much, why don't you become a cop."

Crabs

MY MOTHER didn't mention the way things looked and said there was going to be a bar mitzvah. If I came to it, the relatives "could see" and I could meet her old friends from Miami. Their daughter was a college graduate, beautiful, money up the sunny gazoo. Moreover, it was a double-rabbi affair, one for the Hebrew, one for the English. "Very classy," she said. I had been to such affairs. A paragraph of Hebrew is followed by a paragraph of English. The Hebrew sounds like an interruption. Like jungle talk. I hated the organ music, the hidden choirs, the opulent halls. Besides, I had the crabs. I wasn't in the mood for a Miami bitch who probably had gonorrhea. I said, "No." She said, "Where are your values?"

Smile

IN MEMORIAM I recalled his smile, speedy and horizontal, the corners fleeing one another as if to meet in the back of his head. It suggested pain, great difficulties, failure, gleaming life rot. A smile of "Nevertheless." Sometimes we met on the stairs. He'd smile, yet seem to want to dash the other way, slide into the wall, creep by with no hello. But he smiled. "Nevertheless," he smiled. I would try to seem calm, innocuous, nearly dead. That made him more nevertheless. I would tell him something unfortunate about myself—how I'd overdrawn my checking account, lost my wallet, discovered a boil on my balls—and I would laugh at his self-consciously self-conscious, funny remarks. He nodded gratefully, but he didn't believe I thought he was funny. He didn't believe he was funny. I thought about the murder of complex persons. I thought about his smile, bleeding, beaten to death.

Right Number

A GIRL lived in the apartment below. We became friends. I'd go there any time, early or late. She opened the door and didn't turn on the light. I undressed in darkness, slid in beside her, made a spoon, and she slid into my spoon. She had no work, nothing she had to do, no one expected her to be any place. Money came to her in the mail. She had a body like Goya's whore and a Botticelli face. She was tall, pale, blond, and wavy. I knocked, she let me in. No questions. We talked fast and moved about from bed to chairs to floor. Sometimes I'd pinch her thigh. Once she knocked a coffee cup into my lap. Finally we had sexual intercourse. We made a lot of jokes and she was on her back. I tried to be gentle. She thrashed in a complimentary way and moaned. Later she said to guess how many men she'd had. I said ten. She said fifteen. How does that sound? It sounds more depraved than I feel. After the Turk, she understood the Ottoman Empire. She said people thought of her as manic-depressive. But it wasn't true. She had good reasons for what she feels. Germans are friskier than you'd imagine. The right number is seven or eight. It sounds like a lot, yet it isn't depraved. It's believable. A girl shouldn't say seven or eight, then describe twenty. What if I said more than ten, less than twenty? How does that sound? Six came in one weekend. They count as one. How old do you think I am? Twenty-eight? I'm only twenty-two. With A, it is a way of making something out of nothing. With B, it is a form of conversation. With C, it is letting him believe something about himself. With D, it is a mistake. I've had seventeen. People think I've had fifty or a hundred. Do I want fifty or a hundred? No. I want twenty-five. Twenty-five or thirty. Do you remember what my face is like? I think it looks sluttish. Indians are the nicest. Blacks don't talk to you afterward. I was raped when I was a kid. Then I rode my bicycle around and around the block and talked to myself in a loud voice. All my life I've tried to keep things from getting out of hand, but I get out of hand. Nothing works. Nothing works. I like you very very much, I said, let's try again. I was gentle. She thrashed in a complimentary way and moaned. The next day she knocked at my door, wearing a handsome gray wool suit and high heels. Her hair had been washed and combed into a style. She looked neat, intelligent, and extremely beautiful. She said she was going to a job interview to have something to do. We hugged for good luck and kissed. Somehow she was on her back. We had sexual intercourse. I wasn't gentle. She whipped in the pelvis and screamed murder. Me too.

Animals

HER SKIN was made of animals, exceedingly tiny, compressed like a billion paps in a breathing sponge. Caressing her, my palm was caressed by the smooth resilient motion in her skin. Awake or asleep, angry, bored, loving, made no difference. Her skin was superior to attitudes or words. It implied the most beautiful girl. And the core of my pleasure ached for her, the one she implied.

God

MY MOTHER SAID, "What's new?" I said, "Nothing." She said, "What? You can tell me. Tell me what's new." I said, "Something happened." She said, "I had a feeling. I could tell. What happened?" I said, "Nothing happened." She said, "Thank God."

His Certain Way

IKSTEIN had a certain way of picking up a spoon, asking for the time, getting down the street from here to there. He would pick up his spoon in his certain way, stick it in the soup, lift it to his mouth, stop, then whisper, "Eat, eat, little Ikily." Everything he did was in his certain way. He made an impression of making an impression. I remembered it. I remembered Ikstein. It was no different to remember than to see the living Ikstein, in his certain little ways. For me, he never died. He lived where he always lived, in my impression of Ikstein. I could bring him back any time, essentially, for me. "Eat, eat, little Ikily." When he did his work—he was a book and movie reviewer—he always made himself a "nice" bowl of soup. It sat beside his typewriter. He typed a sentence, stopped, said, "Now I'll have a tasty sip of soup." Essentially, for me, Ikstein had no other life. If he had in fact another life, it was never available for me. I could not pretend to regret it was no longer available for him. "Oh, poor Ikstein" would mean "Oh, poor me, what I have lost. The sights and sound of Ikstein." I lost nothing. His loss, I couldn't appreciate. Neither could he. So I remembered Ikstein and felt no sorrow. I mentioned somebody who had married for the second time. "His second wife looks like the first," I said. "As if he were pursuing something." In his certain way, Ikstein said, "Or as if it were pursuing him." Thus, even his mind lived. I said, "My intention was modest, a bit of chitchat, a germ of sense. I wasn't hoping, when I have a headache and feel sick and unable to think, to illuminate the depths. Must you be such a prick, Ikstein?"

Mournful Girls

Busy naked heels, a rush of silky things, elastic snaps, clicks, a rattle of beads, hangers clinking, humming, her quick consistent breathing as the mattress dipped. Lips touched mine. Paper cracked flat near my head. Wooden heel shafts knocked in the hallway. I opened my eyes. A ten-dollar bill lay on the pillow. I got up, dressed, stuck the bill in my pocket, went to the apartment below, and asked, "Do you want anything?"

She said no. She lay on the bed. On the way back I picked up her mail. "Some letters," I said and dropped them beside her. She lay on the bed, skirt twisted about her hips and belly, blouse open, bra unhooked to ease the spill. Her blanket was smooth. I whispered, "Mona, Melanie, Mildred, Sarah, Nora, Dora, Sadie." She whispered, "Mournful girls." I lost the beginning of the next sentence before I heard the end. She heard as much, glanced at me, quit talking. We undressed. I tugged her off the bed to the mirror. I looked at her. She looked at me. Our arms slipped around them. All had sexual intercourse. I was upstairs when she returned from work. She asked, "Why didn't you go to the grocery?" I said, "It will take five minutes," and dashed out. The street was dark, figures appeared and jerked by. In the grocery I couldn't find the ten-dollar bill. It wasn't in my pockets. It wasn't on the floor. I ran back along the street, neck bent like a dog's, inspecting the flux of cigarette butts, candy wrappers, spittle plops, dog piss, beer cans, broken glass, granular pavement—then remembered—and ran upstairs quietly. She lay on the bed. The milk and meat were warm, butter loose and greasy. Everything except the cream cheese was in the bag beside her bed. She lay on the bed, gnawing cream cheese through the foil. "You should have put the bag in the refrigerator," I said. She gnawed. "It would have been simple to put the bag in the refrigerator," I said. "Shut your hole," she said. I shoved her hand. Cream cheese smeared her nostrils. She lay in the bed, slack, still, breathing through her mouth, as if she wouldn't cry and was not crying. I took the bag of groceries and went upstairs. The table was set. She was sweeping the kitchen floor, crying.

The Hand

I smacked my little boy. My anger was powerful. Like justice. Then I discovered no feeling in the hand. I said, "Listen,

I want to explain the complexities to you." I spoke with seriousness and care, particularly of fathers. He asked, when I finished, if I wanted him to forgive me. I said yes. He said no. Like trumps.

All Right

"I DON'T MIND variations," she said, "but this feels wrong." I said, "It feels all right to me." She said, "To you, wrong is right." I said, "I didn't say right, I said all right." "Big difference," she said. I said, "Yes, I'm critical. My mind never stops. To me almost everything is always wrong. My standard is pleasure. To me, this is all right." She said, "To me it stinks." I said, "What do you like?" She said, "Like I don't like. I'm not interested in being superior to my sensations. I won't live long enough for all right."

Ma

I SAID, "Ma, do you know what happened?" She said, "Oh, my God."

Naked

UGLY OR PLAIN she would have had fewer difficulties cultivating an attractive personality or restricting sex to cortex, but she was so nearly physically perfect as to appear, more than anything, not perfect. Not ugly, not plain, then strikingly not perfect made her also not handsome and not at all sentimentally appealing. In brief, what she was she wasn't, a quality salient in adumbration, unpossessed. She lived a bad metaphor, like the Devil, unable to assimilate paradox to personal life, being no artist and not a religious person, suffering spasms of self-loathing in the lonely, moral night. Finally, she smacked a Coke bottle on the rim of the bathtub, mutilated her wrist, then phoned the cops. So clumsy, yet her dinner parties were splendid, prepared at unbelievable speed. She hated to cook. Chewing gum, cigarettes, candy, drugs, alcohol, and taxicabs took her from Monday to Friday. The ambulance attendant—big ironical black man in baggy white trousers—flipped open the medicine cabinet and yelled, "See those barbiturates. You didn't have to make a mess." He dragged her out of the tub by the hair, naked, bleeding. She considered all that impressive, but if I responded to her with a look or tone, she detected my feelings before I did and made them manifest, like a trout slapped out of water by a bear. "You admire my eyes? How about my ass?" I thrilled to her acuity. But exactly then she'd become a stupid girl loosening into sexual mood, and then, then, if I touched her she offered total sprawl, whimpering, "Call me dirty names." I tried to think of her as a homosexual person, not a faggot. She begged me to wear her underpants and walk on my knees. When I demurred, she pissed on the sheets. "You don't love me," she said. "What a waste getting involved with you." Always playing with her flashy, raglike scar, sliding it along the tendons like a watchband.

Better

I PHONED and said, "I feel good, even wonderful. Everything is great. It's been this way for months and it's getting better. Better, better, better. How are you, Ma?" She said, "Me?" I said, "Yes, how are you?" "Me?" she said. "Don't make me laugh."

—1975

98

Manikin

AT THE UNIVERSITY she met a Turk who studied physics and spoke foreigner's English that in every turn expressed the unnatural desire to seize idiom and make it speak just for himself. He worked nights as a waiter, summers on construction gangs, and shot pool and played bridge with fraternity boys in order to make small change, and did whatever else he could to protect and supplement his university scholarship, living a mile from campus in a room without sink or closet or decent heating and stealing most of the food he ate, and when the University Hotel was robbed it was the Turk who had done it, an act of such speed the night porter couldn't say when it happened or who rushed in from the street to bludgeon him so murderously he took it in a personal way. On weekends the Turk tutored mediocrities in mathematics and French...

He picked her up at her dormitory, took her to a movie, and later, in his borrowed Chevrolet, drove her into the countryside and with heavy, crocodilean sentences communicated his agony amid the alien corn. She attended with quick, encouraging little nods and stared as if each word crept past her eyes and she felt power gathering in their difficult motion as he leaned toward her and with lips still laboring words made indelible sense, raping her, forcing her to variations of what she never heard of though she was a great reader of avantgarde novels and philosophical commentaries on the modern predicament...

In the cracking, desiccated leather of the Chevrolet she was susceptible to a distinction between life and sensibility, and dropped, like Leda by the swan, squirming, arching, so as not to be touched again, inadvertently, as he poked behind the cushions for the ignition key. She discovered it pulling up her pants and, because it required intelligent speech inconsistent

99

with her moaning, couldn't bring it to his attention; nor would she squat, winding about in her privates, though she hated to see him waste time bunched up twisting wires under the dashboard.

Despite her wild compulsion to talk and despite the frightened, ravenous curiosity of her dormitory clique whom she awakened by sobbing over their beds, Melanie wasn't able to say clearly what finished happening half an hour ago. She remembered the Turk suddenly abandoned English and raved at her in furious Turkish, and she told them about that and about the obscene tattoo flashing on his chest when she ripped his shirt open, and that he stopped the car on a country road and there was a tall hedge, maples, sycamores, and a railroad track nearby, and a train was passing, passing, and passing, and beyond it, her moans, and later an animal trotting quickly on the gravel, and then, with no discontinuity, the motor starting its cough and retch and a cigarette waving at her mouth already lighted as if the worst were over and someone had started thinking of her in another way.

The lights of the university town appeared and she smoked the cigarette as the car went down among them through empty streets, through the residential area of the ethical, economic community and twisted into the main street passing store after store. She saw an armless, naked manikin and felt like that, or like a thalidomide baby, all torso and short-circuited, and then they were into the streets around campus, narrow and shaky with trees, and neither of them said a word as he shifted gears, speeding and slowing and working the car through a passage irregular and yet steady, and enclosed within a greater passage as tangible as the internal arcs of their skulls. At the dormitory he stopped the car. She got out running.

Quigley, Berkowitz, and Sax could tell that Melanie Green had been assaulted with insane and exotic cruelty: there were fingerprints on her cheeks the color of tea stains and her stockings hung about her ankles like Hamlet's when he exposed himself to Ophelia and called her a whore. So they sucked cigarettes and urged her to phone the Dean of Women, the police, and the immigration authorities, as if disseminating the story among representatives of order would qualify it toward annihilation or render it accessible to a punitive response consistent with national foreign policy. Though none of them saw positive value in Melanie's experience it was true, nevertheless, in no future conversation would she complain about being nineteen and not yet discovered by the right man, as it happened, to rape with. Given her face and legs, that had always seemed sick, irritating crap, and in the pits of their minds where there were neither words nor ideas but only raging morality, they took the Turk as poetic justice, fatal male, and measure for measure. Especially since he lived now in those pits vis-à-vis Melanie's father, a bearded rabbi with tear bags. "What if your father knew?" asked Quigley, making a gesture of anxious speculation, slender hands turned out flat, palms up, like a Balinese dancer. Melanie felt annoyed, but at least Quigley was there, sticking out her hands, and could be relied on always to be symbolic of whatever she imagined the situation required.

She didn't tell the rabbi, the Dean of Women, police, or immigration authorities, and didn't tell Harry Stone, her fiancé, with whom she had never had all-the-way sexual intercourse because he feared it might destroy the rhythm of his graduate work in Classics. But once, during Christmas vacation, she flew east to visit him and while standing on a stairway in Cambridge, after dinner and cognac, he let her masturbate him and then lay in bed beside her, brooding, saying little except, "I feel like Seymour," and she answering, "I'm sorry." Quigley, Berkowitz, and Sax called him "Harry the fairy," but never in the presence of Melanie who read them his letters, brilliantly exquisite and full of ruthless wit directed at everything, and the girls screamed and could hardly wait till he got his degree and laid her. "It'll be made of porcelain," said Sax, and Melanie couldn't refute the proposition (though the girls always told her everything they did with their boy-friends and she owed them the masturbation story) because they were too hot for physiology and wouldn't listen to the whole story, wouldn't hear its tone or any of its music. They were critical, sophisticated girls and didn't dig mood, didn't savor things. They were too fast, too eager to get the point.

She didn't tell the rabbi or any other authority about the rape, and wouldn't dream of telling Harry Stone because he tended to become irrationally jealous and like homosexual Othello would assume she had gone out with armies of men aside from the Turk, which wasn't true. The Turk had been a casual decision, the only one of its kind, determined by bore-dom with classes and dateless weekends, and partly by a long-distance phone call to Harry Stone in the middle of the night when she needed his voice and he expressed irritation at hav-ing been disturbed while translating a difficult passage of Thucydides for a footnote in his dissertation. Furthermore the Turk was interesting looking, black eyes, a perfect white bite of teeth between a biggish nose and a cleft chin, and be-cause he was pathetic in his tortuous English going out with him seemed merely an act of charity indifferently performed and it was confirmed as such when he arrived in the old Chev-rolet and suggested a cowboy movie. He held the door open for her, which she could never expect Harry to do, and he tried to talk to her. To her, she felt—though it was clear that his effort to talk depended very much on her effort to listen.

She went to parties on the two weekends following the rape and sat in darkened rooms while a hashish pipe went around and said things too deep for syntax and giggled hy-sterically, and in the intimate delirium of faces and darkness asked how one might get in touch with an abortionist if, per chance, one needed one. She didn't talk about the rape but remembered the Turk had held her chin and she felt guilty but resistless and saw that his eyes didn't focus and that, more than anything, lingered in her nerves, like birds screaming and inconsummate. She asked her clique about the signs of pregnancy, then asked herself if she weren't peeing more than usual. It seemed to spear down very hot and hard and longer than before, but she ascribed it to sphincters loosened upon the violent dissolution of the veil between vaginal post and lintel. When she asked the girls about an abortionist they laughed maniacally at the idea that any of them might know such a person, but, one at a time, appeared in her room to whisper names and telephone numbers and tell her about the different techniques and the anesthetic she might expect if the man were considerate or brave enough to give her one. "They're afraid of the cops," said Sax, a tough number from Chicago who had been knocked up twice in her freshman year. "They want you out of the office as soon as possible."

Harry surprised her by coming to town during his intersession break and she was so glad to see him she trembled. She introduced him to her house mother and her clique and he ate dinner with her in the dormitory the first night. The next day he went to classes with her and that evening they ate in the best restaurant in town, which wasn't nearly as good as some Harry knew in the East but it was pretty good, and then they walked in the Midwestern twilight, watching swallows, listening to night hawks whistle, and she felt an accumulation of sympathy in the minutes and the hours that became an urge, a possibility, and then a strong need to tell him, but she chatted mainly about her clique and said, "Quigley has funny nipples and Berkowitz would have a wonderful figure except for her thighs, which have no character. I love Sax's figure. It's like a skinny boy's." Harry made an indifferent face and shrugged in his tweeds, but quick frowns twitched after the facts and she went on, encouraged thus, going on, to go on and on. In his hotel room they had necking and writhing, then lay together breathless, tight, indeterminate, until he began talking about his dissertation. "A revolution in scholarship. The vitiation of many traditional assumptions. They say I write uncommonly well." She told him about the rape. He sat up with words about the impossibility of confidence, the betrayal of expecta-tions, the end of things. He was amazed, he said, the world didn't break and the sky fall down. As far as he was con-cerned the ceremony of innocence was drowned. While he packed she rubbed her knees and stared at him. He noticed her staring and said, "I don't like you."

WANDA CHUNG was always in flight around corners, down hallways, up stairs, into bathrooms, and never spoke to people unless obliged to do so and then with fleeting, terrified smiles and her eyes somewhere else. She appeared at no teas or dances, received no calls and no boys at the reception desk, and Melanie and her clique gradually came to think of her as the most interesting girl in the dormitory. One afternoon after classes they decided to go to her room and introduce themselves. She wasn't in so they entered the room and while waiting for her casually examined her closet, which was packed with dresses and coats carrying the labels of good stores in San Francisco. Under her bed there were boxes of new blouses and sweaters, and they discovered her desk drawers were crammed with candy and empty candy wrap-pers. They left her room, never returned, and never again made any effort to introduce themselves to her, but Wanda, who for months had harbored a secret yearning to meet Melanie, decided, the day after Harry Stone left town, to go to Melanie's room and present herself: "I am Wanda Chung. I live downstairs. I found this fountain pen. Could it be yours?"

She bought a fountain pen and went to Melanie's room and an instant after she knocked at the door she forgot her little speech and her desire to meet Melanie. The door gave way at the vague touch of her knuckles and started opening as if Wanda herself had taken the knob and turned it with the intention of getting into the room and stealing something, which is how she saw it, standing there as the door unbelievably, remorselessly, opened, sucking all motion and feeling out of her limbs and making her more and more thief in the possible eyes of anyone coming along. And then, into her dumb rigidity, swayed naked feet like bell clappers. She saw Melanie Green hanging by the neck, her pelvis twitching. Wanda dashed to the stairs, down to her room, and locked herself inside. She ate candy until she puked in her lap and fell asleep.

When the Turk read about the suicide he said in a slow, sick voice, "She loved me." He got drunk and stumbled through the streets looking for a fight, but bumping strangers and firing clams of spit at their feet wasn't sufficiently provocative, given his debauched and fiercely miserable appearance, to get himself punched or cursed or even shoved a little. He ended the night in a scrubby field tearing at an oak tree with his fingernails, rolling in its roots, hammering grass, cursing the sources of things until, in a shy, gentle way, Melanie drifted up out of the dew. He refused to acknowledge her presence but then couldn't tolerate being looked at in silence and yelled at her in furious Turkish. She came closer. He seized her in his arms and they rolled together in the grass until he found himself screaming through his teeth because, however much of himself he lavished on her, she was dead.

—1969

Reflections of a Wild Kid

MANDELL asked if she had ever been celebrated.

"Celebrated?"

"I mean your body, has your body ever been celebrated?" Then, as if to refine the question: "I mean, like, has your body, like, been celebrated?"

"My body has never been celebrated."

She laughed politely. A laugh qualified by her sense of Liebowitz in the bedroom. She was polite to both of them and good to neither. Certainly not to Liebowitz, who, after all, wanted Mandell out of the apartment. Did she care what he wanted? He was her past, a whimsical recrudescence, trapped in her bedroom. He'd waited in there for an hour. He could wait another hour. As far as she knew, he had cigarettes. But, in that hour, as he smoked his cigarettes, his bladder had begun to feel like a cantaloupe. He strained to lift the window. The more he strained, the more he felt his cantaloupe.

"I mean really celebrated," said Mandell, as if she'd answered nothing.

Perhaps, somehow, she urged Mandell to go on. Perhaps she wanted Liebowitz to hear Mandell's witty questions, his lovemaking. Liebowitz didn't care what she wanted. His last cigarette had been smoked. He wanted to piss. He drew the point of a nail file down the sides of the window, trailing a thin peel, a tiny scream in the paint. Again he strained to lift the window. It wouldn't budge. At that moment he noticed wall-to-wall carpeting. Why did he notice? Because he could not piss on it. "Amazing," he thought, "how we perceive the world. Stand on a mountain and you think it's remarkable that you can't jump off."

"My body," said Mandell, "has been celebrated."

Had that been his object all along? Liebowitz wondered why Mandell hadn't been more direct, ripping off his shirt, flashing nipples in her face: "Let's celebrate." She was going to marry a feeb. But that wasn't Liebowitz's business. He had to piss. He had no other business.

"I mean, you know, like my body, like, has been celebrated," said Mandell, again refining his idea. Despite his pain, it was impossible for Liebowitz not to listen—the sniveling syntax, the whining diction—he tasted every phrase. In that hour, as increasingly he had to piss, he came to know Mandell, through the wall, palpably to know him. Some smell, some look, even something about the way he combed his hair, reached Liebowitz through the wall. Bad blood, thought Liebowitz.

He remembered Nietzsche's autobiographical remark: "I once sensed the proximity of a herd of cows ... merely because milder and more philanthropic thoughts came back to me." How true. Thoughts can be affected by invisible animals. Liebowitz had never even seen Mandell. As for Joyce, a shoe lying on its side, in the middle of her carpet—scuffed, bent, softened by the stride of her uncelebrated body—suffused the bedroom with her presence, the walking foot, strong well-shaped ankle, peasant hips rocking with motive power, elegant neck, fleshy boneless Semitic face. A warm receptive face until she spoke. Then she had personality. That made her seem taller, slightly forbidding, even robust. She was robust—heavy bones, big head, dense yellow-brown hair—and her voice, a flying bird of personality. Years had passed. Seeing the hair again and Joyce still fallow beneath it saddened Liebowitz. But here was Mandell. She had time.

"HAS IT BEEN five years?" asked Liebowitz, figuring seven. "You sound wonderful, Joyce." She said he sounded "good." He regretted "wonderful," but noticed no other reserve in her voice, and just as he remembered, she seemed still to love the telephone, coming at him right through the machine, much the thing, no later than this minute. When his other phone

rang he didn't reach for it, thus letting her hear and understand how complete was his attention. She understood. She
went on directly about some restaurant, insisting let's eat
there. He didn't even consider not. She'd said, almost immediately, she was getting married to Mandell, a professor.

Did Liebowitz feel jealousy? He didn't ask professor of
what or where does he teach. Perhaps he felt jealousy; but,
listening to her and nodding compliments at the wall, he listened less to what she said than to how she spoke in echoes.
Not of former times, but approximately these things, in approximately the same way, he felt, had been said in grand
rooms, by wonderful people. Joyce brought him the authority
of echoes. And she delivered herself, too, a hundred thirty-
five pounds of shank and dazzle, even in her questions: "Have
you seen...? "Have you heard...?" About plays, movies, restaurants, Jacqueline Kennedy. Nothing about his wife, child,
job. Was she indifferent? embarrassed? hostile? In any case, he
liked her impetuosity; she poked, checked his senses. He liked
her. Joyce Wolf, on the telephone. He remembered that cab-
bies and waiters liked her. She could make fast personal jokes
with policemen and bellhops. She tipped big. A hundred no-
bodies knew her name, her style. Always en passant, very
much here and not here at all. He liked her tremendously, he
felt revived. Not reliving a memory, but right now, on the telephone, living again a moment of his former life. For the first
time, as it were, that he didn't have to live it. She has magic,
he thought; art. Merely in her voice, she was an event. She
called him back, through time, to herself. Despite his grip on
the phone, knees under the desk, feet on the floor, he felt like
a man slipping from a height, deliciously. He said he would
meet her uptown in forty minutes. Did he once live this way?
Liebowitz shook his head; smirked. He was a wild kid once.

On his desk lay a manuscript that had to be edited, and a
contract he had to work on. There was also an appointment
with an author ... but, in the toilet with electric shaver and

toothbrush, Liebowitz purged his face of the working day and, shortly thereafter, walked into a chic Hungarian restaurant on the Upper East Side. She arrived twenty minutes later; late; but in a black sleeveless dress. Very smart. It gave her a look that seized the day, the feeling and idea of it. She hadn't just come to meet him; she described their moment and meaning in a garment. She appeared. Late; but who, granted such knowledge, could complain? Liebowitz felt flattered and grateful. He took her hands. She squeezed his hands. He kissed her cheek. "Joyce." The hair, white smile, hips—he remembered, he looked, looked. "It was good of you to call me." He looked at her. He looked into his head. She was there, too, this minute's Joyce Wolf who once got them to the front of lines, to seats when the show was sold out, to tables, tables near windows, to parties. Sold out, you say? At the box office, in her name, two tickets were waiting. Then Liebowitz remembered, once, for a ballet, she had failed to do better than standing room. He hadn't wanted to go. He certainly hadn't wanted to stand. Neither had she. But tickets had been sold out to this ballet. Thousands wanted to go. Liebowitz remembered how she began making phone calls, scratching at the numbers till her fingernail tore. That evening, pelvises pressed to a velvet rope, they stood amid hundreds of ballet lovers jammed into a narrow aisle. The effluvia of alimentary canals hung about their heads. Blindfolded, required to guess, Liebowitz would have said they were in a delicatessen. Lights dimmed. There was a thrilling hush. Joyce whispered, "How in God's name can anyone live outside New York?" She nudged him and pointed at a figure seated in the audience. Liebowitz looked, thrusting his head forward to show appreciation of her excitement, her talent for recognizing anyone in New York in almost total darkness. "See! See!" Liebowitz nodded greedily. His soul poured toward a glint of skull floating amid a thousand skulls. He begged, "Who? Who is it?" He wasn't sure that he looked at the correct glint of skull, yet he felt on the verge of extraordinary illumination. Then a voice wailed into his back, "I can't see." Liebowitz twisted about, glanced down. A short lady, staring up at him, pleaded with her whole face. "I can't see." He twisted forward and said, "Move a little, Joyce. Let her up against the rope." Joyce whispered, "This is the jungle, schmuck. Tell her to grow another head." He was impressed. During the ballet he stood with the velvet rope in his fists, the woman's face between his shoulder blades, and now, as he went uptown in the cab, his mouth was so dry he couldn't smoke. After all these years, still impressed. Joyce got them tickets. She knew. She got. Him, for example—virtually a bum in those days, but nice looking, moody, a complement to her, he supposed. Perhaps a girl with so much needed someone like him—a misery. Not that she was without misery. She worked as a private secretary to an investment broker, a shrewd, ugly Russian with a hunchback and a limp. "Hey, collich girl, make me a phone call." After work she used to meet Liebowitz, hunching, dragging a foot, and she would shout, "Hey collich. Hey, collich girl, kiss my ass." They'd laugh with relief and malice; but sometimes she met Liebowitz in tears. Once the Russian even hit her. "In the Longchamps restaurant, during lunch hour," she said. "He knocked me on the floor in front of all those people eating lunch." Liebowitz remembered her screaming at him: "Even if there had been a reason." He stopped trying to justify the horror. It got to him. "Gratuitous sadism!" Liebowitz raged. He'd go next morning and punch the Russian in the mouth. The next morning, in Italian sunglasses, Joyce left for the office. Alone. Five foot seven, she walked seven foot five, a Jewish girl passing for Jewish in tough financial circles. Liebowitz smoked a cigarette, punched his hand. Liebowitz remembered:

The sunglasses—tough, tragic, fantastically clever—looked terrific. She knew what to wear, precisely the item that said it. Those sunglasses were twenty punches in the mouth. She'd wear them all day, even at the typewriter. The Russian would feel, between himself and the college girl, an immensity. He'd know what he was, compared to her in those black, estranging glasses. Liebowitz felt an intellectual pang; his reflections had gone schmuckway. Beginning again:

Joyce made two hundred and fifty dollars a week. With insults and slaps, the Russian gave tips on the market. The year she lived with Liebowitz, Joyce made more than a hundred thousand dollars. Liebowitz, then a salesman in a shoe store, made eighty dollars a week hunkering over corns. He had rotten moods, no tips on anything; he had a lapsed candidacy for the Ph.D. in philosophy and a girl with access to the pleasures of Manhattan. Her chief pleasure—moody Liebowitz. In truth, he never hated the Russian. He pitied Joyce; for a hundred thousand dollars she ate shit. The sunglasses symbolized shame. Liebowitz remembered:

Twenty-four years old, a virgin when she met Liebowitz, who took her on their first date. "I don't know how it happened," she said. "Two minutes ago I had some idea of myself." Liebowitz replied, "Normal." She'd been surprised, overwhelmed by his intensity. She'd never met a man so hungry. Now he was cool, like a hoodlum. "Where's your shower?" He wondered if he hadn't been worse to her than the Russian. Hidden in the bedroom, crouched in pain, Liebowitz made big eyes and held out his hands, palms up, like a man begging for apples. He'd had certain needs. She'd been good to him—the tickets, the parties, and calling now to announce her forthcoming marriage, invite him to dinner. It was touching. Liebowitz had to piss. He remembered that, walking into the restaurant, he'd had an erection. Perhaps that explained the past; also the present, running to meet her as if today were yesterday. Then they strolled in the park. Then they went to her apartment for a drink. Life is mystery, thought Liebowitz. He wondered if he dared, after all these years, after she'd just told him she was getting married, put his hand

on her knee; her thigh; under the black dress where time, surrendering to truth, ceased to be itself. The doorbell.

"Don't answer," said Liebowitz.

"Maybe it's someone else," she said, her voice as frightened as his.

It wasn't somebody else. Liebowitz opted for the bedroom.
Then he was tearing at the window, wild to piss.

"Didn't you say you were going to work this evening?"

"Did I say that?"

Mandell had had a whimsy impulse. Here he was, body
freak, father of Joyce's unborn children. She could have done
better, thought Liebowitz. Consider himself, Liebowitz. But
seven years had passed since he'd put his hand on her thigh. A
woman begins to feel desperate. Still—Joyce Wolf, her style,
her hips—she could have done better than Mandell, thought
Liebowitz, despite her conviction—her boast—that Mandell
wasn't just any professor of rhetoric and communication art.
"He loves teaching—speech, creative writing, anything—and
every summer at Fire Island he writes a novel of ideas. None
are published yet, but he doesn't care about publication. People say his novels are very good. I couldn't say, but he talks
about his writing all the time. He really cares."

Liebowitz could see Mandell curled over his typewriter.
Forehead presses the keys. Sweat fills his bathing-suit jock.
It's summertime on Fire Island. Mandell is having an idea to
stick in one of his novels. "You know, of course, my firm only
does textbooks." Joyce said she knew, yet looked surprised,
changed the subject. Liebowitz felt ashamed. Of course she
knew. Why had he been crude? Did he suppose that she hadn't
really wanted to telephone him, that she was using him as a
source of tickets? What difference? He had an erection, a purpose; she had Mandell, novelist of ideas, celebrated for his
body. "He is terribly jealous of you," she said. "It was long
ago, I was a kid, and he wasn't even in the picture. But he's
jealous. He's the kind who wonders about a girl's former

lovers. Not that he's weird or anything, just social. He's terrific in bed. I'll bet you two could be friends."

"Does he know I'm seeing you tonight?" Liebowitz's hand
had ached for her knee. Her voice had begun to cause brain
damage and had to be stopped. It was getting late, there was
nothing more to say. She laughed again. Marvelous sound,
thought Liebowitz, almost like laughter. He was nearly convinced now that she deserved Mandell. But why didn't she
send him away or suggest they go out? Was it because Liebowitz's firm didn't do novels? Was he supposed to listen?
burn with jealousy? He burned to piss.

"Is something wrong, Joycie?"

Mandell didn't understand. Did she seem slightly cool, too
polite? Did she laugh too much?

"I wanted to talk to you about my writing, but really,
Joycie, is something, like, wrong?"

"What do you mean? There's nothing wrong. I just thought
you'd be working tonight."

Mandell was embarrassed, a little hurt, unable to leave. Of
course. How could he leave with her behaving that polite
way? Mandell was just as trapped as Liebowitz, who, bent
and drooling, gaped at a shoe, a dressing table, combs, brushes, cosmetics, a roll of insulation tape ... and, before he knew
what he had in mind, Liebowitz seized the tape. He laid two
strips, in an X, across a windowpane, punched the nail file
into the heart of the X, and gently pulled away the tape with
sections of broken glass. Like Robinson Crusoe. Trapped, iso-
lated—yet he could make himself comfortable. Liebowitz
felt proud. Mainly, he felt searing release. Liebowitz pissed.

Through the hole in the windowpane, across an echoing
air shaft, a long shining line—burning, arcing, resonant—as
he listened to Mandell. "I have a friend who says my novels
are like writing, but not real writing, you get it?" Liebowitz
shook his head, thinking, "Some friend," as he splashed brick
wall and a window on the other side of the air shaft, and

114

though he heard yelling, heard nothing relevant to Robinson Crusoe, and though he saw a man's face, continued pissing on that face, yelling from the window, on the other side of the air shaft.

"A good neighborhood," thought Liebowitz. "The police won't take long." He wondered what to say, how to say it, and zipped up hurriedly. In the dressing-table mirror he saw another face, his own, bloated by pressure, trying not to cry. "According to that face," he thought, "a life is at stake." His life was at stake and he couldn't grab a cab. Mandell was still there, whining about his writing. Joyce couldn't interrupt and say go home. Writers are touchy. He might get mad and call off the marriage. Liebowitz had no choice but to prepare a statement. "My name, officers, is Liebowitz." Thus he planned to begin. Not brilliant. Appropriate. He'd chuckle in a jolly, personable way. A regular fellow, not a drunk or a maniac. Mandell was shrill and peevish: "Look here, look here. My name is Mandell. I'm a professor of rhetoric and communication art at a college. And a novelist. This is ironic, but it is only a matter of circumstances and I have no idea what it means."

A strange voice said, "Don't worry, Professor, we'll explain later."

Joyce said, "This is a silly mistake. I'm sure you chaps have a lot to do—"

Mandell cut in: "Take your hands off me. And you shut up, Joyce. I've had enough of this crap. Like, show me the lousy warrant or, like, get the hell out. No Nazi cops push me around. Joyce, call someone. I'm not without friends. Call someone."

The strange voice said, "Hold the creep."

With hatred Mandell was screaming, "No, no, don't come with me. I don't want you to come with me, you stupid bitch. Call someone. Get help." The hall door shut. The bedroom door opened. Joyce was staring at Liebowitz. "You hear what happened? How can you sit there and stare at me? I've never felt this way in my life. Look at you. Lepers could be screwing at your feet. Do you realize what happened?"

Liebowitz shrugged yes mixed a little with no.

"I see," she said. "I see. You're furious because you had to sit in here. What could I do? What could I say? You're furious as hell, aren't you?"

Liebowitz didn't answer. He felt a bitter strength in his position. Joyce began pinching her thighs to express suffering. Unable to deal with herself across the room from him, she came closer to where he sat on the bed. Liebowitz said, "The cops took the putz away." His tone revealed no anger and let her sit down beside him. "It's horrible. It's humiliating," she said. "They think he pissed out the window. He called me a stupid bitch." Liebowitz said, "You might be a stupid bitch, but you look as good to me now as years ago. In some ways, better." His hand was on her knee. It seemed to him a big hand, full of genius and power. He felt proud to consider how these qualities converged in himself. Joyce's mouth and eyes grew slow, as if the girl behind them had stopped jumping. She glanced at his hand. "I must make a phone call," she said softly, a little urgently, and started to rise. Liebowitz pressed down. She sat. "It wouldn't be right," she said, and then, imploringly, "Would you like to smoke a joint?"

"No."

She has middle-class habits, he thought.

"It wouldn't be right," she said, as if to remind him of something, not to insist on it. But what's right, what's wrong, to a genius? Liebowitz, forty years old, screwed her like a nineteen-year-old genius.

—1975

Mildred

MILDRED was at the mirror all morning, cutting and shaping her hair. Then, every hour or so, she came up to me with her head tipped like this, like that, cheeks sucked in, a shine licked across her lips. I said, "Very nice," and finally I said, "Very, very nice."

"I'm not pretty."

"Yes; you're pretty."

"I know I'm attractive in a way, but basically I'm ugly."

"Your hair is very nice."

"Basically, I hate my type. When I was little I used to wish my name were Terry. Do you like my hair?"

"Your hair is very nice."

"I think you're stupid looking."

"That's life."

"You're the only stupid-looking boyfriend I ever had. I've had stupid boyfriends, but none of them looked stupid. You look stupid."

"I like your looks."

"You're also incompetent, indifferent, a liar, a crook, and a coward."

"I like your looks."

"I was told that except for my nose my face is perfect. It's true."

"What's wrong with your nose?"

"I don't have to say it, Miller."

"What's wrong with it?"

"My nose, I've been told, is a millimeter too long. Isn't it?"

"I like your nose."

"Coward. I can forgive you for some things, but cowardice is unforgivable. And I'll get you for this, Miller. I'll make you cry."

"I like your legs."

"You're the only boyfriend I've ever had who was a coward. It's easy to like my legs."

"They're beautiful. I like both of them."

"Ha. Ha. What about my nose?"

"I'm crazy about your big nose."

"You dirty, fuck'n aardvark. What about yours, Miller? Tell me ..."

The phone rang.

"His master's voice," she said and snatched it away from me. "Me, this time. Hello." She smacked it down.

"What was that about?"

"A man."

"What did he say?"

"He asked how much I charged ... I don't care to talk about it."

"To what?"

"It was disgusting. I don't care to talk about it, understand. Answer the fuck'n phone yourself next time."

She dropped onto the bed. "Hideous."

"Did you recognize the voice?"

"I was humiliated."

"Tell me what he said."

"It must have been one of your stinking friends. I'm going to rip that phone out of the wall. Just hideous, hideous."

I lay down beside her.

"He asked how much I charged to suck assholes."

I shut my eyes.

"Did you hear what I said, Miller?"

"Big deal."

"I was humiliated."

"You can't stand intimacy."

"I'll rip out the phone if it happens once more. You can make your calls across the street in the bar."

"He was trying to say he loves you."

She thrashed into one position, then another, then another. I opened my eyes and said, "Let's play our game."

"No; I want to sleep."

"All right, lie still. I want to sleep, too."

"Then sleep."

I shut my eyes.

"I'll play once. You send."

"Never mind. Let me sleep."

"You suggested it."

"I've changed my mind."

"Son of a bitch. Always the same damn shit."

"I'm sending. Go on."

"Do you see it clearly?"

"Yes."

"I see a triangle."

I didn't say anything.

"A triangle, that's all. I see a triangle, Miller. What are you sending?"

"Jesus Christ. Jee-zuss Chrice. I've got chills everywhere."

"Tell me what you were sending."

"A diamond. First a sailboat with a white, triangular sail, then a diamond. I sent the diamond."

I turned. Her eyes were waiting for me.

"You and me," I whispered.

"We're the same, Miller. Aren't we?"

I kissed her on the mouth. "If you want to change your mind, say so."

"I am you," she whispered, kissing me. "Let's play more."

"I'll call Max and tell him not to come."

"He isn't coming, anyway. Let's play more."

"I'm sleepy."

"It's my turn to send."

"I'm very sleepy."

"You are a son of a bitch."

"Enough. I haven't slept for days."

"What about me? Don't you ever think about me? I warn you, Miller, don't go to sleep. I'll do something."

"I want to sleep."

"Miller, I see something. Quick. Please."

"A flower."

"You see a flower?"

"It's red."

"What kind of flower? I was sending a parachute."

"That's it, Mildred. A parachute flower."

"Fuck you, Miller."

"You, too. Let me sleep."

"Miller, I still see something. Hurry. Try again."

I lay still, eyes shut. Nothing came to me except a knock at the door, so quiet I imagined I hadn't heard it. She said, "Was that a knock?"

I sat up and listened, then got out of bed and went to the door. It was Max and Sleek. Max nodded hello. Sleek stepped backward, but a smile moved in his pallor. I said, "Hi." I heard Mildred rushing to the kitchen sink and held them at the door. "Only one room and a kitchen," I said. Max nodded again. The smile faded slowly in Sleek's pale, flat face. Water crashed, then she was shooting to the closet, jamming into heels, scrambling a blouse on her back. A light went on. She slashed her mouth with lipstick. "Come in, come in."

They came in.

"Please sit down."

Max sat down in his coat, looked into the folds across his lap, and began to roll a cigarette. Sleek sat down in his coat, too, watching Max. Both of them glanced once at Mildred, then at each other. I said, then Max said. Sleek laughed feebly as if suppressing a cough. Then they both stared at her. Max offered her the first drag on the cigarette. She said quickly, but in a soft voice, cool, shy. They looked at one another, Max and Sleek, and agreed with their eyes: she was a smart little girl. I sat down. I told them she might be pregnant. We were thinking about getting married, I said. I was going to look for a new job. Everyone laughed at something. Max said, Sleek said. They took off their coats. She was now shining awake, feeling herself, being looked at.

"Do you want some coffee?" She tossed her hair slightly with the question.

Max said, "Do you have milk?"

Sleek said, "Coffee."

She curled tightly in her chair, legs underneath, making knees, shins, ankles to look at. They looked. I stood up and went into the kitchen for the coffee and milk. Max was saying and Sleek added. She was quick again, laughing, doing all right for herself. I took my time, then came back in with the coffee and milk. I asked what they were into lately, imports, exports, hustlers, what. Sleek sucked the cigarette. Max rolled another and was looking at Mildred. He asked if she had considered an abortion. She smiled. Sleek said I was an old friend. He would get us a discount. They wouldn't take their cut until I had a new job. They shook their heads. No cut. Max mentioned a doctor in Jersey, a chiropractor on Seventy-second Street. He said his own girl had had an abortion and died. Almost drove him nuts. He drank like a pleeb. You have to get a clean doctor. Otherwise it can be discouraging. His stable was clean. Sleek nodded shrewdly, something tight in his face, as if he knew. "Of course," he said. "Of course." He opened his hand and showed Mildred some pills. She raised an eyebrow, shrugged, looked at me. I was grinning, almost blind.

"Do what you like."

She took a pill. I took a pill, too. Max talked about the egg-beater they use and what comes out, little fingers, little feet.

Mildred squirmed, showed a line of thigh, feel of hip, ankles shaped like fire.

"Abortions are safe," I said and waved a hand.

"Right," said Max. He tossed a pill into his mouth.

Sleek said he had a new kind of pill. Mildred asked shyly with her eyes. He offered immediately. She took it. "The whole country shoves pills up itself," he said. "My mother takes stoppies at night and goies in the morning." He gleamed, sucked the cigarette, and sat back as if something had been achieved.

Max frowned, mentioned his dead girl, and said it hadn't been his baby. He shook his head, grinding pity, and said, "Discouraging."

"Your mother?" asked Mildred.

Sleek said she lived in Brooklyn. I nodded as if to confirm that he had a mother. He whispered, "The womb is resilient. Always recovers." Max said, "Made of steel." "Of course," said Sleek, "chicks are tough." Mildred agreed, sat up, showed us her womb. Max took it, squeezed, passed it to Sleek. He suppressed a laugh, then glanced at me.

"Squeeze, squeeze," I said.

He said, "Tough number. Like steel."

I said it looked edible. Sleek stared at Mildred. She got up and took her womb to the stove. I had a bite. Max munched and let his eyelids fall to show his pleasure. Sleek took a sharp little bite and made a smacking noise in his mouth. I felt embarrassed, happy. Mildred seemed happy, seeing us eat. I noticed her grope furtively for something else to eat. But it was late now. Rain banged like hammers, no traffic moved in the street. They waited for a few more minutes, then Max yawned, belched, stood up. "We'll get a cab on Sixth Avenue," he said to Sleek. I said we would decide, then get in touch with him right away. We thanked them for the visit. I apologized for not being more definite. Max shrugged. They were

in the neighborhood, anyway. Sleek said take a couple of days
to think about it. Gay things were said at the door. Max said,
Sleek said, Mildred laughed goodbye. Their voices and feet
went down the stairs.

Mildred kicked off her shoes. I turned out the light. We
kissed. I put my hand between her legs. She began to cry.

"You may not love me, Miller, but you'll cry when I'm
gone."

"Stop it," I said.

She cried. I made fists and pummeled my head. She cried. I
pummeled until my head slipped into my neck. She stopped
crying. I smashed my mouth with my knee. She smiled a
little.

"Do it again."

I started eating my face. She watched, then her eyes grew
lazy, lids like gulls, sailing down. She lay back and spread underneath like a parachute. I lay beside her and looked at the
window. It was black and shining with rain. I said, "I like
your hair, Mildred, your eyes, your nose, your legs. I love your
voice." She breathed plateaus and shallow, ragged gullies. She
slept on her back, mouth open, hands at her sides, turned up.
Rain drilled the window. Thunder burdened the air.

—1969

Some Laughed

T. T. MANDELL locked his office door, then read letters from experts advising the press against publishing his book, *The Enduring Southey*. One letter was insulting, another expressed hatred. All agreed *The Enduring Southey*—"an examination of the life and writing of Robert Southey"—should not be published. Every letter was exceedingly personal and impeccably anonymous. Mandell, an assistant professor of rhetoric and communication art at Bronx Community State Extension, had hoped to win a permanent position at the college. But no published book, no job. In effect, the experts said T. T. Mandell should be fired. But in every negative lives a positive. Mandell could read the letters; Mandell could revise *The Enduring Southey*. Where he'd previously said "yes" or "no," he now said "perhaps yes," "perhaps no." Miss Nugent, the department secretary, retyped the manuscript, then mailed it to another press. It was rejected.

T. T. Mandell locked his office door, then read the letters. All different, yet one conclusion: *The Enduring Southey* must not be published. Again there were insults: "To publish this book would represent an attack on the mind." Mandell wasn't troubled by insults. His life had been shaped by them. Two criticisms, however, were troubling:

> The introductory chapter is full of errors of fact and judgment, and the prose is like that of a foreigner who has no feeling for English and probably not much more for his indigenous bush tongue.

The other:

> The introductory chapter, where Mandell says he approaches Southey from the inside, is bad. The rest of the manuscript falls below its level.

Mandell realized, considering these criticisms, "Even experts can't agree." More important, a contradiction implied intellectual space. He could perhaps shoot *The Enduring Southey* through that space into publication. He corrected the facts wherever he sensed them. With commas he jerked his style toward elegance. Because an expert had said the introductory chapter was best, Mandell put it last. Miss Nugent retyped, then mailed *The Enduring Southey* to another press. It was rejected.

T. T. Mandell locked his office door and thought: "I went to required schools, received required degrees, made changes required by experts. What then do they want?" It struck him: "A man can't be rejected. He can only reject himself." Thus he recovered will and, to the new criticisms, responded with vigorous compliance. He eradicated paragraphs and pages as if they contained nothing. Though he worried about leaving breaks in his argument, time was short. He could not say, when required to state his achievements, that for a long while he had been rewriting a book that he had been rewriting. Anyone could say that. Even a moron. The manuscript—retyped, mailed to a scholarly press called Injured Merit—was returned with a letter from an editor: "Chop *Southey* in half. Put in pictures."

T. T. Mandell locked his office door, removed his clothes; silently, he rolled on the floor.

To colleagues he showed the letter—not with pride but by the way, as if unsure of its tone. They said it urged, without committing the editor to a promise of publication, that Mandell rewrite and resubmit. He frowned, puckered, and said, "Hmmm." His colleagues stared. He himself wondered, fleetingly, if he wasn't a prick.

Mandell cut *The Enduring Southey* in half and inserted a photo of the library in the Bronx where he'd done research. Below the photo he wrote, "Thanks." It occurred to him to insert a photo of himself. That might seem presumptuous, but he remembered scholarly books where the author's photo appeared—an old book on Southey, for example. In the library he found that book again, but no photo, only a drawing, and not of the author, but Southey. Mandell nearly cried. Instead, he laughed and told people. Some laughed.

The Enduring Southey was not resubmitted to Injured Merit. It had become too good. Miss Nugent mailed it to a university press. It was rejected.

T. T. Mandell locked his office door, then telephoned a number he had prepared for this eventuality. A moment later he spoke to a lawyer who specialized in outrage. Mandell told the lawyer what degrees he held and where he had been teaching, as an assistant professor, for several years, while he tried to fulfill the publication requirements of a scholar as well as the general institution of requirements as such. He spoke of his faith in the system. He said he wasn't a troublemaker or a critic of prevailing values but the author of a proper book rewritten according to the criticism of experts. There had been a time, Mandell said, when he wore sneakers to class, but upon noticing that no other faculty members wore sneakers, he quit doing so. There were other things of this nature, but, Mandell believed, the lawyer had the picture. The lawyer then explained: "Professor, there's no action in this crap." Mandell read the letters, revised the manuscript, threw out the photo. Miss Nugent retyped, mailed. The Enduring Southey was rejected.

T. T. Mandell locked his office door. As if from the abyss of authenticity, a voice came: "It doesn't matter if you're a nice guy." Mandell listened. The voice continued: "I made the whale." Mandell felt depressed—or deepened. In this mood, he made revisions.

Miss Nugent now wore glasses and walked faster. Leaving her typewriter to go pee, she always glanced at her wristwatch as if to confirm her need. She retyped *The Enduring Southey,* mailed it away again, then again. Mandell's face had a greasy, dissatisfied quality now, impossible to wash or shave away, and his manner had gained spasmodic vigor. Once he interrupted a conversation between two colleagues, rushing up to their lunch table, driving a bread knife into the Formica top, and shouting, "You were talking about *Moby Dick,* right?"

The Enduring Southey had been mailed away for the last time. To Stuttgart. Miss Nugent believed the finest scholarly books were published there. Mandell could afford no more rejections, certainly none that might take long in coming, but Miss Nugent felt *The Enduring Southey* was hers as much as his. She wanted the last rejection to come from the best. *The Enduring Southey* was accepted.

A VW mechanic in Mandell's neighborhood translated the letter for him. Mandell waved it at Miss Nugent and flung into a dance before her typewriter. She pummeled the keys and hissed, "Don't let them have it. Tell them to screw off." He gave her a look of terror and fled.

Der andauernde Southey was published. Mandell was given permanency. He mastered the ho-ho style of laughter and, at department meetings, said things like, "What fun." Discussing the book with students who, someday, would write one like it, he said it wrote itself. Nasty reviews appeared, but they were in German. Mandell was considered an expert and received manuscripts from university presses with requests for his opinion. His letters were always written with uncompromising and incisive hatred.

—1975

The Deal

TWENTY were jammed together on the stoop; tiers of heads made one central head, and the wings rested along the banisters: a raggedy monster of boys studying her approach. Her white face and legs. She passed without looking, poked her sunglasses against the bridge of her nose, and tucked her bag between her arm and ribs. She carried it at her hip like a rifle stock. On her spine forty eyes hung like poison berries. Bone dissolved beneath her lank beige silk, and the damp circle of her belt cut her in half. Independent legs struck toward the points of her shoes. Her breasts lifted and rode the air like porpoises. She would cross to the grocery as usual, buy cigarettes, then cross back despite their eyes. As if the neighborhood hadn't changed one bit. She slipped the bag forward to crack it against her belly and pluck out keys and change. In the gesture she was home from work. Her keys jangled in the sun as if they opened everything and the air received her. The monster, watching, saw the glove fall away.

Pigeons looped down to whirl between buildings, and a ten-wheel truck came slowly up the street. As it passed she emerged from the grocery, then stood at the curb opposite the faces. She glanced along the street where she had crossed it. No glove. Tar reticulated between the cobbles. A braid of murky water ran against the curb, twisting bits of flotsam toward the drain. She took off her sunglasses, dropped them with her keys into the bag, then stepped off the curb toward the faces. Addressing them with a high, friendly voice, she said: "Did you guys see a glove? I dropped it a moment ago."

The small ones squinted up at her from the bottom step. On the middle steps sat boys fourteen or fifteen years old. The oldest ones made the wings. Dandies and introverts, they sprawled, as if with a common corruption in their bones. In

129

the center, his eyes level with hers, a boy waited for her attention in the matter of gloves. To his right sat a very thin boy
with a pocked face. A narrow-brimmed hat tipped toward his
nose and shaded the continuous activity of his eyes. She spoke
to the green eyes of the boy in the center and held up the glove
she had: "Like this."

Teeth appeared below the hat, then everywhere as the
boys laughed. Did she hold up a fish? Green eyes said: "Hello,
Miss Calile."

She looked around at the faces, then laughed with them at
her surprise. "You know my name?"

"I see it on the mailbox," said the hat. "He can't read. I see
it."

"My name is Duke Francisco," said the illiterate.

"My name is Abbe Carlyle," she said to him.

The hat smirked. "His name Francisco Lopez."

Green eyes turned to the hat. "Shut you mouth. I tell her
my name, not you."

"His name Francisco Lopez," the hat repeated.

She saw pocks and teeth, the thin oily face and the hat, as
he spoke again, nicely to her: "My name Francisco Pacheco,
the Prince. I seen you name on the mailbox."

"Did either of you . . ."

"You name is shit," said green eyes to the hat.

"My name is Tito." A small one on the bottom step looked
up for the effect of his name. She looked down at him. "I am
Tito," he said.

"Did you see my glove, Tito?"

"This is Tomato," he answered, unable to bear her attention. He nudged the boy to his left. Tomato nudged back,
stared at the ground.

"I am happy to know you, Tito," she said, "and you, Tomato. Both of you." She looked back up to green eyes and the hat.
The hat acknowledged her courtesy. He tilted back to show

her his eyes, narrow and black except for bits of white reflected in the corners. His face was thin, high boned, and
fragile. She pitied the riddled skin.

"This guy," he said, pointing his thumb to the right, "is
Monkey," and then to the left beyond green eyes, "and this
guy is Beans." She nodded to the hat, then Monkey, then
Beans, measuring the respect she offered, doling it out in split
seconds. Only one of them had the glove.

"Well, did any of you guys see my glove?"

Every tier grew still, like birds in a tree waiting for a sign
that would move them all at once.

Tito's small dark head snapped forward. She heard the
slap an instant late. The body lurched after the head and
pitched off the stoop at her feet. She saw green eyes sitting
back slowly. Tito gaped up at her from the concrete. A sacri-
fice to the lady. She stepped back as if rejecting it and
frowned at green eyes. He gazed indifferently at Tito, who
was up, facing him with coffee-bean fists. Tito screamed, "I
tell her you got it, dick-head."

The green eyes swelled in themselves like a light blooming
in the ocean. Tito's fists opened, he turned, folded quickly,
and sat back into the mass. He began to rub his knees.

"May I have my glove, Francisco?" Her voice was still
pleasant and high. She now held her purse in the crook of her
arm and pressed it against her side.

Some fop had a thought and giggled in the wings. She
glanced up at him immediately. He produced a toothpick.
With great delicacy he stuck it into his ear. She looked away.
Green eyes again waited for her. A cup of darkness formed in
the hollow that crowned his chestbone. His soiled gray polo
shirt hooked below it. "You think I have you glove?" She
didn't answer. He stared between his knees, between heads
and shoulders to the top of Tito's head. "Hey, Tito, you tell
her I got the glove?"

"I didn't tell nothing," muttered Tito, rubbing his knees harder as if they were still bitter from his fall.

"He's full of shit, Miss Calile. I break his head later. What kind of glove you want?"

"This kind," she said wearily, "a white glove like this."

"Too hot." He grinned.

"Yes, too hot, but I need it."

"What for? Too hot." He gave her full green concern.

"It's much too hot, but the glove is mine, mister."

She rested her weight on one leg and wiped her brow with the glove she had. They watched her do it, the smallest of them watched her, and she moved the glove slowly to her brow again and drew it down her cheek and neck. She could think of nothing to say, nothing to do without expressing impatience. Green eyes changed the subject. "You live there." He pointed toward her building.

"That's right."

A wooden front door with a window in it showed part of the shadowy lobby, mailboxes, and a second door. Beyond her building and down the next street were warehouses. Beyond them, the river. A meat truck started toward them from a packing house near the river. It came slowly, bug-eyed with power. The driver saw the lady standing in front of the boys. He yelled as the truck went past. Gears yowled, twisting the sound of his voice. She let her strength out abruptly: "Give me the glove, Francisco."

The boy shook his head at the truck, at her lack of civilization. "What you give me?"

That tickled the hat. "*Vaya.* What she give you, eh?" He spoke fast, his tone decorous and filthy.

"All right," she said fast as the hat, "what do you want?" The question had New York and much man in it. The hat swiveled to the new sound. A man of honor, let him understand the terms. He squinted at her beneath the hat brim.

"Come on, Francisco, make your deal." She presented brave, beautiful teeth, smiling hard as a skull.

"Tell her, Duke. Make the deal." The hat lingered on "deal," grateful to the lady for this word.

The sun shone in his face and the acknowledged duke sat dull, green eyes blank with possibilities. Her question, not "deal," held him. It had come too hard, too fast. He laughed in contempt of something and glanced around at the wings. They offered nothing. "I want a dollar," he said.

That seemed obvious to the hat: he sneered, "He wants a dollar." She had to be stupid not to see it.

"No deal. Twenty-five cents." Her gloves were worth twenty dollars. She had paid ten for them at a sale. At the moment they were worth green eyes' life.

"I want ten dollars," said green eyes, flashing the words like extravagant meaningless things; gloves of his own. He lifted his arms, clasped his hands behind his head, and leaned against the knees behind him. His belly filled with air, the polo shirt rolled out on its curve. He made a fat man doing business. "Ten dollars." Ten fingers popped up behind his head like grimy spikes. Keeper of the glove, cocky duke of the stoop. The number made him happy: it bothered her. He drummed the spikes against his head: "I wan' you ten dol-lar." Beans caught the beat in his hips and rocked it on the stoop.

"Francisco," she said, hesitated, then said, "dig me, please. You will get twenty-five cents. Now let's have the glove." Her bag snapped open, her fingers hooked, stiffened on the clasp. Monkey leered at her and bongoed his knees with fists. "The number is ten dol-lar." She waited, said noth-ing. The spikes continued drumming, Monkey rocked his hips, Beans pummeled his knees. The hat sang sadly: "Twany fyiv not d'nummer, not d'nummer, not d'nummer." He made claves of his fingers and palms, tocked, clicked his tongue against the

beat. "Twan-ny fyiv—na t'nomma." She watched green eyes.
He was quiet now in the center of the stoop, sitting motionless, waiting, as though seconds back in time his mind still
touched the question: what did he want? He seemed to won-
der, now that he had the formula, what did he want? The
faces around him, dopey in the music, wondered nothing,
grinned at her, nodded, clicked, whined the chorus: "Twany
fyiv not t'nomma, twany fyiv not t'nomma."

Her silk blouse stained and stuck flat to her breasts and
shoulders. Water chilled her sides.

"Ten dol-lar iss t'nomma."

She spread her feet slightly, taking better possession of the
sidewalk and resting on them evenly, the bag held open for
green eyes. She could see he didn't want that, but she insisted
in her silence he did. Tito spread his little feet and lined the
points of his shoes against hers. Tomato noticed the imitation
and cackled at the concrete. The music went on, the beat feed-
ing on itself, pulverizing words, smearing them into liquid
submission: "Iss t'nomma twany fyiv? Dat iss not t'nomma."

"Twenty-five cents," she said again.

Tito whined, "Gimme twenty-five cents."

"Shut you mouth," said the hat, and turned a grim face to
his friend. In the darkness of his eyes there were deals. The
music ceased. "Hey, you got no manners? Tell what you want."
He spoke in a dreamy voice, as if to a girl.

"I want a kiss," said green eyes.

She glanced down with this at Tito and studied the small
shining head. "Tell him to give me my glove, Tito," she said
cutely, nervously. The wings shuffled and looked down,
bored. Nothing was happening. Twisting backward Tito
shouted up to green eyes, "Give her the glove." He twisted
front again and crouched over his knees. He shoved Tomato
for approval and smiled. Tomato shoved him back, snarled at
the concrete, and spit between his feet at a face that had
taken shape in the grains.

"I want a kiss," said the boy again.

She sighed, giving another second to helplessness. The sun was low above the river and the street three quarters steeped in shade. Sunlight cut across the building tops where pigeons swept by loosely and fluttered in to pack the stone foliage of the eaves. Her bag snapped shut. Her voice was business: "Come on, Francisco. I'll give you the kiss."

He looked shot among the faces.

"Come on," she said, "it's a deal."

The hat laughed out loud with childish insanity. The others shrieked and jiggled, except for the wings. But they ceased to sprawl, and seemed to be getting bigger, to fill with imminent motion. "Gimme a kiss, gimme a kiss," said the little ones on the lowest step. Green eyes sat with a quiet, open mouth.

"Let's go," she said. "I haven't all day."

"Where I go?"

"That doorway." She pointed to her building and took a step toward it. "You know where I live, don't you?"

"I don't want no kiss."

"What's the matter now?"

"You scared?" asked the hat. "Hey, Duke, you scared?"

The wings leaned toward the center, where green eyes hugged himself and made a face.

"Look, Mr. Francisco, you made a deal."

"Yeah," said the wings.

"Now come along."

"I'm not scared," he shouted and stood up among them. He sat down. "I don't want no kiss."

"You're scared?" she said.

"You scared chicken," said the hat.

"Yeah," said the wings. "Hey, punk. Fairy. Hey, Duke Chicken."

"Duke scared," mumbled Tito. Green eyes stood up again. The shoulders below him separated. Tito leaped clear of the stoop and trotted into the street. Green eyes passed through the place he had vacated and stood at her side, his head not so high as her shoulder. She nodded at him, tucked her bag up and began walking toward her building. A few others stood up on the stoop and the hat started down. She turned. "Just him." Green eyes shuffled after her. The hat stopped on the sidewalk. Someone pushed him forward. He resisted, but called after them, "He's my cousin." She walked on, the boy came slowly after her. They were yelling from the stoop, the hat yelling his special point, "He's my brother." He stepped after them and the others swarmed behind him down the stoop and onto the sidewalk. Tito jumped out of the street and ran alongside the hat. He yelled, "He's got the glove." They all moved down the block, the wings trailing sluggishly, the young ones jostling, punching each other, laughing, shrieking things in Spanish after green eyes and the lady. She heard him, a step behind her. "I give you the glove and take off."

She put her hand out to the side a little. The smaller hand touched hers and took it. "You made a deal."

She tugged him through the doorway into the tight, square lobby. The hand snapped free and he swung by, twisting to face her as if to meet a blow. He put his back against the second door, crouched a little. His hands pressed the sides of his legs. The front door shut slowly and the shadows deepened in the lobby. He crouched lower, his eyes level with her breasts, as she took a step toward him. The hat appeared, a black rock in the door window. Green eyes saw it, straightened up, one hand moving quickly toward his pants pocket. The second and third head, thick dark bulbs, lifted beside the hat in the window. Bodies piled against the door behind her. Green eyes held up the glove. "Here, you lousy glove."

She smiled and put out her hand. The hat screamed, "Hey, you made a deal. Hey, you got no manners."

"Don't be scared," she whispered, stepping closer.

The glove lifted toward her and hung in the air between them, gray, languid as smoke. She took it and bent toward his face. "I won't kiss you. Run." The window went black behind her, the lobby solid in darkness, silent but for his breathing, the door breathing against the pressure of the bodies, and the scraping of fingers spread about them like rats in the walls. She felt his shoulder, touched the side of his neck, bent the last inch, and kissed him. White light cut the walls. They tumbled behind it, screams and bright teeth. Spinning to face them she was struck, pitched against green eyes and the second door. He twisted hard, shoved away from her as the faces piled forward popping eyes and lights, their fingers accumulating in the air, coming at her. She raised the bag, brought it down swishing into the faces, and wrenched and twisted to get free of the fingers, screaming against their shrieks, "Stop it, stop it, stop it." The bag sprayed papers and coins, and the sunglasses flew over their heads and cracked against the brass mailboxes. She dropped amid shrieks, "Gimme a kiss, gimme a kiss," squirming down the door onto her knees to get fingers out from under her and she thrust up with the bag into bellies and thighs until a fist banged her mouth. She cursed, flailed at nothing.

There was a light in the lobby and leather scraping on concrete as they crashed out the door into the street. She shut her eyes instantly as the fist came again, big as her face. Then she heard running in the street. The lobby was silent. The door shut slowly, the shadows deepened. She could feel the darkness getting thicker. She opened her eyes. Standing in front of her was the hat.

He bowed slightly. "I get those guys for you. They got no manners." The hat shook amid the shadows, slowly, sadly.

She pressed the smooth leather of her bag against her cheek where the mouths had kissed it. Then she tested the clasp, snapping it open and shut. The hat shifted his posture and waited. "You hit me," she whispered, and did not look up at him. The hat bent and picked up her keys and the papers. He handed the keys to her, then the papers, and bent again for the coins. She dropped the papers into her bag and stuffed them together in the bottom. "Help me up!" She took his hands and got to her feet without looking at him. As she put the key against the lock of the second door she began to shiver. The key rattled against the slot. "Help me!" The hat leaned over the lock, his long thin fingers squeezing the key. It caught, angled with a click. She pushed him aside. "You give me something? Hey, you give me something?" The door shut on his voice.

—1969

Going Places

BECKMAN, a day out of the hospital, barely strong enough to walk the streets for a job, carrying a ruined face that wouldn't heal for weeks and probably would never look the same, was shocked to find himself hired at the first place he tried, as assistant to a paint contractor, and thought to tell his parents and write his girl to come back from Chicago and marry him, but, recalling disappointments with jobs in the past, decided to wait, not say anything, and see how things went; to see if they continued to be real as the hard, substantial hand that had enveloped and strongly shaken his hand, less rough and hairy, but masculine, calloused by the wheel and stick of his trade, and a substantial hand, too; if not in muscle and bone, certainly in spirit, for in that shake Beckman was welcomed to the end of a successful interview, the end of a life made wretched by rattling kidneys, the stench of gasoline, of cigarettes, of perfume and alcohol and vomit, the end of surly toughs, drunken women, whoring soldiers, vagrant blacks and whites, all the streaming, fearsome, pathetic riffraff refuse of the city's dark going places, though places in hell, while he, Beckman, driver of the cab, went merely everyplace, anyplace, until the sun returned the day and he stopped, parked, dropped his head against the seat, and lay mindless, cramped, chilled in a damp sweater and mucky underwear, lay seized by the leather seat, debauched by the night's long, winding, resonant passage and the abuse of a thousand streets.

Everyplace Beckman, anyplace Beckman, he went noplace until two figures in misty, dismal twilight hailed his cab—a man with a pencil mustache; a woman with big, slick, black eyes, orange lipstick, and Indian cheekbones—got in and beat him up while he begged, shrieking, "Take my money." They did and they left him for dead.

They left him for dead, Beckman, who revived in a hospital and asked for a newspaper with his first deliberate words, and read want ads and thought about his life, so nearly his death, with a powerful, urgent thrust of mind entirely unlike the vague motions it had been given to while drifting through the dark streets of the city.

Something dreadful—running over a drunk, a collision with another car—might have happened sooner or later, but the beating, the beating, was precisely what he deserved, what he needed after years scouring the avenues like a dog, waiting for change to come into his life as if it might hail him from a corner like another fare. Indeed it had. Deserved, too, because he, Beckman, unlike the average misérable, could understand his own experience and, not without pride, he acknowledged the deity that had hailed him in the shape of twilight creatures and presented his face to their fists—as an omen, as a reminder of who he was—Beckman, son of good people who, when he pulled up before their two-story house in Riverdale on his monthly visit, became literally sick.

They were happy of course to see their son, but Beckman, winner of second place in an all-city essay contest celebrating fire prevention week, open to every child in New York, Beckman, the college graduate, history and economics major, risking life with strangers, ruining health in a filthy machine, it literally made them sick.

Laughing, telling stories, even a bit cocky, Beckman would finger the badge with his taxi number on it while his mother's eyes, with unblinking persistence, told him he was miserable, and his father, puffing a cigar against doctor's orders, sat quietly, politely killing himself, nodding, chuckling at the stories until Beckman left and he could stagger out of the room and grope down the wall to his bed. Behind the wheel, Beckman flicked the ignition key, squinted his mind's eye, and saw his father prostrate with a headache, and Beckman gunned the motor, gunned house and street, his mother's eyes and father's rotten heart and headache.

There had been omens in his life not so damaging, if hair loss, shortness of breath, and wrinkles around the eyes and mouth were omens, but death had never been so close and tangible, and Beckman had never thought "I am going to die" as he had, sprawled begging, writhing on the floor of his cab. He had felt the proximity of annihilation just passing a strange man on a dark street or making love to his girl, but the thrill of imminent nothing always came to nothing, gone before he might study it, leaving him merely angry or vacant and low. But now, like Pascal emerging from the carriage after nearly falling from it to his death; like Dostoevsky collapsed against the wall scribbling notes as the firing squad, dissolved by the witty czar, walked off giggling; like Lazarus rising, Beckman was revived, forever qualified and so profoundly reminded of himself he felt like someone else.

Hitting him, the woman cried, "Hey, hey, Beckman," a series of words chanted with the flat exuberance and dull inertia of a work song, repeated without change in pitch or intensity while fists rocked his skull and Beckman thrashed in the darkness, flapped his hands, and begged them to take his money and continued begging as they dragged him by his hair over the front seat and onto the floor in back where the mat reeked of whiskey, stale butts, the corruption of lungs, and a million yards of bowel. "Hell your lousy money, Beckman," said the woman, her spikes in his face and ribs as the man, squealing with effort, pummeled straight down into Beckman's groin. But the punches and kicks were heralds, however brutal, bearing oracles of his genius, the bludgeoning shapers of himself if properly understood. Years ago he should have had this job with the paint contractor, a steady salary, and his nights to sleep in.

He would write his girl this first day after work, thought

Beckman, a letter of impressions, feelings, hopes, and the specific promise of their future, for now he wanted to get married, and his small, gray eyes saw themselves reading that line
as he leaned toward the mirror and shaved around the welts
and scabs. His brows showed the puffed ridges of a pug's dis-
colored, brutalized flesh where a billion capillaries had been
mashed and meat-hammered to the consistency of stone.
Ugly, but not meaningless, and Beckman could even feel glad
there had been nothing worse, no brain damage, no broken
eardrum, no blindness, and could indeed see qualities that
pleased him in the petrified, moiled meat, Hardness and Danger, not in his face or in his soul before the beating, but there
now as in the faces of junkies, whores, bums, pimps, and bar
fighters, the city's most deeply kicked, stabbed, and slashed,
whom he had carried to and fro in his cab; memento moris
twisted into living flesh reflected in his rear-view mirror, reflected now in his bathroom mirror, like the rock formations
of aboriginal desert and plateau where snakes, lizards, and
eagles subsist and life is true and bleak, where all things move
in pure, deep knowledge of right and wrong or else they die.
Beckman whispered, "They die," and the ruined flesh gave
substance to the cocky twist of his head, his manner of speaking out of the side of his mouth and twisting his head as
though whomever he addressed lived on his hip, though he
himself was a few inches less than average height. The sense
of his small hands flapped suddenly in his mind as the furies
dragged him over the seat like a dumb, insentient bag, though
he shrieked take his money, which they would take anyway,
and his body refused to yield its hideous residue of consciousness even as they mercilessly refused to grant it any. He could
not remember when he had passed out or ceased to feel pain
or his voice had stopped, but thought now that he had continued screaming after he had stopped thinking or moving, and
that they had continued beating him until his undeliberate,

importunate voice stopped of its own. They couldn't have been human and so persisted, but had to have been sublime things that had seized Beckman as the spirit seizes the prophet, twists his bones and makes him bleed in agonies of knowledge. Beckman, so gifted, saw himself like the Trojan Cassandra, battered, raped on the rowing benches by Agamemnon's men, and she was Apollo's thing. But then he looked into the mirror, looked at the lumps above his eyes and at the flesh burned green and blue around his mouth. Not a shaman's face. He pulled his tongue through space once filled by an eyetooth and molar, licked sheer, delicate gum.

Enough, this was another Beckman. In truth, no prophet, but neither a bag scrunched into leather, glass, and steel, commanded by anyone to stop, go, ache, count change out of nasty fingers, breathe gas, and hear youth ticked away in nickels. This was Beckman among painters, learning the business, gallon can in each hand, surveying the great hollow vault of the factory that he and the men were come to paint. High brick walls seemed not to restrict but merely to pose theoretical demarcations in all the space now his. He and the gang of painters trudged with cans, brushes, and ropes up a wall toward the sky and the factory's clangor dropped beneath them to a dull, general boom like a distant sea. The light they rose toward grew sharper and whiter as they entered it climbing the narrow stairway that shivered beneath their feet. Paint cans knocked the sides of Beckman's legs, the loops cut thin channels into his palms. At the top of the factory, against the white, skylighted morning, they settled their equipment on a steel platform. The men stirred cans of paint, attached ropes to the pipes that ran along beneath the skylight, and moved out on swings into the voluminous air. Beckman stood back on the platform trying to look shrewdly into the nature of these things and feel his relevance. The sun drifted toward the vertical and blazed through the skylight. It drilled the top of his

head as he concentrated on a painter swinging ten feet out
from the edge of the platform, his arm and trunk like a heavy
appendage dangling from his hand. His feet jerked in vast
nothing. His swing was suspended from a pipe running beside
the one he painted, and as he moved farther from the platform
he left yards of gleaming orange behind him. Beckman felt his
breathing quicken as he leaned after the long smack and drag
of the painter's brush. Repeated, overlapped, and soon, between Beckman and the painter, burned thirty feet of the hot,
brilliant color. Beckman yearned to participate, confront un-
painted steel, paint it, see it become a fresh, different thing as
he dissolved in the ritual of strokes. The painter stopped
working and looked at him. A vein split the man's temple
down the center and forked like the root of a tree. Flecks of
orange dazzled on his cheeks. He pointed with his brush to a
can near the edge of the platform and Beckman snapped it up,
stepped to the edge, and held it out into the air toward the
painter. Thus, delivering the can, he delivered himself,
grabbed life in the loop, and hoisted it like a gallon of his own
blood, swinging it out like a mighty bowler into the future.
Concrete floor, towering walls, steeping light hosannaed
while Beckman's arm stiffened and shuddered from wrist to
mooring tendons in his neck as he held the stance, leaned
with the heavy can like an allegorical statue: Man Reaching.
The painter grinned, shook his head, and Beckman saw in a
flash blinding blindness that his effort to reach thirty feet
was imbecilic. His head wrenched back for the cocky vantage
of height and relieved his stance of allegory. He shuffled
backward with a self-mocking shrug and set down the can as
if lifting it in the first place had been a mistake. The painter's
grin became a smile and he tapped the pipe to which his swing
was attached. Beckman understood—deliver the can by
crawling down the pipe. Aggravation ripped his heart. A
sense of his life constituted of moments like this, inept and

freakish, when spirit, muscle, and bone failed to levels less than thing, a black lump of time went streaming down the inside of his skull with the creepy feel of slapstick spills, twitches, flops, and farts of the mind. But the painter had resumed his good work and Beckman, relieved and gratified, was instantly himself again, immune to himself, and snapped up the can. At the edge of the platform he stooped, laid his free hand on the pipe, then straddled the pipe. He clutched the loop in his right hand, shoved off the platform, tipped forward, and dragged with his knees, thighs, and elbows down toward the painter. His feet dangled, his eyes dug into the pipe, and he pushed. He dragged like a worm and didn't think or feel what he did. Fifteen feet from the edge of the platform he stopped to adjust his grip on the can, heavier now and swinging enough to make him feel uneasy about his right side and make him tighten his grip on the left so hard he pitched left. The can jerked up, both legs squeezed the pipe, and a tremor set into his calves and shanks, moving toward his buttocks and lower back.

Beckman squeezed the pipe with his legs and arms and slipped his left hand gradually under the pipe to cup its belly. His right hand, clutching the loop of the can, hung straight down, and Beckman leaned his chin against the pipe and listened to his shirt buttons rasp against steel. He breathed slowly to minimize the rasping and gaped down the pipe at the hard, curved flare of morning light. His knees felt through cloth to steel and the pipe's belly was slick in his palm. The tremor, in his shoulders now, moved up toward the muscles of his neck. Against his mouth he smelled, then tasted, steel as it turned rancid with sweat and spit. He felt water pour slowly, beyond his will, into his pants as it had when they hit him for no reason and he twisted and shrieked on the floor of his cab. He felt the impulse to move and did not want to look around into the vacuous air, nor to imagine the beating or the possibility that the tremor in his chin and lips would become a long, fine scream spinning out the thread of his life as he dropped toward the machines and the concrete floor. He felt the impulse to move and he could remember how motion felt gathering in his body to move his body, how it felt gathering, droning in the motor of his cab, to move him through the dark avenues of the city. He stared down the pipe, clung to it, and saw the painter stop working to look at him, looking at him with surprise, saying as if only with lips, slowly, again and again, "Hold on, Beckman." He clung to the pipe, squeezed life against his chest, and would neither let go nor drag toward the painter. He heard men shout from the platform, "Don't let go, Beckman." He did not let go. The tremor passed into muscle as rigid as the steel it squeezed.

—1969

Tell Me Everything

CLAUDE RUE had a wide face with yellowish green eyes and a long aristocratic nose. The mouth was a line, pointed in the center, lifted slightly at the ends, curving in a faint smile, almost cruelly sensual. He dragged his right foot like a stone, and used a cane, digging it into the floor as he walked. His dark blue suit, cut in the French style, arm holes up near the neck, made him look small in the shoulder, and made his head look too big. I liked nothing about the man that I could see.

"What a face," I whispered to Margaret, "Who would take anything he says seriously?"

She said, "Who wouldn't? Gorgeous. Just gorgeous. And the way he dresses. Such style."

After that, I didn't say much. I hadn't really wanted to go to the lecture in the first place.

Every seat in the auditorium was taken long before Rue appeared onstage. People must have come in from San Francisco, Oakland, Marin, and beyond. There were even sad creatures from the Berkeley streets, some loonies among them, in filthy clothes, open sores on their faces like badges. I supposed few in the audience knew that Claude Rue was a professor of Chinese history who taught at the Sorbonne, but everyone knew he'd written *The Mists of Shanghai*, a thousand-page, best-selling novel.

Onstage, Rue looked lonely and baffled. Did all these people actually care to hear his lecture on the loss of classical Chinese? He glanced about, as if there had been a mistake and he was searching for his replacement, the star of the show, the real Claude Rue. I approved of his modesty, and I might have enjoyed listening to him. But then, as if seized by an irrational impulse, Rue lifted the pages of his lecture for all to witness, and ripped them in half. "I will speak from my heart," he said.

The crowd gasped. I groaned. Margaret leaned toward him, straining, as if to pick up his odor. She squeezed my hand and checked my eyes to see whether I understood her feelings. She needed a reference point, a consciousness aside from her own to slow the rush of her being toward Rue.

"You're terrible," I said.

"Don't spoil my fantasy. Be quiet, okay?"

She then flattened her thigh against mine, holding me there while she joined him in her feelings, onstage, fifty feet away. Rue began his speech without pages or notes. The crowd grew still. Many who couldn't find seats stood in the aisles, some with bowed heads, staring at the floor as if they'd been beaten on the shoulders into penitential silence. For me it was also penitential. I work nights. I didn't like wasting a free evening in a crowded lecture hall when I could have been alone with Margaret.

I SHOWED up at her loft an hour before the lecture. She said to her face in the bathroom mirror, "I can hardly wait to see the man. How do I look?"

"Chinese." I put the lid down on the toilet seat, sat on it.

"Answer me. Do I look all right, Herman?"

"You know what the ancient Greeks said about perfume?"

"I'm about to find out."

"To smell sweet is to stink."

"I use very little perfume. There's a reception afterwards, a party. It's in honor of the novel. A thousand pages and I could have kept reading it for another week. I didn't want it to end. I'll tell you the story later."

"Maybe I'll read it, too," I said, trying not to sound the way I felt. "But why must you see what the man looks like? I couldn't care less."

"You won't go with me?" She turned from the mirror, as if, at last, I'd provoked her into full attention.

"I'm not saying I won't."

"What are you saying?"

"Nothing. I asked a question, that's all. It isn't important. Forget it."

"Don't slither. You have another plan for the evening? You'd rather go somewhere else?"

"I have no other plan. I'm asking why should anyone care what an author looks like."

"I'm interested. I have been for months."

"Why?"

"Why not? He made me feel something. His book was an experience. Everybody wants to see him. Besides, my sister met him in Beijing. She knows him. Didn't I read you her letter?"

"I still don't see why ..."

"Herman, what do you want me to say? I'm interested, I'm curious. I'm going to his lecture. If you don't want to go, don't go."

That is, leave the bathroom. Shut the door. Get out of sight.

MARGARET can be too abrupt, too decisive. It's her business style carried into personal life. She buys buildings, has them fixed up, then rents or sells, and buys again. She has supported herself this way since her divorce from Sloan Pierson, professor of linguistics. He told her about Claude Rue's lecture, invited her to the reception, and put my name on the guest list. Their divorce, compared to some, wasn't bad. No lingering bitterness. They have remained connected—not quite friends—through small courtesies, like the invitation; also, of course, through their daughter, Gracie, ten years old. She lives with Sloan except when Margaret wants her, which is often. Margaret's business doesn't allow a strict schedule of visits. She appears at Sloan's door without notice. "I need her," she says. Gracie scampers to her room, collects school books for the next day, and packs a duffel bag with clothes and woolly animals.

Sloan sighs, shakes his head. "Really, Margaret. Gracie has needs, too. She needs a predictable daily life." Margaret says, "I'll phone you later. We'll discuss our needs."

She comes out of the house with Gracie. Sloan shouts, "Wait. Gracie's pills."

There's always one more word, one more thing to collect. "Goodbye. Wait." I wait. We all wait. Margaret and Gracie go back into the house, and I stand outside. I'm uncomfortable inside the house, around Sloan. He's friendly, but I know too much about him. I can't help thinking things, making judg-ments, and then I feel guilty. He's a fussy type, does every-thing right. If he'd only fight Margaret, not be so good, so cor-rect. Sloan could make trouble about Margaret's unscheduled appearances, even go to court, but he thinks if Margaret doesn't have her way, Gracie will have no mother. Above all things, Sloan fears chaos. Gracie senses her daddy's fear, shares it. Margaret would die for Gracie, but it's a difficult love, measured by intensities. Would Margaret remember, in such love, about the pills?

Sloan finds the pills, brings them to the foyer, hands them to Margaret. There. He did another correct thing. She and Gracie leave the house. We start down the path to the side-walk. Gracie hands me her books and duffel bag, gives me a kiss, and says, "Hi, Herman German. I have an ear infection. I have to take pills four times a day." She's instructing Mar-garet, indirectly.

Margaret glares at me to show that she's angry. Her ten-year-old giving her instructions. I pretend not to notice. Gra-cie is a little version of Margaret, not much like Sloan. Chi-nese chemistry is dominant. Sloan thinks Gracie is lucky. "That's what I call a face," he says. He thinks he looks like his name—much too white.

I say, "Hi, Gracie Spacey." We get into my Volvo. I drive us away.

Gracie sits back. Margaret, sitting beside me, stares straight ahead, silent, still pissed, but after a while she turns, looks at Gracie. Gracie reads her mind, gives her a hug. Margaret feels better, everyone feels better.

WHILE Margaret's houses are being fixed up, she lives in one, part of which becomes her studio where she does her painting. Years ago, at the university, studying with the wonderful painters Joan Brown and Elmer Bischoff, Margaret never discovered a serious commitment in herself. Later, when she married and had Gracie, and her time was limited, seriousness arrived. Then came the divorce, the real estate business, and she had even less time. She paints whenever she can, and she reads fifty or sixty novels a year; also what she calls "philosophy," which is religious literature. Her imagery in paintings comes from mythic, visionary works. From the Kumulipo, the Hawaiian cosmological chant, she took visions of land and sea, where creatures of the different realms are mysteriously related. Margaret doesn't own a television set or go to movies. She denies herself common entertainment for the same reason that Rilke refused to be analyzed by Freud. "I don't want my soul diluted," she says.

Sometimes, I sit with her in her loft in Emeryville—in a four-story brick building, her latest purchase—while she paints. "Are you bored?" she asks.

I'm never bored, I like being with her. I like the painting odors, the drag and scratch of brush against canvas. She applies color, I feel it in my eyes. Tingling starts along my forearms, hairs lift and stiffen. We don't talk. Sometimes not a word for hours, yet the time lacks nothing.

I say, "Let's get married."

She says, "We are married."

Another hour goes by.

She asks, "Is that a painting?"

I make a sound to suggest that it is.

"Is it good?"

She knows.

When one of her paintings, hanging in a corner of a New York gallery owned by a friend, sold—without a formal show, and without reviews—I became upset. She'll soon be famous, I thought.

"I'll lose you," I said.

She gave me nine paintings, all she had in the loft. "Take this one, this one, this one ..."

"Why?"

"Take them, take them."

She wanted to prove, maybe, that our friendship was inviolable; she had no ambition to succeed, only to be good. I took the paintings grudgingly, as if I were doing her a favor. In fact, that's how I felt. I was doing her a favor. But I wanted the paintings. They were compensation for her future disappearance from my life. We're best friends, very close. I have no vocation. She owed me the paintings.

I QUIT graduate school twenty years ago, and began waiting tables at Gemma's, a San Francisco restaurant. From year to year, I expected to find other work or to write professionally. My one book, *Local Greens*, which is about salads, was published by a small press in San Francisco. Not a best-seller, but it made money. Margaret told me to invest in a condominium and she found one for me, the top floor of a brown-shingle house, architect unknown, in the Berkeley hills. I'd been living in Oakland, in a one-room apartment on Harrison Street, near the freeway. I have a sedentary nature. I'd never have moved out. Never really have known, if not for Margaret, that I could have a nicer place, be happier. "I'm happy," I said. "This place is fine." She said my room was squalid. She said the street was noisy and dangerous. She insisted that I talk to a realtor or check the newspapers for another place, exert myself, do something. Suddenly, it seemed, I had two bedrooms, living room, new kitchen, hardwood floors, a deck, a bay view, monthly payments—property.

It didn't seem. I actually lived in a new place, nicer than anything I'd ever known.

My partner, so to speak, lives downstairs. Eighty-year-old Belinda Forster. She gardens once a week by instructing Pilar, a silent Mexican woman who lives with Belinda, where to put the different new plants, where to prune the apple trees. Belinda also lunches with a church group, reviews her will, smokes cigarettes. She told me, if I find her unconscious in the garden, or in the driveway, or wherever, to do nothing to revive her. She looks not very shrunken, not extremely frail. Her eyes are beautifully clear. Her skin is without the soft, puffy surface you often see in old people.

Belinda's husband, a professor of plant pathology, died about fifteen years ago, shortly after his retirement. Belinda talks about his work, their travels in Asia, and his mother. Not a word about herself. She might consider that impolite, or boastful, claiming she too had a life, or a self. She has qualities of reserve, much out of style these days, that I admire greatly, but I become awkward talking to her. I don't quite feel that I say what I mean. Does she intend this effect? Is she protecting herself against the assertions, the assault, of younger energies?

Upstairs, from the deck of my apartment, I see sailboats tilted in the wind. Oil tankers go sliding slowly by Alcatraz Island. Hovering in the fuchsias there are hummingbirds. Squirrels fly through the black, light-streaked canopies of Monterey pines. If my temperament were religious, I'd believe there had to be a cause, a divinity in the fantastic theater of clouds above San Francisco Bay.

Rue spoke with urgency, his head and upper body lifting and settling to the rhythm of his sentences. His straight, blond hair, combed straight back, fell toward his eyes. He swept it aside. It fell. He swept it aside, a bravely feminine gesture, vain, distracting. I sighed.

Margaret pinched my elbow. "I want to hear him, not your opinions."

"I only sighed."

"That's an opinion."

I sat quietly. Rue carried on. His subject was the loss to the Chinese people, and to the world, of the classical Chinese language. "I am saying that, after the revolution, the ancients, the great Chinese dead, were torn from their graves. I am saying they have been murdered word by word. And this in the name of nationhood, and a social justice which annihilates language, as well as justice, and anything the world has known as social."

End.

The image of ancient corpses, torn from their graves and murdered, aroused loonies in the audience. They whistled and cried out. Others applauded for a whole minute. Rue had said nothing subversive of America. Even so, Berkeley adored him. Really because of the novel, not the lecture. On the way to the lecture, Margaret talked about the novel, giving me the whole story, not merely the gist, as if to defend it against my negative opinion. She was also apologizing, I think, by talking so much, for having been angry and abrupt earlier. Couldn't just say "I'm sorry." Not Margaret. I drove and said nothing, still slightly injured, but soothed by her voice, giving me the story; giving a good deal, really, more than the story.

She said *The Mists of Shanghai* takes place in nineteenth-century China during the opium wars, when low-quality opium, harvested from British poppy fields in India, was thrust upon the Chinese people. "Isn't that interesting?" she said. "A novel should teach you something. I learned that the production, transportation, and distribution of opium, just as today, was controlled by western military and intelligence agencies, there were black slaves in Macao, and eunuchs were very powerful figures in government."

The central story of the novel, said Margaret, which is told by an evil eunuch named Jujuzi, who is an addict and a dealer, is about two lovers—a woman named Neiping and a man named Goo. First we hear about Neiping's childhood. She is the youngest in a large, very poor family. Her parents sell her to an elegant brothel in Shanghai, where the madam buys little girls, selected for brains and beauty. She tells Neiping that she will be taught to read, and, eventually, she will participate in conversation with patrons. Though only eight years old, Neiping has strong character, learns quickly, and becomes psychologically mature. One day a new girl arrives and refuses to talk to anyone. She cries quietly to herself at night. Neiping listens to her crying and begins to feel sorry for herself. But she refuses to cry. She leaves her bed and crawls into bed with the crying girl, who then grows quiet. Neiping hugs her and says, "I am Neiping. What's your name?"

She says, "Dulu."

They talk for hours until they both fall asleep. She and Neiping become dear friends.

It happens that a man named Kang, a longtime patron of the brothel, arrives one evening. He is a Shanghai business-man, dealing in Mexican silver. He also owns an ironworks, and has initiated a lucrative trade in persons, sending laborers to a hellish life in the cane fields of Pacific Islands and Cuba. Kang confesses to the madam that he is very unhappy. He can't find anyone to replace his recently deceased wife as his opponent in the ancient game of wei-ch'i. The madam tells

Kang not to be unhappy. She has purchased a clever girl who will make a good replacement. Kang can come to the brothel and play wei-ch'i. She brings little Neiping into the room, sits her at a table with Kang, a playing board between them. Kang has a blind eye that looks smoky and gray. He is unashamedly flatulent, and he is garishly tattooed. All in all, rather a monster. Pretty little Neiping is terrified. She nods yes, yes, yes as he tells her the rules of the game, and he explains how one surrounds the opponent's pieces and holds territory on the board. When he asks if she has understood everything, she nods yes again. He says to Neiping, "If you lose, I will eat you the way a snake eats a monkey."

Margaret said, "This is supposed to be a little joke, see? But, since Kang looks sort of like a snake, it's frightening."

Kang takes the black stones and makes the first move. Neiping, in a trance of fear, recalls his explanation of the rules, then places a white stone on the board far from his black stone. They play until Kang becomes sleepy. He goes home. The game resumes the next night and the next. In the end, Kang counts the captured stones, white and black. It appears that Neiping has captured more than he. The madam says, "Let me count them." It also appears that Neiping controls more territory than Kang. The madam counts, then looks almost frightened. She twitters apologies, and she coos, begging Kang to forgive Neiping for taking advantage of his kindness, his willingness to let Neiping seem to have done well in the first game. Kang says, "This is how it was with my wife. Sometimes she seemed to win. I will buy this girl."

The madam had been saving Neiping for a courtier, highly placed, close to the emperor, but Kang is a powerful man. She doesn't dare reject the sale. "The potential value of Neiping is immeasurable," she says. Kang says Neiping will cost a great deal before she returns a profit. "The price I am willing to pay is exceptionally good."

The madam says, "In silver?"

Kang says, "Mexican coins."

She bows to Kang, then tells Neiping to say goodbye to the other girls.

Margaret says, "I'll never forget how the madam bows to Kang."

Neiping and Dulu embrace. Dulu cries. Neiping says they will meet again someday. Neiping returns to Kang. He takes her hand. The monster and Neiping walk through the night-time streets of Shanghai to Kang's house.

For the next seven years, Neiping plays wei-ch'i with Kang. He has her educated by monks, and she is taught to play musical instruments by the evil eunuch, Jujuzi, the one who is telling the story. Kang gives Neiping privileges of a daughter. She learns how he runs his businesses. He discusses problems with her. "If somebody were in my position, how might such a person reflect on the matters I have described?" While they talk, Kang asks Neiping to comb his hair. He never touches her. His manner is formal and gentle. He gives everything. Neiping asks for nothing. Kang is a happy monster, but then Neiping falls in love with Goo, the son of a business associate of Kang. Kang discovers this love and he threatens to undo Neiping, sell her back to the brothel, or send her to work in the cane fields at the end of the world. Neiping flees Kang's house that night with Goo. Kang wanders the streets of Shanghai in a stupor of misery, looking for Neiping.

Years pass. Unable to find a way to live, Goo and Neiping fall in with a guerrilla triad. Neiping becomes its leader. In-spired by Neiping, who'd become expert in metals while liv-ing with Kang, the triad undertakes to study British war technology. Neiping says they can produce cannons, which could be used against opium merchants. The emperor will be pleased. In fact, he will someday have tons of opium seized and destroyed. But there is no way to approach the emperor until Neiping learns that Dulu, her dear friend in the brothel, is now the emperor's consort. Neiping goes to Dulu.

"The recognition scene," said Margaret, "is heartbreaking. Dulu has become an icy woman who moves slowly beneath layers of silk. But she remembers herself as the little girl who once cried in the arms of Neiping. She and Neiping are now about twenty-three."

Through Dulu's help, Neiping gains the emperor's support. This enrages Jujuzi, the evil eunuch. Opium trade is in his interest, since he is an addict and a dealer. Everything is threatened by Neiping's cannons, which are superior to the originals, but the triad's military strategy is betrayed by Jujuzi. Neiping and Goo are captured by British sailors and jailed.

Margaret said, "Guess what happens next. Kang appears. He has vanished for three hundred pages, but he's back in the action."

The British allow Kang to speak to Neiping. He offers to buy her freedom. Neiping says he must also buy Goo's freedom. Kang says she has no right to ask him to buy her lover's freedom. Neiping accepts Kang's offer, and she is freed from jail. She then goes to Dulu and appeals for the emperor's help in freeing Goo. Jujuzi, frustrated by Neiping's escape, demands justice for Goo. The British, who are in debt to Jujuzi, look the other way while he tortures Goo to death.

The emperor, who has heard Neiping's appeal through Dulu, asks to see Neiping. The emperor knows Goo is dead. He was told by Jujuzi. But the emperor is moved by Neiping's beauty and her poignant concern to save the already dead Goo. The emperor tells her that he will save him, but she must forget Goo. Then he says that Neiping, like Dulu, will be his consort. In the final chapter, Neiping is heavy with the emperor's child. She and Dulu wander in the palace gardens. Jujuzi watches the lovely consorts passing amid flowers, and he remembers in slow, microscopic detail the execution of Neiping's lover.

"What a story."

"I left most of it out."

"Is that so?"

"You think it's boring."

"No."

"You do."

"Don't tell me what I think. That's annoying."

"Do you think it's boring?"

"Yes, but how can I know unless I read the book?"

"Well, I liked it a lot. The last chapter is horribly dazzling and so beautiful. Jujuzi watches Neiping and Dulu stroll in the garden, and he remembers Goo in chains, bleeding from the hundred knives Jujuzi stuck in him. To Jujuzi, everything is aesthetic, knives, consorts, even feelings. He has no balls so he collects feelings. You see? Like jewels in a box."

LIGHTS went up in the midst of the applause. Margaret said, "Aren't you glad you came?" Claude Rue bowed. Waves of praise poured onto his head. I applauded, too, a concession to the community. Besides, Margaret loved the lecture. She watched me from the corners of her eyes, suspicious of my enthusiasm. I nodded, as if to say yes, yes. Mainly, I needed to go to the toilet, but I didn't want to do anything that might look like a negative comment on the lecture. I'd go when we arrived at the reception for Rue. This decision was fateful. At the reception, in the Faculty Club, I carried a glass of white wine from the bar to Margaret, then went to the men's room. I stood beside a man who had leaned his cane against the urinal. He patted his straight blond hair with one hand, holding his cock with the other, shaking it. The man was, I suddenly realized, himself, Claude Rue. Surprised into speech, I said I loved his lecture. He said, "You work here?"

Things now seemed to be happening quickly, making thought impossible. I was unable to answer. Exactly what was Rue asking—was I a professor? a men's room attendant?

a toilet cruiser? Not waiting for my answer, he said he'd been promised a certain figure for the lecture. A check, made out to him from the regents of the university, had been delivered to his hotel room. The check shocked him. He'd almost canceled the lecture. He was still distressed, unable to contain himself. He'd hurried to the men's room, after the lecture, to look at his check again. The figure was less than promised. I was the first to hear about it. Me. A stranger. He was hysterical, maybe, but I felt very privileged. Money talk is personal, especially in a toilet. "You follow me?" he said.

"Yes. You were promised a certain figure. They gave you a check. It was delivered to your hotel room."

"Precisely. But the figure inscribed on the check is less than promised."

"Somebody made a mistake."

"No mistake. Taxes have been deducted. But I came from Paris with a certain understanding. I was to be paid a certain figure. I have the letter of agreement, and the contract." His green stare, fraught with helpless reproach, held me as he zipped up. He felt that he'd been cheated. He dragged to a sink. His cane, lacquered mahogany, with a black, iron ferrule, clacked the tile floor. He washed his hands. Water raged in the sink.

"It's a mistake, and it can be easily corrected," I said, speaking to his face in the mirror above the sink. "Don't worry, Mr. Rue. You'll get every penny they promised."

"Will you speak to somebody?" he said, taking his cane. "I'm very upset."

"Count on it, Mr. Rue."

"But will you speak to somebody about this matter?"

"Before the evening is over, I'll have their attention."

"But will you speak to a person?"

"Definitely."

I could see, standing close to him, that his teeth were heavily stained by cigarette smoke. They looked rotten. I asked if I might introduce him to a friend of mine. Margaret would get a kick out of meeting Claude Rue, I figured, but I mainly wanted her to see his teeth. He seemed thrown off balance, reluctant to meet someone described as a friend. "My time is heavily scheduled," he muttered; but, since he'd just asked me for a favor, he shrugged, shouldering obligation. I led him to Margaret. Rue's green eyes gained brightness. Margaret quickened within, but offered a mere "Hello," no more, not even the wisp of a smile. She didn't say she loved his lecture. Was she overwhelmed, having Claude Rue thrust at her like this? The silence was difficult for me, if not for them. Lacking anything else to say, I started to tell Margaret about Rue's problem with the university check. "It wasn't the promised amount." Rue cut me off:

"Money is offal. Not to be discussed."

His voice was unnaturally high, operatic and crowing at once. He told Margaret, speaking to her eyes—as if I'd ceased to exist—that he would spend the next three days in Berkeley. He was expected at lunches, cocktail parties, and dinner par-ties. He'd been invited to conduct a seminar, and to address a small gathering at the Asian Art Museum.

"But my lecture is over. I have fulfilled my contract. I owe nothing to anybody."

Margaret said, "No point, then, cheapening yourself, is there?"

"I will cancel every engagement."

"How convenient," she said, hesitated, then gambled, "for us."

Her voice was flat and black as an ice slick on asphalt, but I could hear, beneath the surface, a faint trembling. I prayed that she would look at Rue's teeth, which were practically biting her face. She seemed not to notice.

"Do you drive a car?"

She said, "Yes," holding her hand out to the side, toward me, blindly. I slipped the keys to my Volvo into her palm. Tomorrow, I'd ride to her place on my bike and retrieve the car. Margaret wouldn't remember that she'd taken it. She and Rue walked away, but I felt it was I who grew smaller in the gathering distance. Margaret glanced back at me to say goodbye. Rue, staring at Margaret, lost peripheral vision, thus annihilating me. I might have felt insulted, but he'd been seized by hormonal ferocity, and was focused on a woman. I'd have treated him similarly.

MONTHS earlier, I'd heard about Rue from Margaret. She'd heard about him from her sister May, who had a Ph.D. in library science from Berkeley and worked at the university library in Beijing. In a letter to Margaret, May said she'd met Professor Claude Rue, the linguistic historian. He was known in academic circles, but not yet an international celebrity. Rue was in Beijing completing his research for *The Mists of Shanghai*. May said, in her letter, that Rue was a "womanizer." He had bastard children in France and Tahiti. She didn't find him attractive, but other women might. "If you said Claude Rue is charming or has pretty green eyes, I wouldn't disagree, but as I write to you, I have trouble remembering what he looks like."

Margaret said the word *womanizer* tells more about May than Rue. "She's jealous. She thinks Rue is fucking every woman except her."

"She says she doesn't find him attractive, doesn't even know what he looks like."

"She finds him very attractive, and she knows what he looks like, what he sounds like, smells like, feels like. May has no respect for personal space. She touches people when she talks to them. She's a shark, with taste sensors in her skin. When May takes your hand, or brushes up against you, she's tasting you. Nobody but sharks and cannibals can do that. She shakes somebody's hand, then tells me, 'Needs salt and a little curry.'"

"All right. Maybe *womanizer* says something about May, but the word has a meaning. Regardless of May, *womanizer* means something."

"What?"

"You kidding?"

"Tell me. What does it mean?"

"What do you think? It means a man who sits on the side of the bed at two in the morning, putting on his shoes."

"What do you call women who do that? Don't patronize me, Herman. Don't you tell me what *womanizer* means."

"Why did you ask?"

"To see if you'd tell me. So patronizing. I know exactly what the word means. *Womanizer* means my sister May wants Claude Rue to fuck her."

"Get a dictionary. I want to see where it mentions your sis-ter and Claude Rue."

"The dictionary is a cemetery of dead words. All words are dead until somebody uses them. *Womanizer* is dead. If you use it, it lives, uses you."

"Nonsense."

"People once talked about nymphomaniacs, right? Remem-ber that word? Would you ever use it without feeling it said something embarrassing about you? Get real, Herman. Every-one is constantly on the make—even May. Even you."

"Not me."

"Maybe that's because you're old-fashioned, which is to say narrow-minded. Self-righteous. Incapable of seeing your-self. You disappoint me, Herman. You really do. What about famous men who had bastards? Rousseau, Byron, Shelley, Wordsworth, the Earl of Gloucester, Edward VII."

"I don't care who had bastards. That isn't pertinent. You're trying to make a case for bad behavior."

"Rodin, Hegel, Marx, Castro—they all had bastards. If

they are all bad, that's pertinent. My uncle Chan wasn't famous, but he had two families. God knows what else he had.
Neither family knew of the other until he died. Then it became pertinent, everyone squabbling over property."

"What's your point, if you have one, which I seriously
doubt?"

"And what about Kafka, Camus, Sartre, Picasso, Charlie
Chaplin, Charlie Parker, J.F.K., M.L.K.? What about Chinese
emperors and warlords, Arab sheiks, movie actors, thousands
of Mormons? Everybody collects women. That's why there
are prostitutes, whores, courtesans, consorts, concubines,
bimbos, mistresses, wives, flirts, hussies, sluts, et cetera, et
cetera. How many words are there for man? Not one equivalent for *cunt*, which can mean a woman. *Prick* means some
kind of jerk. Look at magazine covers, month after month.
They're selling clothes and cosmetics? They sell women, stupid. You know you're stupid. Stupid Herman, that's you."

"They're selling happiness, not women."

"It's the same thing. Lions, monkeys, horses, goats, people
... many, many, many animals collect women animals. When
they stop, they become unhappy and they die. Married men
live longer than single men. This has long been true. The truth
is the truth. What am I talking about? Hug me, please."

"The truth is you're madly in love with Claude Rue."

"I've never met the man. Don't depress me."

"Your sister mentions him in a letter, you imagine she
wants him. She wants him, you want him. You're in love,
you're jealous."

"You're more jealous."

"You admit it? You've never before conceded anything in an
argument. I feel like running in the streets, shrieking the
news."

"I admit nothing. After reading my sister May's gossipy,
puritanical letter, I find that I dislike Claude Rue intensely."

"You never met the man."

"How can that have any bearing on the matter?"

As FOR the people in the large reception room at the Faculty Club—deans, department heads, assistant professors, students, wives, husbands—gathered to honor Claude Rue— he'd flicked us off like a light. I admired Rue for that, and I wished his plane back to Paris would crash. Behind me, a woman whispered in the exact tone Margaret had used, "I dislike him intensely."

A second woman said, "You know him?"

"Of course not. I've heard things, and his novel is very sexist."

"You read the novel. Good for you."

"I haven't read it. I saw a review in a magazine at my hairdresser's. I have the magazine. I'll look for it tonight when I get home."

"Sexist?" said the first woman. "Odd. I heard he's gay."

"Gay?" said a man. "How interesting. I suppose one can be gay and sexist, but I'd never have guessed he was gay. He looks straight to me. Who told you he's gay? Someone who knows him?"

"Well, not with a capital K, if that's what you mean by 'knows,' but he was told by a friend of Rue's that he agreed to fly here and give this lecture only because of the Sanfran bath houses. That's what he was told. Gossip in this town spreads quick as genital warts."

"Ho, ho, ho. People are so dreadfully bored. Can you blame them? They have no lives, just careers and Volvos."

"That's good. I intend to use it. Do look for conversational citations in the near future. But who is the Chinese thing? I'll die if I don't find out. She's somebody, isn't she? Ask him."

"Who?"

"Him, him. That man. He was standing with her." Someone plucked my jacket sleeve. I turned. A face desiccated by propriety leaned close, old eyes, shimmering liquid gray, bulging, rims hanging open like thin crimson labia. It spoke:

"Pardon me, sir. Could you please tell us the name of the Chinese woman who, it now seems, is leaving the reception with Professor Rue?"

"Go fuck yourself."

MARGARET said the success of his lecture left Rue giddily deranged, expecting something more palpable from the night. He said, she said, that he couldn't have returned to his hotel room, watched TV, and gone to sleep. "'Why is it like this for me, do you think?'" he said, she said. "'It would have no style. You were loved,'" she said, she said, sensing his need to be reminded of the blatant sycophancy of his herdlike audience. "'Then you appeared,'" he said, she said. "'You were magnificently cold.'"

Voilà! Margaret. She is cold. She is attentive. She is determined to fuck him. He likes her quickness, and her legs. He says that to her. He also likes the way she drives, and her hair—the familiar black Asian kind, but which, because of its dim coppery strain, is rather unusual. He likes her eyes, too. I said: "Margaret, let me. Your gray-tinted glasses give a sensuous glow to your sharply tipped Chinese eyes, which are like precious black glittering pebbles washed by the Yangtze. Also the Yalu."

Margaret said, "Please shut up, dog-eyed white devil. I'm in no mood for jokes."

Her eyes want never to leave Rue's face, she said, but she must concentrate on the road as she drives. The thing is underway for them. I could feel it as she talked, how she was thrilled by the momentum, the invincible rush, the necessity. Resentment built in my sad heart. I thought, Margaret is over thirty years old. She has been around the block. But it's never enough. Once more around the block, up the stairs, into the room, and there lies happiness.

"'Why shouldn't I have abandoned the party for you?'" he said, she said, imitating his tone, plaintive and arrogant. "'I wrote a novel.'" He laughs at himself. Margaret laughs, imitating him, an ironic self-deprecatory laugh. The moment seemed to her phony and real at once, said Margaret. He was nervous, as he'd been onstage, unsure of his stardom, unconvinced even by the flood of abject adoration. "'Would a man write a novel except for love?'" he said, she said, as if he didn't really know. He was sincerely diffident, she said, an amazing quality considering that he'd slept with every woman in the world. But what the hell, he was human. With Margaret, sex will be more meaningful. "'Except for love?'" she said, she said, gaily, wondering if he'd slept with her sister. "'How about your check from the university?'"

"'You think I'm inconsistent?'" He'd laughed. Spittle shot from his lips and rotten teeth. She saw everything except the trouble, what lay deep in the psychic plasma that rushed between them.

She drove him to her loft, in the warehouse and small factory district of Emeryville, near the bay, where she lived and worked, and bought and sold. Canvases, drawings, clothes— everything was flung about. She apologized.

He said, "'A great disorder is an order.'"

"Did you make that up?"

He kissed her. She kissed him.

"'Yes,'" he said. Margaret stared at me, begging for pity. He didn't make that up. A bit of an ass, then, but really, who isn't? She expected Rue to get right down to love. He wanted a drink first. He wanted to look at her paintings, wanted to use the bathroom and stayed inside a long time, wanted something to eat, then wanted to read poetry. It was close to midnight. He was reading poems aloud, ravished by beauties of

LEONARD MICHAELS

phrasing, shaken by their music. He'd done graduate work at
Oxford. Hours passed. Margaret sat on the couch, her legs
folded under her. She thought it wasn't going to happen, after
all. Ten feet away, he watched her from a low-slung, leather
chair. The frame was a steel tube bent to form legs, arms, and
backrest. A book of modern poetry lay open in his lap. He was
about to read another poem when Margaret said, in the flat
black voice, "'Do you want me to drive you to your hotel?'"

He let the book slide to the floor. Stood up slowly, strug-
gling with the leather-wheezing-ass-adhesive chair seat, then
came toward her, pulling stone foot. Leaning down to where
she sat on the couch, he kissed her. Her hand went up, lightly,
slowly, between his legs.

"He wasn't a very great lover," she said.

She had to make him stop, give her time to regather powers
of feeling and smoke a joint before trying again. Then, him inside, "working on me," she said, she fingered her clitoris to
make herself come. "There would have been no payoff otherwise," she said. "He'd talked too much, maybe. Then he was a
tourist looking for sensations in the landscape. He couldn't
give. It was like he had a camera. Collecting memories. Savoring the sex, you know what I mean? I could have been in another city." Finally, Margaret said, she screamed, "'What
keeps you from loving me?'" He fell away, damaged.

"'You didn't enjoy it?'" he said, she said.

She turned on the lamp to roll another joint, and told him
to lie still while she studied his cock, which was oddly discol-
ored and twisted left. In the next three days, the sex got better, not great. She'd say, "'You're losing me.'" He'd moan.

When she left him at the airport, she felt relieved, but driving back to town, she began to miss him. She thought to
phone her psychotherapist, but this wasn't a medical problem.
The pain surprised her and it wouldn't quit. She couldn't
work, couldn't think. Despite strong reservations—he hadn't

168

been very nice to her—she was in love, had been since she saw him onstage. Yes; definitely love. Now he was gone. She was alone. In the supermarket, she wandered the aisles, unable to remember what she needed. She was disoriented—her books, her plants, her clothes, her hands—nothing seemed really hers. At night, the loneliness was very bad. Sexual. Hurt terribly. She cried herself to sleep.

"Why didn't you phone me?"

"I knew you weren't too sympathetic. I couldn't talk to you. I took Gracie out of school. She's been here for the last couple of days."

"She likes school."

"That's just what you'd say, isn't it? You know, Herman, you are a kind of person who makes me feel like shit. If Gracie misses a couple of days it's no big deal. She's got a lot of high Q's. I found out she also has head lice. Her father doesn't notice anything. Gracie would have to have convulsions before he'd notice. Too busy advancing himself, writing another ten books that nobody will read, except his pathetic graduate students."

"That isn't fair."

"Yes, it is. It's fair."

"No, it isn't."

"You defending Sloan? Whose friend are you?"

"Talking to you is like cracking nuts with my teeth."

SHE TOLD ME Rue had asked if she knew Chinese. She said she didn't. He proposed to teach her, and said, "'The emperor forbid foreigners to learn Chinese, except imperfectly, only for purposes of trade. Did you know that?'"

"'No. Let's begin.'"

Minutes into the lesson, he said, "'You're pretending not to know Chinese. I am a serious person. Deceive your American lovers. Not me.'"

169

She said, "Nobody ever talked to me like that. He was furious."

"Didn't you tell him to go to hell?"

"I felt sorry for him."

She told him that she really didn't know a word of Chinese. Her family had lived in America for more than a hundred years. She was raised in Sacramento. Her parents spoke only English. All her friends had been white. Her father was a partner in a construction firm. His associates were white. When the Asian population of the Bay Area greatly increased, she saw herself, for the first time, as distinctly Chinese. She thought of joining Chinese cultural organizations, but was too busy. She sent money.

"'You don't know who you are,'" said Rue.

"'But that's who I am. What do you mean?'"

"'Where are my cigarettes?'"

"Arrogant bastard. Did you?"

"What I did is irrelevant. He felt ridiculed. He thought I was being contemptuous. I was in love. I could have learned anything. Chinese is only a language. It didn't occur to me to act stupid."

"What you did is relevant. Did you get his cigarettes?"

"He has a bald spot in the middle of his head."

"Is there anything really interesting about Rue?"

"There's a small blue tattoo on his right shoulder. I liked it. Black moles are scattered on his back like buckshot. The tattoo is an ideograph. I saw him minutely, you know what I mean? I was on the verge of hatred, really in love. But you wouldn't understand. I won't tell you anymore."

"Answer my question."

She didn't.

"You felt sorry for him. I feel sorry for you. Is it over now?"

"Did it begin? I don't really know. Anyhow, so what?"

"Don't you want to tell me? I want to know. Tell me everything."

"I must keep a little for myself. Do you mind? It's my life. I want to keep my feelings. You can be slightly insensitive, Herman."

"I never dumped YOU at a party in front of the whole town. You want to keep your feelings? Good. If you talk, you'll remember feelings you don't know you had. It's the way to keep them."

"No, it isn't. They go out of you. Then they're not even feelings anymore. They're chit-chat commodities. Some ass-hole like Claude will stick them in a novel."

"Why don't you just fly to Paris? Live with him."

"He's married. I liked him for not saying that he doesn't get along with his wife, or they're separated. I asked if he had an open marriage."

"What did he say?"

"He said, 'Of course not.'"

MARGARET spoke more ill than good of Rue. Nevertheless, she was in love. Felt it every minute, she said, and wanted to phone him, but his wife might answer. He'd promised to write a letter, telling her where they would meet. There were going to be publication parties for his book in Rome and Madrid. He said that his letter would contain airline tickets and notification about her hotel.

"Then you pack a bag? You run out the door?"

"And up into the sky. To Rome. To Madrid."

"Just like that? What about your work? What about Gracie?"

"Just like that."

I bought a copy of *The Mists of Shanghai* and began reading with primitive, fiendish curiosity. Who the hell was Claude Rue? The morning passed, then the afternoon. I quit reading at twilight, when I had to leave for work. I'd reached the point where Dulu comes to the brothel. It was an old-fash-ioned novel, something like Dickens, lots of characters and sentimental situations, but carefully written to seem mind-less, and so clear that you hardly feel you're reading. Jujuzi's voice gives a weird edge to the story. Neiping suffers terribly, he says, but she imagines life in the brothel is not real, and that someday she will go home and her mother will be happy to see her. Just as I began to think Rue was a nitwit, Jujuzi re-flects on Neiping's pain. He says she will never go home, and a child's pain is more terrible than an adult's, but it is the nour-ishment of sublime dreaming. When Dulu arrives, Neiping wishes the new girl would stop crying. It makes Neiping sad. She can't sleep. She stands beside the new girl, staring down through the dark, listening to her sob, wanting to smack her, make her be quiet. But then Neiping slides under the blanket and hugs the new girl. They tell each other their names. They talk. Dulu begins slowly to turn. She hugs Neiping. The little bodies lie in each other's arms, face to face. They talk until they fall asleep.

Did Claude Rue imagine himself as Neiping? Considering Rue's limp, he'd known pain. But maybe pain had made him cold, like Jujuzi, master of sentimental feelings, master of cru-elty. Was Claude Rue like Jujuzi?

A week passed. Margaret called, told me to come to her loft. She sounded low. I didn't ask why. When I arrived, she gave me a brutal greeting. "How come you and me never hap-pened?"

"What do you mean?"

"How come we never fucked?"

She had a torn-looking smile.

"We're best friends, aren't we?"

I sat on the couch. She followed, plopped beside me. We sat beside each other, beside ourselves. Dumb. She leaned against me, put her head on my shoulder. I loved her so much it hurt my teeth. Light went down in the tall, steel-mullioned fac-tory windows. The air of the loft grew chilly.

"Why did you phone?" I asked.

"I needed you to be here."

"Do you want to talk?"

"No."

The perfume of her dark hair came to me. I saw dents on the side of her nose, left by her eyeglasses. They made her eyes look naked, vulnerable. She'd removed her glasses to see less clearly. Twisted the ends of her hair. Chewed her lip. I stood up, unable to continue doing nothing, crossed to a lamp, then didn't turn it on. Electric light was violent. Besides, it wasn't very dark in the loft, and the shadows were pleasant. I looked back. Her eyes had followed me. She asked what I'd like to drink.

"What do you have?"

"Black tea?"

"All right."

She put on her glasses and walked to the kitchen area. The cup and saucer rattled as she set them on the low table. I took her hands. "Sit," I said. "Talk."

She sat, but said nothing.

"Do you want to go out somewhere? Take a walk, maybe."

"We were together for three days," she said.

"Did he write to you?"

"We were together for hours and hours. There was so much feeling. Then I get this letter."

"What does he say? Rome? Barcelona?"

"He says I stole his watch. He says I behaved like a whore, going through his pockets when he was asleep."

"Literally, he says that?"

"Read it yourself."

"It's in French." I handed it back to her.

"An heirloom, he says. His most precious material possession, he says. He understands my motive and finds it contemptible. He wants his watch back. He'll pay. How much am I asking?"

"You have his heirloom?"

"I never saw it."

"Let's look."

"Please, Herman, don't be tedious. There is no watch."

With the chaos of art materials scattered on the vast floor, and on table tops, dressers, chairs, and couch, it took twenty minutes before she found Claude Rue's watch jammed between a bedpost and the wall.

I laughed. She didn't laugh. I wished I could redeem the moment. Her fist closed around the watch, then opened slowly. She said, "Why did he write that letter?"

"Send him the watch and forget it."

"He'll believe he was right about me."

"Who cares what he believes?"

"He hurt me."

"Oh, just send him the watch."

"He hurt me, really hurt me. Three days of feeling, then that letter."

"Send it to him," I said.

But there was a set look in Margaret's eyes. She seemed to hear nothing.

—1992

Honeymoon

ONE SUMMER, at a honeymoon resort in the Catskill Mountains, I saw a young woman named Sheila Kahn fall in love with her waiter. She had been married a few hours earlier in the city. This was her first night at dinner. The waiter bent beside her and asked if she wanted the steak or the chicken. She stared at him with big sick eyes. Her husband said, "Sheila?" Three other couples at the table, all just married, looked at Sheila as if waiting for the punch line of a joke. She sat like a dummy.

The waiter, Larry Starker, a tall fellow with Nordic cheekbones and an icy, gray stare, was considered dangerously handsome. In fact, he'd modeled for the covers of cheap paperbacks, appearing as a Teutonic barbarian about to molest a semi-naked female who lay at his feet, manacled, writhing in terror-pleasure. He'd also appeared chained to a post, watching the approach of a whip-queen in leather regalia. But the real Larry Starker, twenty-two years old, didn't have a clue about exotic sex. He'd completed a year of dental school and hoped to have an office someday in Brighton Beach, where he'd grown up playing handball with the neighborhood guys. Like everyone else on the dining-room staff, he was working to make money for books and tuition.

I was eighteen years old, Larry's busboy. This was my first job in a good resort. The previous three summers, I'd worked in a schlock-house where, aside from heavy meals and a lake with a rowboat, there were few amenities, and the dining-room staff slept two to a bed. Husbands arrived on weekends, set a card table on the lawn and played pinochle, ignoring the women and children they'd come to visit. My own family used to go to a place like that every summer, and my father was one of the men playing pinochle. He never once took me fishing or hunting, like an American dad, but then he never went fishing or hunting. The only place he ever took me was to the stone-cutter's, one Sunday afternoon, when he ordered his grave-stone.

As Larry's busboy, I cleared away dishes, poured coffee, served desserts, then set the tables for the next meal. Between breakfast and lunch, we had an hour break and we all lay about dozing in the bunkhouse or sat on our narrow beds writing letters home. Between lunch and dinner, there was a two-and-a-half-hour break. Some of us slept through the af-ternoon heat, others spent the time reading, and others played cards, or handball, or basketball, or went swimming. After we worked dinner, nobody wanted to sleep. It was then about 9:00 PM. We'd taken orders from strangers in the dining room, and chefs had screamed at us from behind a steam table. We should have been exhausted, but the nighttime air smelled good, the starry mountain skies were exhilarating, and we were young.

As we showered and dressed, the fine strain of a flute came through the darkness. It meant the Latin dance band was play-ing. In clean shirts and sport jackets, we left the bunkhouse, hurrying toward the lights of the casino where we danced the mambo. Our partners were the young brides. When that be-came depressing, we took off for another resort and danced with free women, governesses, chambermaids, or guests who were unmarried or whose husbands were in the city.

There may have been waitresses in the Catskill resorts, but I never met one. Since women guests far outnumbered the men, waiters and busboys were expected to show up at night on the dance floor. At the honeymoon resort there was no shortage, but the dining-room staff was all men, anyway. I don't know why. Maybe the atmosphere of newly married bliss forbade hanky-panky among the help.

Latin music was the rage in the early fifties. You would hear the dining-room staff singing in Spanish: rumbas, mambos, cha-cha-chas. We understood the feeling in the words, not the words. We called Latin music "Jewish." The wailing melodies were reminiscent of Hebraic and Arabic chanting, but we only meant the music was exciting to us. A fusion music, conflating Europe and Africa. In mambo, Spanish passion throbs to Nigerian syncopation. In Yiddish, the German, Hebrew, Spanish, Polish, and English words are assimilated to a culture and a system of sound. The foxtrot and lindy hop we called "American." They had a touch of Nigeria, too, but compared to mambo or Yiddish, they felt like "Jingle Bells."

Handsome Larry Starker, with his straight dark blond hair and long bones, danced the mambo as well as anyone at the Palladium in Manhattan, great hall of the conga drum and Machito. Other dancers made a space when Larry stepped onto the floor. The music welcomed him, horns became more brilliant, congas and timbales talked to his belly. He did no fancy steps, but in the least of his motions he was wonderful, displaying the woman who danced in his arms, turning her around and around for the world to see.

Larry gave me forty percent of his tips, the customary waiter-busboy split. On Sundays after lunch, guests checked out and tipped the waiter six dollars and the busboy four. Sometimes they put money directly in my hand, but more often they gave it to Larry. We shoved the money into the pockets of our black sweaty trousers. Later, in the bunkhouse, each of us went off alone and pulled out sticky wads by the fistful, peeling away bills, counting as they fluttered to the bed. At the end of the summer, having worked ten- to fourteen-hour days, sometimes seven days a week, I expected to make between eight and twelve hundred dollars.

I'd have done a little better working with a waiter who didn't have icy eyes and a face like a cliff above the North Sea, beaten by freezing winds. Larry spoke Yiddish and was fluent in the mambo, but he looked like an SS officer. Not a good way to look after World War II, especially in the Catskills where

177

the shadow of death, extending from millions of corpses in Europe, darkened the consciousness of surviving millions in New York.

Comedians, called tummlers, who played the Catskills were even stranger in their effects than Larry. Masters of Jewish self-mockery, they filled casino theaters with a noise never previously heard in the human universe—to my ears, anyway—the happy shrieks of unghosted yiddim. "What does not destroy me makes me stronger," says Nietzsche. We laughed. We danced the mambo. Because we weren't dead, we lived.

Entertainers came streaming up from the city—actors, magicians, hypnotists, jugglers, acrobats, impersonators, singers. But with or without entertainment, there was always dancing. After the dancing, we sometimes drove to a late-night Chinese restaurant called Corey's, ate sweet-and-sour spareribs, and listened to a small Latin band. Piano, bass, horn, congas, and a black-haired Latina in a tight red dress who played maracas and sang so beautifully you wanted to die at the table, lips shining with grease, cigarette forgotten, burning your fingers. She played maracas as she sang and danced, taking small steps, her shoulders level, hips subtly swaying to intimate the grandeurs and devastations of love. Pleasure was in the air, day and night.

The newly married couple, Sheila and Morris Kahn, took meals in their honeymoon suite for two days after their embarrassment. Larry said, ironically, "I don't expect them to tip big." I thought they had checked out of the resort and we'd never see them again, but the evening of the third day, they returned to the dining room.

Wearing a bright blue dress and high heels, Sheila looked neat, cool, and invulnerable. She took her seat, greeted everyone at the table, plucked her napkin out of the water glass, where I'd propped it up like a tall white iris, and placed it in her lap. But she didn't make it past the soup. Larry set down her bowl. She stood up clutching the napkin and hurried away. Morris gaped after her, his ears like flames of shame, his cheeks pale. An urgent question struggled to shape his lips, then perished. The blue dress of happiness fled among the tables. Larry muttered, "I didn't do anything," and strode off to the kitchen to pick up the next course. I collected Sheila's soup bowl, contents untasted, and put it out of sight.

Morris lingered through the meal. I heard him talking, in a loud, officious voice, about Hitler. "According to my sources," said Morris, "Hitler isn't dead." Nobody disagreed with his sources. The flight of Sheila, the only subject, wasn't mentioned.

Larry read one book all summer, which was about the mechanics and pathology of the human mouth. Otherwise, he was dedicated to Latin dancing and handball. He took on challengers at handball every week—lifeguards, tennis instructors, waiters, and bellhops—first-class players who often came from resorts miles away. Some referred to him as "the Nazi," even to his face. Catskill resorts weren't polite society, and conversation could be blunt and cruel. To call Larry a Nazi wasn't fair, but he looked the way he looked. It had an alienating effect, despite his Yiddish, despite his being a Jew.

The hard black rubber ball, banging the backboard, sounded like gunfire as Larry annihilated challengers. I didn't root for Larry, because he always won anyway, and I felt sorry for the others. They wanted badly to beat him, as if more than a game and a couple of dollars were at stake. He knew what they felt, men with strength and speedy reflexes who had come from miles away to beat the Nazi. He beat them week after week.

There was another great handball player, "Hairy Murray," also know as "the maniac from Hackensack." He worked the resort circuit as a tummler. He'd challenged Larry, and a date had been set for a game. The odds were usually around ten to one against the challenger, but against Hairy Murray there were no odds. People wanted to see these competitors in the flesh, the way people want to see horses before a race. I assumed Larry would win. He played like the God of Isaiah, an insatiable destroyer. Larry's dancing wasn't altogether different. He moved without a smile or the dopey rictus of ballroom professionals, his body seized by rhythms of the earth. I could live with his inhuman sublimity, and even his good looks, but I couldn't think that I'd ever have Larry's effect on a woman.

I felt envy, a primitive feeling. Also a sin. But go not feel it. According to Melanie Klein, envy is among the foundation stones of Brain House. Nobody is free of it. I believed envy is the chief principle of life: what one man has, another lacks. Sam is smart; hence, you are stupid. Joey is tall; hence, you are a midget. Kill Sam and Joey, you are smart and tall. Such sublogical thoughts applied also to eating. The first two bites satisfy a person's hunger. After that comes eating, which satisfies more than hunger. Seeing hundreds of people eat three times a day in the dining room brought to mind the Yiddish expression, "Eating is nothing to sneeze at," which is no joke. Guests looked serious in the dining room, as if they had come to eat what life denied them—power, brains, beauty, love, wealth—in the form of borscht, boiled beef, chopped liver, sour cream, etc. In the bunkhouse at night, falling asleep, I saw hundreds of faces *geshtupt*, like chewing machines in a factory that ingests dreams.

I also saw Sheila's light brown curly hair and her appealing face, with its pointy lips and small, sweet chin, and her nice figure, today called a "body." Like a sculptor's vision, it was nearly palpable, an image in my hands. I remembered her agony, too, how she stood up clutching her napkin, how she seemed transfigured, going from mere appealingness to divinity. She got to me, though she wasn't my type, and I'd have felt nothing, maybe, if she hadn't been deranged by Larry.

The morning after she fled the dining room, Morris Kahn arrived for breakfast alone. He carried the *Times*. It was to suggest that he was an intelligent man, with interests beyond personal life. He opened the *Times* and began to read. Larry approached like a robot waiter, wordless. Not looking up, Morris said, "Scrambled eggs."

Larry spun away, returned with scrambled eggs.

Morris said, "These eggs are cold."

Larry took away the eggs.

Morris said, "Fuck eggs. Bring pancakes."

Larry quick-marched to the kitchen, reappeared with pancakes.

Morris let them get cold, then ordered more.

I stepped forward, took away cold pancakes.

Larry set down warm pancakes.

Morris read the newspaper, ate nothing. Larry's white rayon shirt, gray with sweat, sucked his chest. Hair, pressing up against the rayon, was a dark scribble of lines.

Morris, about thirty years old, maybe ten or twelve years older than Sheila, was almost completely bald, and he had a pink, youthful, placid face that showed no anguish. He ordered pancakes five times. He wanted to make a bad scene, but, like a round-headed dog, he was hopelessly affectionate and at a loss for an appropriate violence. Larry and I sped back and forth, rolling our eyes at each other as we passed, in opposite directions, through the swinging doors of the kitchen. At last Morris was content. He rose and walked out, the *Times* folded under his arm, like one who has completed important business and is at leisure to amble in the sunlight.

That morning, he checked out of the resort with Sheila. At the desk, he left an envelope with Larry's name scrawled across the front. It contained a thirty-five-dollar tip, much more than he'd have left if they'd stayed a week and never missed a meal. The tip was an apology. Had Morris been a Catskill gangster, Larry Starker would have disappeared, dumped in a mountain lake.

In the following weeks, Larry received phone calls from

the city, sometimes in the middle of the night. It was no secret who was calling. He stayed long on the phone and never discussed the calls. Sheila had spent only a few days at the resort, and if she and Larry had found moments to talk, nobody noticed. Lovers are sly, making do in circumstances less convenient than the buildings and grounds of a resort in the Catskills.

One afternoon, in the break after lunch, I was lying in my bunk, groggy with fatigue and heat, unable to sleep or to sit up and finish reading *The Stranger*, in which Camus's hero mysteriously murders an Arab, on a blindingly sunny beach in Algiers, and feels no remorse, feels hardly anything else, and has no convictions. A modern believer, I supposed, different from the traditional kind, like Saint Teresa, who draws conviction from feeling. I thought the book couldn't have been written before the Holocaust.

Larry was lying in the bed next to mine. I heard his voice: "What do you say?"

"All right," I answered, hearing my own voice, as I sprawled in stuporous languor after lunch, a dairy meal, which was always the hardest of the day. Guests had to sample everything. Busboy trays became mountains of dirty dishes. The dining room was too warm. The kitchen was hot, and the wooden floors were soft and slick, dangerous when rushing with a heavy tray on your shoulder. The chefs, boiling behind the steam counter, screamed at you for no reason. In the middle of the meal, the dishwasher cut himself on broken glass. He couldn't stop working. More and more dishes were arriving, and there was blood everywhere.

"Then get up."

"Doing it," I said.

I'd agreed to play handball, surprised and flattered by Larry's invitation, never before offered, but my body got up reluctantly, lifting from the clutch of mud. I followed him out of the bunkhouse. He'd brought a ball and two gloves. "You lefty or righty?" he asked. I mumbled, "Righty," as if not sure. He said, "Here. Take both gloves." He didn't really need them, since he could hit killers with his iron-hard, naked hands. In the glare and stillness, the ball boomed off the back-board. As we warmed up, my body returned to itself. I hit a few good shots, then said, "I'm ready." We played one game. Larry beat me by eighteen points. It felt like an insult. He'd slammed the ball unnecessarily on every play. My palms were burning and swollen. Walking back to the bunkhouse, he said, "Sheila Kahn has a sister. Adele. Would you like a date with her? They live in Riverdale."

"Too far."

"I'm talking about later, in the city. Not now, not in the Catskills, moron. She's seventeen, goes to Barnard, a chem-istry major. Sheila says Adele is pretty. You and Adele. Me and Sheila. A double date."

"Double-shmubble. I don't have wheels, and I don't want to sit in the subway for an hour and a half to meet a chemist."

"Ever hear of Glock Brothers Manufacturing?"

"No. Go alone."

"I'll pick you up on my way from Brooklyn. You never heard of Glock Manufacturing?"

"You think, if I go with you, it will be easier to face Sheila's parents. Since you ruined her life."

Larry said, "Don't *hock mir a chinek*, which means, "Don't bang me a tea kettle," or, without the Yiddish compression, "Don't bug me with empty chatter." He continued: "You don't know shit. You'll never get anywhere."

"Fuck you. I don't like to be used."

"Sheila's father is Herschel Glock."

"Fuck him, too."

"Glock Manufacturing makes airplane parts for Boeing and McDonnell Douglas. Her father owns the company."

"So he's a rich man. So his daughters are rich girls. Big deal."

LEONARD MICHAELS

"I can't talk to you."

"You want to talk to me? Why didn't you tell me?"

To go out with Sheila's sister would have been kicks, but Larry let me score only three points and used me like a dog to retrieve the ball for him so he could hit it again too hard and fast for me. Besides, I had no car and didn't want charity. Who knows what the date would cost? Maybe twenty bucks. It took a week, serving a married couple, to make fifteen. I planned to go alone the next day to the courts and slam the ball till the pain was unbearable. It was near the end of the season, not enough time to improve much, and I'd never beat Larry anyway. But if I could win five points, I'd say I twisted my ankle, and quit in the middle of the game, and never play him again. He wouldn't know for sure if he could beat me. The sunlight was unbearable. And I was too mixed up with feeling to know what I wanted, but I could refuse to go out with Sheila's sister. That was a powerful response, disappointing to Larry and hurtful to me because I wanted to go with Sheila's sister. In the bunkhouse we flopped on our beds, two feet apart, and lay shining with sweat. I reviewed the game in memory, making myself more depressed and angry. I couldn't stop thinking about it, couldn't relax. Larry said, "Is it raining?"

"It's the sunniest day on record," I said, and my hurt feelings grabbed my voice. "You want to know something, Larry. We're different. We don't look like each other. We don't think like each other. We don't nothing like each other. It's a miracle that we can even speak and understand what's said, either in English or Yiddish."

He groaned.

I glanced at him and saw eyes without pupils, showing only whites. A horrible face, as if he were tortured by my remarks or he'd remembered something extremely important that he hadn't done.

I sat up, saying, "You're making me sick, you freak," then realized he couldn't hear me. He was foaming at the corners of his mouth, and his body was thrashing like a live wire. Foam pinkish with blood streamed down his chin. I shouted for help. Nobody came. I heard voices in the next room. I ran into the next room. A bed was strewn with dollars and quarters and playing cards. Two guys sat on the adjacent bed to the left, facing three on the bed to the right. Nobody noticed me until I brought both fists down on the cards and dollars. Quarters flew up in the air. I shouted, "Larry is having a fit."

They rushed after me into my room. Larry, still thrashing, was sidling up the wall against his back, as if to escape a snake on his mattress. His face was blue. Bloody foam was running down his neck. Someone said, "He's swallowing his tongue. Do something." I saw a comb on the window ledge above Larry's bed and snatched it. Two guys seized Larry's arms and forced him down flat onto the bed. I straddled his chest and pried his mouth open with the edge of the comb, clenching it in my fists at either end. I said, "Open, open, open," as I forced the edge of the comb between his teeth, trying to press his tongue down. He went limp abruptly. The guys let go of his arms. I slid off his chest. We backed away. His head rolled to one side, then slowly to the other, as if to shake away the seizure. He opened his eyes, seeing, and said, "What?" The word was dim, from far away. I said, "Are you all right, Larry? You had a seizure."

"When?"

I TOOK OVER his station at dinner, waiting his tables. Busboys came shooting from nearby stations to clear dishes, doing double work. We'd have done the same at breakfast, but he insisted on returning to his station. He made it through the day with no help. That night, in the casino bar, drinking beers, he said he felt fine. He didn't remember the seizure. I described it to him, feeling nervous and guilty, as if I shouldn't be telling him about himself. He said it had happened before. Only his parents knew.

"I'm worried," he said.

"Of course."

"Hairy Murray the tummler is driving up to play handball tomorrow afternoon."

"You're worried about that? Call off the game."

"I'll rip his head off."

"Sure. But not tomorrow."

"I put money down."

"Forfeit. Tell him you're sick. Hairy Murray doesn't need your money. He'll let you keep it."

"He hangs out with hard guys. He won't let me keep one cent. It's a question of honor."

"It's a question of you being sick."

"I can play."

"You want to be king of the little black ball."

"Yeah."

We sat for a while in silence. Then I said, "Because of Sheila?"

"That's over."

"Yesterday you were fixing me up with her sister, the great chemist."

"I phoned Sheila last night. I told her what happened and said to stay out of my life."

"What did she say?"

"She was crying."

"I'm sorry. So why are you playing?"

"I want to win."

"You want to lose."

"If I need a psychiatrist, I'll give you a ring."

"Do that. I'll have you put in a straitjacket. You had a fit right in my face. *El gran mambo.*"

Hᴀɪʀʏ Mᴜʀʀᴀʏ arrived like a boxer, with an entourage. He was on the short side, with a thick neck, wide and deeply sloping shoulders, and short arms. He wore a white linen suit, white shoes, and sunglasses. He looked tropical. When he stepped out of his Cadillac, he began limping heavily toward the handball court, then, suddenly, he became a blind man, walking in the wrong direction. His entourage, five guys in flashy, gabardine slacks, were laughing their heads off. The dining-room and kitchen staff were already in the stands, along with the musicians and a lot of the guests. When people arrived from other resorts, they sat on the grass. Everyone knew about Larry's seizure. It made the game more interesting.

Hairy Murray waved to the crowd, then began to strip. One of the gabardine men held his shorts and sneakers. It was another joke, changing in public. When Hairy Murray dropped his pants, he snapped them back up again instantly. He had no underwear. He pretended to be confused, shamed by his forgetfulness. Everyone had seen his big cock slop free of his pants. Men cheered and booed. Women stared wildly at each other, smiling with disgust. Hairy Murray's entourage, virtually in tears, was laughing as they made a circle around him, shielding him from view while he changed.

Larry ignored the spectacle and warmed up, serving the ball to himself, slamming righty, then lefty. He looked thoughtful, faintly slower. He wouldn't even glance at Hairy Murray, whose legs, arms, back, and neck were covered with black hair. A gold star of David, on a fine gold chain, floated on the black sea of chest hair. I thought maybe he would beat Larry. A man couldn't have so much hair without being exceptionally gifted. His arms were stumpy but looked powerful. The question was, could he move fast? Larry's hope was to hit wide angles, make Hairy Murray chase the ball.

The coin was tossed. Larry called tails. It came down tails.

Hairy Murray quit joking, took his position on the court, and braced to receive the first serve, a tremendous boom off the board, speeding back low and at a wide angle to the left side-line. Hairy Murray was after it with a blur of short steps. He sent the ball back with the least flick of his left wrist, a soft, high lob. Larry went drifting to the endline, where he returned hard, but no slam was possible. They played even for seventeen points. Neither was clearly superior. Then Hairy Murray served, won four straight points, and the game was over. There wasn't a sound from the stands and nobody moved to pay off bets. Hairy Murray said, "Double or nothing?"

Larry shrugged. "I don't think so."

"I'll spot you the four points you lost and triple the bet."

"Thanks, no."

"You don't have the cash?"

"Not today."

"You'll owe me."

"You want to play me that bad?"

"I want to kill you." He said this smiling.

Larry looked vague, as if he didn't remember he was a Teutonic barbarian, handball ace, mambo genius, future dentist, and the man Sheila Kahn had been smitten by so hard it ruined her life. I wanted to go to the bunkhouse, go to sleep. Seeing him like this was a kind of betrayal. Nameless, creepy feelings swarmed about my heart. I wished he would say goodbye, go. He couldn't say anything, and couldn't go. He bounced the ball, caught it, bounced it. Hairy Murray put his hands on his hips, waiting, patience and contempt in his posture.

Then another man walked onto the court. A bald man. He looked so different from Hairy Murray that, oddly enough, they looked like brothers. It was Morris Kahn. I hadn't noticed him arrive. "Take the bet," he said. "I'll cover it." Morris looked haggard, with dark, puffy crescents under his eyes.

Hairy Murray said, "Hey Starker, you hear this cat?"

"I don't want to lose your money," said Larry to Morris.

"So don't lose it." Morris's voice was quick and definitive. "Do you think I drove up here, two hours from the city, to see a loser?"

Hairy Murray grinning, said, "Four points, kid. Beat me." He twitched faintly, enough to suggest epilepsy, then grinned, holding his hands out, palms up, to suggest no harm intended. Morris said, *"Khazar fisl kosher,"* meaning, more or less, Hairy Murray is a pig showing us clean little feet. Hairy Murray laughed, exhibiting every tooth and a flare of crimson gums. In his thickness and vigor, he was pleased; didn't feel injured. Smiling at Larry, he said, "What's shaking? You'll take a four-point spot?"

He looked at Morris; said nothing.

"A four-point spot is for losers," said Morris. "Larry plays even. Double or nothing." Morris reached into his pants pocket, came up with a quarter, tossed it high and said, "Call, Larry." The coin hit the ground and rolled away too far to make out how it landed. Hairy Murray looked at Larry and said, *"Nu, boychick,* you call it, or I'll call it."

Larry said, "Tails." I heard a sort of keening in his voice, high and miserable. It came neither from fear nor defiance, but, like the wind of Golgotha, from desolation. In that instant, I knew the difference between winners and losers has no relation to talent or beauty or personal will, what athletes call "desire," but only to a will beyond ourselves. Larry had just established his connection to it. If I weren't exceedingly frugal, I'd have bet every cent I made that summer on Larry. He slipped off his wristwatch and T-shirt, handed them to me, then returned to the court. His eyes were lonely, remotely seeing, unlike the blind man a day ago, torso electrified and thrashing. Charged with cold control, he looked grim and invincible. I wasn't the only one who felt it. People were making new bets even before the first serve. Hairy Murray took in the change. He chuckled, as if he'd thought of something funny but decided not to say it. I think he felt fear. Between himself and Larry, the air had become glass. Hairy Murray would play against himself, his limits.

Morris went to the coin to see how it lay. He said, "Larry serves." Morris then picked up the coin and walked off the court, returning to the stands where he'd left his newspaper. He began reading as he had that morning in the dining room. The moments of the game were of no concern.

Larry bent low to serve. His long naked arm swept back, then flashed forward. He slapped the ball, and it boomed off the wood face of the backboard. Hairy Murray returned boom for boom. Larry then hit a killer. Murray couldn't return it without tearing his knuckles on the concrete. He let it go. Larry served again, stronger, faster. Near the end of the game, Morris looked up from his newspaper. There was no excitement in his eyes and hardly much interest. He looked back at the newspaper, its bad news. From the way his shoulders slumped, I felt his resignation. Larry won by eleven points. People were counting money, passing it back and forth. Morris put the paper down. His expression was tired and neither pleased nor displeased. He rose and walked toward Larry.

What Morris and Sheila had said to each other can't be known, but I imagined fifty conversations, how Sheila called Morris after Larry told her to stay out of his life, how she cried. It was inconceivable that she had asked Morris to help her with Larry, but I knew she had. Morris must have loved her a lot. In his pain and disappointment, he drove up from the city to talk to Larry and heard about the game. Afterward, he and Larry walked away together. Morris's round, youthful face was turned toward Larry. Larry stared at the ground. Their conversation was brief. Morris extended his hand. Larry extended his. I didn't want to watch them and walked away to the bunkhouse, carrying Larry's T-shirt bunched up in my fist with the watch.

A FEW days later, the season ended, and the dining-room staff went home. I didn't go out on any double dates with Larry. I didn't see him again until three summers later. I'd been promoted to waiter at the honeymoon resort. Larry appeared in the casino bar one night, drinking alone. He wore a dark blue suit, white-on-white shirt with sapphire-studded cuff links, and a yellow silk tie. He looked elegant as a gangster. In his chest and face, he was slightly heavier. "Larry Starker," I said. He looked at me without a word as he shook my hand, offering only a little smile, as if he were remembering his opinion of me.

"Sigmund Freud, right?"

The hotel tummler, master of ceremonies at the resort, thrust between us before we could talk, slapping Larry on the shoulder, saying, "Let's go, Doctor. Where's the wife?" Walking away, Larry glanced at me and said, "Hang around. Come backstage later." Then the tummler was onstage, introducing a dance team. They had won a Latin dance contest in Brooklyn and were touring the Catskills. "Larry, the dentist, and beautiful Sheila. Give these kids a hand."

The first number, a triple mambo, was wild with congas, bongos, and timbales. Cowbells were clanging *gidong-gidong-gidong-dong*. The beat could make dancers look frantic, but Larry and Sheila were smooth and cool. He in his dark suit and yellow tie. She in spike heels and a black, supremely elegant cocktail dress. A moment ago, she might have been sipping an exquisitely dry martini. In the stage light, in this music, they were king and queen. I ached with admiration and primitive envy, and applauded madly. Afterward in a room backstage, I shook hands with Larry again, told him he and Sheila were fantastic, and reminded him that I'd once been his busboy.

He said, "I know."

"I'm waiting tables now. Our old station."

To my own ears, I sounded a little false, pressing our con-

nection too happily. My feelings were impure. I'd never actually been able to love him as a friend. He introduced me to
Sheila, his wife, and said she was almost four months pregnant. It didn't show. She sat in a folding chair, legs crossed,
smoking a cigarette.

I said, "Hi."

She said, "Hi."

I didn't feel invited to step closer and shake her hand, but
she nodded to me with an empty smile, then looked at Larry.
The moment was strangely awkward, nobody saying anything. I felt intrusive. Then Larry said he had his dental degree.

"Not everyone in my class made it. You need hand-eye coor-
dination. Like a fighter pilot. You're always looking in a tiny
mirror to see what your hands are doing—in reverse—inside
somebody's mouth."

"Are you still playing handball?"

Sheila's father had bought him into an office in Brighton
Beach, he said, walking distance to the handball courts, but
he didn't play much. He was too busy, too tired at the end of
the day. Then he talked about their dance routine.

"We're working a story into it. The man dances in place.
He is almost motionless. The woman dances for his pleasure,
like she is exhibiting herself. He watches, but still dancing in
place. Suspense is building, building, until the woman can't
hold back, can't stay away. She goes to him. It's a chase, but
different."

He worked himself up as he talked, and began to clap out
the clave rhythm—one, two three—one, two—doing the
steps in place, carrying himself like a tall, smooth, arrogant
seducer. Sheila, sitting in her chair, watched with no expression until she realized he was seriously involved in the routine
and expected her to join him. She said, "Aw, Larry. Enough
already. I just finished dancing my ass off."

Larry looked good, even when almost motionless; he had the music inside him. He ignored her protest, and kept dancing in place, clapping out the clave sharp and loud, and he raised an eyebrow the least degree, and, faintly, he curled his lip. Barbarian lights flashed in his teeth. He said, "Dance, bitch."

Sheila sighed, dropped her cigarette on the floor, looked down, and stepped on it. She looked back up at him with the face of a sweet, pathetic dummy and whimpered, "No."

Larry kept on dancing, clapping out the beat, staring at her. The tension was unbearable. I wanted to say, "I'll see you two do it another time," or, "Leave her alone," but I didn't know if I was looking at a dance routine or real life. As if in a trance, Sheila was then rising from her chair, beginning to move toward Larry, tentatively, moving to the beat in a deliberately broken, mechanical way. She said, "No," once more but was now very close to him, face to face, then leaning into him, pressing against his chest. He had stopped clapping, and they were pressed flat together from chest to thigh, dancing. There was silence in the room, except for the rhythm of their feet sliding along the floor, perfectly together.

As I watched, gooseflesh swept along my arms, like a breeze across the surface of a Catskill lake. At the bottom of the lake, in the shimmering murk, I made out Larry Starker, ankles chained to cinder blocks, straight blond hair streaming up, wavy in the water, slow as smoke. His arms were flailing at his sides. There was a bullet hole in his forehead.

—1993

Viva la Tropicana

BEFORE World War II, Cuba was known mainly for sugar and sex, but there was also a popular beach with sand imported from Florida, and grand hotels like the Nacional where you could get a room with a harbor view for ten dollars, and there were gambling casinos managed by American gangsters whose faces appeared in *Life* magazine, like Meyer Lansky and my uncle, Zev Golenpolsky Lurie, who could multiply giant numbers in his head and crack open a padlock with his hands. Habaneros, however, celebrated Zev for his dancing—rhumba, mambo, cha-cha—rhythms heard nightly in New York, Miami, Paris, Mexico City, and everywhere in Central America and much of South America, where Zev had toured as an exhibition dancer until he caught the fancy of big shots in the mob, and soon was doing more than dancing.

When he came up from Havana, Zev stayed with us in Manhattan. He loved my mother, Rosey, widow of Zev's twin, my father. When he died in a plane crash returning from a convention of trade-magazine publishers in Chicago, Zev grieved more than I did. I hardly knew my father. He and my mother, who was a mute, had lived apart from the time I was about five. So I didn't much grieve, but to see my uncle where I'd once seen my father was morally unsettling, especially since they looked alike. The quiet businessman was replaced by the dancer and gangster. Unsettling, but it almost seemed natural because Zev had been coming around for as long as I could remember. I think Zev always loved my mother, or loved his brother so much that he couldn't keep his hands off the widow. He spent no time in Brooklyn with his own wife and son.

After dinner, I went to my room to do homework. Zev continued sitting with Rosey at the kitchen table. They smoked and he talked. I heard a match being struck, a spoon clink against a saucer, and the rough slow drone of Zev's voice. My mother let him talk half the night, though she had to rise early to get to work at Ludmilla's, a dress manufacturer. She was a tailor who could reproduce from memory whatever she saw at fashion shows, and make design changes with no loss to style. She also made decisions about fabrics and construction that saved on manufacturing costs.

When Zev stayed overnight, I ate breakfast alone, but my mother would hear me leaving for school and then come out of her bedroom and catch me at the door. She rebuttoned my coat, or insisted that I wear a scarf, or looked at me with the question: Don't you need a sweater? Then she kissed me and I smelled the odors of their sleep and vestiges of the perfume she'd worn the previous night. I understood that the ritual goodbye in the morning was mainly a reminder (to both of us) that I had a mother. Sometimes Zev took her out and they wouldn't return for days. I'd find money on the kitchen table along with the phone number of a hotel. I never called the number.

When Zev was out of town, my mother saw other men. She was attractive, and never lacked suitors. Zev wasn't jealous, but if she began to care for another man, Zev could tell and she would go about with bruises until he won back her affections. I don't think he ever hit her in the face.

Their relationship was passionate and otherwise incomprehensible, at least to me. I think they felt they looked too good together to break up. Zev's tall figure and Slavic facial bones and thick yellow hair, and her red hair, tight skirts slit up the side, legs flashing as he spun her about the floor. Not that I ever saw them dancing, but I imagined them rising from their table at the edge of the dance floor, and other couples surrendering the floor to them, as in a romantic movie.

Zev gave me things like watches, cameras, fountain pens, and bikes. He was always giving me things. He gave and gave, and he took my mother away whenever he liked.

THE FIRST time I heard their dancing music, I was in a Chevy Bel Air, driving to Brooklyn with my cousin Chester. I was about fifteen. He was eighteen. He was taking me to a pool room on Kings Highway, Brooklyn, where World War II veterans hung out. Among them, Chester felt important because they knew his name and praised his skill at shooting pool. He was left handed, and a natural at any sport he tried.

Chester wore alligator shoes, like Zev's dancing shoes, and a chain bracelet of heavy silver, with a name tag, which was a high school fashion, like penny loafers and bobby socks. He imitated Zev, and liked to boast of his father's connections in Havana. After a trip to Havana, Chester boasted of an adventure with a Cuban prostitute, a young black woman who, said Chester, told him she would be proud to have his baby. I was impressed by his story, and believed it completely but still felt sorry for him. Zev didn't love his wife or son too much, and I suspected this accounted for the eccentric, showy element in Chester's personality that made him a charming ass, irresistible to girls, obnoxious to boys.

As we drove, Chester flicked on the radio and the deejay, Symphony Sid, began talking to us. His voice was full of knowing in the manner of New York, and he said we could catch Tito Puente this Wednesday at the Palladium, home of Latin music, Fifty-third and Broadway, up the street from Birdland, home of jazz. Then Symphony Sid played a tune by Puente called "Ran Kan Kan." Chester pulled the Chevy to the curb, cut the motor, turned up the volume, and said, "You know what this music is, Herman?"

I knew only that he'd do something show-offy. He lunged out of the car and began dancing on the asphalt, his alligator shoes making a dull dazzle. "Cuban mambo," he said, pressing his right palm to his belly, showing me the source of the music, and how it streams down through your hips and legs into your feet. He danced as if he held a woman in his arms, or the music itself was a magnificent woman, like Abbe Lane or

Rita Hayworth, with the mammalian substance and heat much favored in the late forties and early fifties. Chester displayed this woman with formal and fiery adoration. His back was straight, shoulders level, and his head held high in the arrogant posture of flamenco dancers, but he moved in a less angular way, and his mambo was marked by a different hesitations.

"Cuban mambo, Herman. *Ritmo caliente.*"

The spectacle of Chester dancing in the middle of New York, in the midst of traffic, was embarrassing, but he could dance and it gave me pleasure. He looked very macho, and I could see why girls liked him, but he was showing off to please me, as if to make me admire and like him, which was pathetic because he was older. Chester wouldn't stop urging me to get out of the car that minute and dance with him in the street. It mattered to him. He had to do this, and insist that I do it.

"Come on, I'll teach you."

"Not in the street."

"Who gives a fuck? Come on."

"Get back in the car, Chester."

"Dance, Herman."

"I can't."

"You can walk, you can dance. I'll show you."

The way his feet caressed the ground, I knew he was a born dancer. He knew I wasn't. Chester did his mambo and wouldn't stop urging me until, finally, I was doing it, too—self-conscious, intimidated by Chester's talent—but I succumbed to Chester's love of this music and this dancing in which I saw the shadow of Uncle Zev, who moved in a greater life, far away in the elegant casinos of Havana where glamorous women and dangerous men took their nightly pleasure.

ONE AFTERNOON, with a hundred and forty-five dollars of Zev's money, I went to a pet shop and bought a beagle. It wasn't a puppy, but still young and untrained. In Riverside Park, I unleashed the beagle and it took off trailing a scent. I hadn't given it a name so I was just yelling "Come here." It was deaf to my yelling. Nose to the sidewalk in a sniffing delirium, the beagle bolted into traffic, and was hit by a truck. It popped about fifteen feet in the air, then lay still. Dead. The beagle went from excited to dead. I was shocked and embarrassed, and turned away, as if it weren't mine.

It's ridiculous, but the sniffing beagle reminds me that I hated the smell of Zev's cigars, which lingered thickly in the bathroom, like an insalubrious mist. He took his time in there, reading a newspaper, having a smoke.

I'd come home from school and see his beat-up yellowish leather Gladstone suitcases, pasted all over with Caribbean travel tags, standing in the foyer. They announced Zev's presence, and his presence filled the rooms. His smoke and droning voice at the kitchen table, and the sound of his stride along the wooden floor of the hallway outside my room, made me feel small and forgotten, as if I had no place actually to be. Zev took Rosey away, and I was always crying for her until another person began growing inside me, a secret mourner to whom I referred all pain.

OVER the years, I wanted to go to Cuba, but, if not for Nana, my girlfriend, I might not have made the trip. She was doing her residency in a San Francisco hospital, becoming a gastroenterologist. She had a narrow, definite, purpose in life. It depressed me to think I had only a vague interest in writing magazine articles. Then, as if to give me purpose, came an invitation to a film festival in Havana, expenses paid. However trivial, I suddenly felt that I had a purpose—Cuba. I suspected that the person at The Cuban Film Institute who issued the invitation assumed I was somebody important. I had no screen credits, but my name had appeared in *Variety*, a tiny notice saying I was writing a screenplay about a European voyage of discovery in the Pacific Islands. In fact I'd been hired to write a treatment, not a screenplay, based on an article I wrote about Captain Cook and Hawaii, which appeared in the travel section of a San Francisco newspaper.

I'd written about the mystical genius of Captain Cook, his courage, and his terrible death. The article caught the eye of the director, Leigh Armitage, and he thought it could become a movie, and went about touting me as a Captain Cook scholar. I'd merely read Cook's journals, and knew that he was killed during a scuffle on a beach with some natives. Presumably, they ate him. A sack of bones was given to his fellow officers, but not until they shelled the island, setting fire to a village. This would be a major scene in the movie. The warship was carrying Hawaiian women. It's reported that they were thrilled, not terrified, by the beauty of the flames and devastation.

I wrote about Cook's uncanny relation to the water and sky, his gift for knowing where he was in seas he'd never sailed, and, without maps, knowing land was nearby. He was my hero, maybe, because I carried unknown seas within. Leigh hired me to write a treatment, my name appeared in *Variety*, and I was invited to a film festival in Havana. I felt happy, just as if I'd achieved something or was on the verge of achieving it. Life in the movie business seemed as good as a real life. Nana began calling me Captain Cook, which she thought was hilarious.

I REMEMBER Zev grumbling, "I can smell it." He had detected a disturbing change in his psychological environment, because my mother was mad about some other guy. She assumed Zev had women in Miami or Cuba, but that didn't stop him from accusing her of putting horns on him. He'd worked himself into a destructive fit, smashing vases and pictures. She pointed at him to say, "You, not me."

I came back from school into this scene. She was scared, and looked as if she hadn't slept for days. I went to Zev's suit-cases and found his gun. He said, "You think I would hit Rosey?" He'd hit her plenty, but that's what he said, and for an instant I suffered a doubt. "Never point a gun at anyone you don't intend to kill," he said. "Put it down." I aimed the gun at his face. My hands didn't shake. I wasn't crying. Then Zev said, "I'll show you how to release the safety later. Now put it back in the suitcase while I talk to Rosey."

MY MOTHER had been in love with Santos for almost a year. He was a lawyer whom she'd met at a business lunch that she attended with her boss. Santos's eyes were Asian, and his skin had a bronze-like coloring. He was beautiful in a way that was neither masculine nor feminine. Transcendent beauty, or god-like in effect. He wore hand-tailored suits and white shirts and a wide-brimmed gray hat, a tiny black-and-green feather in the band. He smoked thin black cigarillos. His hands were slender, long, finely shaped. He was learning sign language so that my mother could speak to him. Zev never bothered to learn.

As for me, I didn't have to learn. I could hear my mother. Like hearing a voice in dreams, soundless, yet it speaks any language or none, and you understand. I never wondered about the mystery of hearing her. Before language, people com-municated. Otherwise, there could be no language, only men-tal telepathy, maybe, and such primitive powers. It's said lan-guage was invented to hide our thoughts. My mother hid noth-ing from me. She talked to me in music, or something that gave me pleasure. No sound, no words, only a flow of pure mean-ings. I was anxious when she was anxious. I felt good if she was happy. No sound, just a sensuous flow of pure meaning even if she said the most banal sort of thing. Saint Augustine and Tol-stoy believed wordless communion is basic to love.

I'd forget we were in a public place, and reproach her, saying "Not now," or "I can't," which would attract puzzled attention. I'd then realize I'd heard her tell me to button my coat collar, or blow my nose, or comb my hair, or come home early, or go out for Chinese food, or help her complete her income tax returns. I didn't know when she'd actually said anything. Her moods and requests and desires seeped into my mind. I found myself annoyed, or blowing my nose, or, mechanically, combing my hair. Once, she began talking to me during a movie. Movies bored her. I cried out, "Please shut up. You didn't have to come with me." People nearby moved to distant seats. She was embarrassed and wounded. I had to beg her to forgive me.

ONE EVENING Zev intercepted Santos in the building's lobby. The doorman phoned and told me to tell my mother to come down. When we arrived, Zev was gone and Santos was seated on the tile floor near the elevator. His delicate, slightly hooked nose had been smashed. Blood bubbled in an ear and went running down the side of his neck, staining his collar red. His eyes and mouth were red and pulpy. For the first time, I feared Zev; and even hated him a little, but there was a fine strain of awe mixed in, what you might feel watching a building burn with people jumping out of the windows. Not a good sensation, even shameful, but it had nothing to do with me in particular, and would have been aroused in anyone. A function of fear and hate. Feel one thing, you feel another.

Ten days later, after she and Santos got the results of their Wassermann tests, they were married. In those days, you needed proof that you didn't have syphilis. Maybe nothing is more relevant to marriage. Santos was a good man, sensitive, courteous, religious, well-off, etc. I had nothing against him, but nasty thoughts about my mother gathered so thick and scary that I believed I should leave town, go far away, and never see her again. As it happened, she and Santos left town. I never saw them again.

It had been many years since we'd last spoken, but I recognized the voice instantly.

"You're going to Havana," he said.

"How do you know, Uncle Zev?"

"I know. I need a favor."

"Anything."

"There's a woman in Havana. Consuela Delacruz. I am saying this once, so listen good. Go to Consuela. Identify yourself. Get down on your knees."

"Knees?"

"Say your uncle Zev continues to worship the ground upon which she walks. Say he kisses her feet and she is more dear to him than his life. You have a pencil? I'll tell you how to say it in Spanish."

"I don't understand."

"I'm talking to you about undying love in the heart of an old man. You heard about love? What the hell is there to understand?"

"Can you be sure I'll find her?"

"She works at the Tropicana."

"What's the story? Shouldn't I know?"

"You don't have to know," he said, but then said a little more.

In 1959, when Fidel made his triumphant progress through the streets, with Che Guevara and Celia Sanchez, a doctor and the daughter of a doctor, Zev stood in the cheering crowds, wondering what to do with his life. He was indifferent to the revolution, except that it put an end to his mob income. He'd have left Cuba with his colleagues in the gambling business, but he was in love with Consuela Delacruz, and she refused to leave. To struggle with English, buying bread and eggs in an American grocery store, would be an insufferable humiliation. Besides, Zev was married, which disturbed Consuela greatly.

I said, "I'll find her."

SANTOS and my mother bought a house in a Chicago suburb, where Santos had family and belonged to a cult called "Followers." Their symbol was the sunflower, which follows the arc of the sun. The cult combined the Christian story—Sun is a pun on son—with other ancient myths of virgin births and sacrificed gods. The cult also had a pantheistic theology drawn from Spinoza. In services, they used drummers. A priest would chant in African tongues. The services might last two or three days. I know about the cult, which was secretive, only because when Santos and my mother got married in New York, I attended the ceremony and asked a lot of questions of Santos. My mother, to my confusion, couldn't not confess to being a believer.

Santos restricted his legal work to the cult. My mother quit the garment industry. Santos preached to gatherings in the Midwest. He and my mother became priests. Now and then, before and after her death, my mother reached out to me. I'd stop in the middle of saying something to listen. Nana saw my suddenly flat abstracted expression, and would say, "Make her quit doing that to you. It's like being with half a person. Tell the witch to stop."

"I don't know if I can," I said.

It would have frightened Nana if I told her that my mother and Santos had been murdered, in an internecine cult war, years previously. (She answered the door one evening and was shot dead where she stood. The killer or killers then found Santos.)

"Make her stop," said Nana. "I won't share your mind with another woman. It's worse than sexual infidelity. I'll never trust you until get free of her, Herman."

There was a kind of satisfaction in letting her rave in ignorance, but Nana's protesting also made me despair. I'd never be free of my mother's voice.

I'D REMAINED in New York, alone in the apartment when my mother left town with Santos. The apartment had been put up for sale. Nana thought the apartment was haunted. "I feel as if I'm being watched," she said, and wouldn't let me touch her until we went somewhere else. One evening, after a shower, I left the bathroom window open, and a pigeon flew in. I tried to shoo it back to the bathroom window. The pigeon was frantic, flapping from room to room, banging into furniture and walls. I was afraid it would break a wing or bash out its tiny brain against a wall.

It wasn't the first time I lived alone, but with my mother gone, I'd been living alone for weeks, and Nana wouldn't have sex in the apartment, and now the hysterical bird. I opened every window. The pigeon swooshed about my head making its noises. I finally shrieked at it, told it go away and die.

WHEN NANA got the residency in the San Francisco hospital, I was working at a trade magazine, an editorial job I'd gotten through a friend of my father. I quit the job and followed Nana to San Francisco and found an apartment near hers, but I hardly saw her except when she was in the mood. It put her off when I wanted to make love because she suspected that I had another girlfriend and was seeing her on the sly, which made no sense. Nana's residency kept her so busy I could have had ten girlfriends.

I got a job as a waiter, and then a bicycle messenger. On weekends, I tried to write articles for magazines and newspapers. Then came Captain Cook, then the invitation to Cuba. I thought Nana would be impressed.

"I've been invited to a film festival in Cuba."

"I'll get you Tetracycline. Take it with you. You might get sick, Captain Cook."

"Thanks. Don't you want to know if I'm going to accept the invitation?"

"Of course you'll accept, Cap'n."

Her attitude was infuriating. I said, "Nobody wants medicine from a tattooed doctor. I wish you'd have it removed."

"When you tell your witch doctor mother to stop talking to you, I'll think about having it removed. Right now I like it and I'm keeping it."

As FOR Zev's story, he lingered in Havana, working as a bartender at the Tropicana, a club where he'd once delighted the crowd with his dancing. He didn't leave Cuba until obliged to do so by the revolutionary government.

In 1966, the ministry of economics unearthed ledgers in the Hotel Capri, and discovered Zev's initials beside certain figures again and again right up to New Year's Eve, 1959, indicating that he had been responsible for great sums of gambling money, not only from the Capri, but the Nacional and Tropicana, too. The revolution wanted to know where this money had gone. When Batista fled to the Dominican Republic, there hadn't been enough time to collect all the casino earnings. Zev produced copies of the receipts he'd sent to the mob in Miami, proving he'd turned over the casino money to Batista before his flight. In a fit of disgust, Fidel ordered Zev's expulsion.

Fidel said, "I wanted the money only to burn it in your face."

Zev had been a runner between the casinos and Batista's officers. On the night Batista fled Havana, Zev drove down O'Reilly Street to the docks and then into a receiving shed. In the trunk of the car he had several suitcases each bulging with casino profits, in dollars and bank certificates, that Batista hadn't collected and that hadn't been slipped out of Cuba before Castro took over. The money was expected in Miami. The soldiers gave Zev a photo of Batista. Across the eyes of the photo, Batista always signed his mother's name. The photo was signed, but across the mouth, not the eyes, and Batista was spelled with three T's instead of two. Zev under-

stood that the soldiers, whom he'd never seen before, intended to make a fool out of him and keep the money. He asked in
a pleasant manner, as if amused by their little joke, for the authentic receipt. They laughed and slapped him on the back,
congratulating Zev on his sharp eyesight and towering intelligence. They said he could have no use for the authentic receipt. They intended to hand the money over to the revolution
and thereby escape Fidel's tribunals and the firing squad. Zev
had to present the authentic receipt to parties in New York
who also had firing squads. Zev laughed, too, and broke the
neck of one soldier with his elbow and disemboweled the
other with a knife even as their laughter resonated in the
shed. Other soldiers were present. They didn't move while
Zev searched the uniform pockets of the soldiers he'd killed,
found the authentic receipt, and then, turning his back on the
other soldiers, lit a cigarette, took a few drags, then ground it
out beneath his heel. He opened one suitcase, took out a stack
of bills and dropped it on the ground, then put all of the suitcases into the car and drove away. Zev spent that night with
Consuela.

"Return the money, or give it to the revolution," she said.

"I have the receipt. The money is for you and the child."

"Cuba will be a socialist state. Nobody will need money."

Zev told me all this. It was very like the old days when he
told me how he got the most desirable tables in night clubs.
Now, 1987, considering the economic misfortunes of the revolution, Zev figured Consuela would be glad to have the money,
and come to the States. I was to explain this to Consuela, reading from the Spanish dictated to me by Zev over the phone.
She knew about the money. She didn't know what Zev had
done with it. That night in Havana, twenty-eight years ago,
lying in the arms of Consuela, Zev made a plan that would be
put into effect if he continued to love Consuela.

"I am a realistic person. Feeling dies," he said.

Seven years later, a few weeks before Zev was deported,

he was still in love with Consuela. Their child was five years old.

From the pattern of whorls in the child's small thumb-print, Zev had worked out a formula. It translated into a graph. This graph described the proportionate distances be-tween the whorls of the thumbprint, which could be extrapo-lated into the distances between peaks and valleys along the shaft of a key that opened one lock of a bank box in Zurich. The second lock of the bank box could be opened only by a key held by the bank.

Zev's original key, fashioned by himself, along with the lock, was destroyed after the lock had been tested. To recon-struct the key, Zev's child—now twenty-seven years old— had to supply the thumbprint. Only one person, his Cuban love child, could walk into the bank in Zurich and present her thumbprint. The bank would then make the key to open the box, which contained certificates of deposit. They had in-creased in value and could be redeemed for many more mil-lions than Zev had carried away from the Cuban gambling parlors. He'd waited seven years in Cuba and loved Consuela. He'd waited more than twenty years away from her. He loved her no less.

On December 17, at ten PM, two hours prior to the celebra-tion of the birthday of San Lazaro, I walked into the Trop-icana looking for Consuela Delacruz to tell her that she and the child were rich in dollars and the undying love of my uncle. I imagined Zev huddled in a heavy black coat, his face bent against the blades of winter, hustling across a freezing sidewalk in New York from his office to his limousine. My heart went out to him, though I knew he could be a cruel bad-tempered son of a bitch. But he was old, no longer his former self, and I owed him something in the way of sentiment. I was delivering warmth to the lonely winter of his life. I'd even felt honored when Uncle Zev asked me for this favor. Maybe I was betraying certain memories, or an allegiance to my mother. I'm not sure what I was supposed to feel. I felt what I felt.

It would have useful to have a photo of Consuela, and I asked for one, but there was no time to get it to me, and besides, Zev had only some photos of his love child that had been sent through The American Interest Section in Havana. As relations between America and Cuba became worse, photos stopped arriving. Of course Zev knew what Consuela and his love child looked like. He made no effort to describe them to me.

I passed through an entranceway of pointed arches, then a lobby, and entered the largest outdoor night club in the world. Tiers of white tablecloths, in a great sweep of concentric semi-circles, descended toward a vast curved stage. There were trees all about, tall palms and flamboyants amid the walls of a natural cathedral open to the nighttime sky. I went to a table near the edge of the stage. A waiter approached. I pulled out my notebook and asked, *"Donde puedo encontrar,* Consuela Delacruz?"

"Ron y Coca-Cola," he said.

Music started, lights began flashing, dancers appeared on the central stage.

I raised my voice. "Consuela Delacruz. *Ella trabaja aqui."*
"Cuba libre?"

"Okay," I shouted, a word like Coca-Cola, universally understood. I'd try again when the drink came. He left. Was I reading incorrectly? Mispronouncing?

Karl Marx said, in the spirit of his master Hegel, "Nothing can stop the course of history," but here was the Tropicana, in a Havana suburb, an airy and geometrical marvel of fifties architecture. Onstage, as in pre-revolutionary days, was the glitzy artificiality of a Las Vegas tits-and-ass dance routine, a spectacle of lush and gorgeous vulgarity, the heritage of bacchanalian sensationalism cultivated by Italo-Judaic American gangsters. The communist regime allowed the Tropicana to exist for the sake of tourist dollars, but gambling was forbidden. Tables had been destroyed in one casino after another by rampaging mobs. Prostitutes no longer walked the streets, but the stages of the Tropicana had been left intact for nearly naked women to dance upon.

Viva La Tropicana, I said to myself and looked about for my waiter and my drink. It was coming to me in the hand of a tall, slender, black woman, very handsome, in her late forties. There was a hard light in her eyes, and an expression of distaste in the line of her lips as she stood before me and then set the drink on the table. I got down on my knees and started reading the Spanish in my notebook. She touched my shoulder to make me stop. I glanced up, she was half-smiling, her eyes softly inquisitive.

"Zev?"

I nodded. She then tugged me to my feet, kissed my cheek, and pulled me after her along the aisle that curved with the stage front, and then behind it into darkness tangled with wires that streamed along the floor, stopping only to turn and gape at me, to see what couldn't be said, and she asked about fifteen questions. Cuban Spanish is faster than most languages, but if she'd spoken with the slow lips of death, I'd have understood none of them. She continued to hold my hand, squeezing it in her eagerness to know what I couldn't tell her. Gradually, she made out in my eyes no hope, no Spanish, but she persisted:

"*Norteamericano?* Brook-leen?"

Then, tugging hard, she drew me after her through the aisle toward the side of the stage and around behind the stage into an alley, like another part of the city, no longer the Tropicana. She tugged me toward two near-naked women, their heads glorified by mountains of colorful feathers, their bodices all spangles. They were practicing dance steps together, and didn't notice us until Consuela thrust me in front of one of them. To me she said, "*La niña*. Zeva." To her she said, "*Tu padre lo mando. Anda habla con el. Hablale.*" La Niña looked from her mother to me, then just at me, her large dark eyes rich in incomprehension. Words came, as if experimentally, "You are from Zev?"

"Yes."

She was Chester's half-sister, Zev's love child, my cousin. I had to tell it to myself, before saying, "I'm your cousin." She repeated it to her mother who, while she'd had no trouble kissing me earlier, was now strangely reserved, though she smiled and said, "Ah."

Zeva stepped toward me. In a sweetly formal way, she kissed my cheek, whispering, "Did he send us money?"

I whispered, "More than you can imagine."

AFTER the last show, I waited for them at the front gate. Zeva emerged wearing blue jeans, a white T-shirt, and sandals, looking like an American college student. Consuela had gone ahead to get their car, an old Chevy, like the one Chester drove years ago, but with rusted fenders and doors, battered. It was a loud and rocky ride. The car produced sickening gasoline odors as we banged along the Malecon. To the left, waves smashed against the sea wall and stood high in the air before hitting the parapet and sliding backward, collapsing along the sidewalk and the avenue. To the right, facing the ocean, stood rows of old, grim, suffering facades, buildings with colonnades and baroque ornamentation, much decayed; tragically beautiful in decay. I had glimpses of Arabic tile work and the complicated glass of chandeliers hanging, glittering pendants dripping amid clotheslines strung across rooms where the rich once dined and danced. We turned right, entering a large square, then a long empty narrow street where there were few lights. The Chevy sounded louder, echoing off buildings in the dark shadows. There was no other sound but the raucous metallic rattle, no voices, no music. There was nobody about.

This was the Old Town. Zeva and Consuela had an apartment in a three-story building with a much-broken face, elaborate mortar work along the balconies, pieces fallen away, iron railings loose in their moorings, and tall windows eaten by water and fungus. The apartment was long and very narrow, with a linoleum floor, rather like what they used to call "shotgun" in the States. Lights hung from the ceiling by naked wires. Chests and tables were loaded with porcelain figurines, ashtrays, framed photos, and innumerable bright little cheap glass nameless things, like junk shop memorabilia. We sat in the kitchen at an oval formica-topped table. The surface was imitation gray marble embraced by an aluminum band. The pipe legs were also aluminum. In an L.A. antique shop, I figured, it with the four chairs would sell for about a thousand bucks as an authentic fifties antique.

Zeva looked at her hands when I finished the story Zev told me. "Which thumb?"

"Aren't they the same?"

"Maybe only one is good. I'll give you impressions of both thumbs, or I could cut them off. You bring them to him."

"He wants all of you," I said.

Consuela, respectful of our deliberations, waited for us to conclude. Zeva told her the story and an argument started. I couldn't understand it, but guessed that it touched old disagreements—Zeva wanted to go to the States, and Consuela didn't. Consuela rose, stood with arms folded across her chest, looking down at us. Then, from her angry rigid height, she bent abruptly and hugged me. The same with Zeva, then she walked away down the narrow hall.

Zeva said, "She's tired. She's going to sleep. You stay here tonight. She wants you to. I'll fix a bed by the windows, or take my room. I won't be able to sleep, anyway. This is terrible. Terrible. I don't know Zev, but he must be a thoughtless man. How could he do this to me? To us? We have lived for years with promises. This apartment is ours. Almost ours. We are buying it slowly. Now you bring new promises from him. She wants to tell everything to the authorities. It won't be too good for you. I'm sure you'll be detained. Come, I'll show you."

I followed her to the window.

The street was dark and seemed empty, but then as I stared into the darkness the moonlight revealed a man at the corner, ordinary looking, wearing a nicely molded, white, straw hat, brim pulled down front and back.

"The police?"

"He is their neighborhood representative. He will tell the police about your visit. They will want to know what we talked about."

"We're cousins. We talked about Zev. You told me about yourself, your work, your studies. Where you learned English. Where did you learn English?"

"I don't know."

"You don't?"

"After Zev was deported, my mother was in ill favor. She lost her job at the Tropicana. They gave it back to her later, but for years she did other work, mainly cooking and cleaning for the family of a Dutch diplomat. She took me with her every day. I played with their children. The family spoke English and Spanish to make sure the children learned them both. Like the children, I also spoke English. When they switched to Spanish, so did I. There were also other languages. The diplomat's family had lived in Indonesia. To me, it was pure meaning. The particular language was irrelevant."

"You don't speak a child's English."

"I studied it later in school."

"Changing languages is like changing lovers."

"Have you changed many lovers?"

"Have you?"

"I can count them on one thumb. Do you grow and mature from one to the next, and the next? With the first, are you always a child? I wanted to work in the foreign service, so I studied English. I would like to travel. I'm good at languages, but I'm a little too black, and a little too much like a woman. Opportunities don't come my way. My mother says Zev speaks nine languages. She refuses to admit she understands a word of English. She obliged him to speak to her in Spanish. If a man loves you, she says, he must prove it every day. When Zev spoke to her, always in Spanish, he reminded himself of what he felt for my mother. She's a real Cuban, very warm and loving, but when she tells me what Zev did to Batista's soldiers, there is no pity in her voice. I ask her why not. She says your father is a man. Tell me how much money there is for us?"

The man in the street lit a cigarette and glanced up, and the flare of the match reflected in his eyes. I waved to him. He looked away.

She said, "Americans think anything can be made into a joke."

"What can he do to me?"

"You like rice and beans? You might eat rice and beans for a long time."

We stood near each other, easy in our nearness; familial. It wasn't an American feeling. I could hear her breathing quicken when I said "A couple of million dollars." She took my hand and said, "It's the truth?"

My cousin was very attractive. I put my arm around her shoulder. She leaned against me, as if we'd grown up together, two Latin kids, always touching.

"I like rice and beans," I said.

I WASN'T detained in Cuba. Nothing was done to me; nobody asked questions. I went back to the Tropicana, but one night

Zeva told me it was unwise for us to talk to each other any-more.

"What should I tell Uncle Zev?" I asked, as if my feelings weren't hurt.

"You will know before you leave. They will communicate."

"Who will?"

"Our leader. Now go."

On the last night of the film festival, I was invited to a grand dinner, with hundreds of others, at the Palacio de la Revolucion. Long tables in parallel lines, with wide aisles be-tween them, were laid out with Cuban foods. Guests walked the length of the tables, loading their plates, then returned for more. At the end, they served cakes and excellent Cuban ice cream. Without announcement, Fidel appeared and the crowd swarmed toward him, surrounding him, but this was an ele-gant crowd of well-dressed people, and they felt the necessity of leaving him a little space in front. I couldn't approach close-ly, but I could see his head and shoulders, the top of his green army uniform, his beard and intense black eyes. He was the tallest man in the hall, perhaps six-foot-five. His head was large, leonine, heroic, bending slightly toward those who asked questions, listening with utter seriousness. I saw a mon-ument. The man called Fidel was the living monument of him-self. For a moment, while talking to a man in the crowd, he seemed to be talking beyond him. "Of course," he said, "we would publish the complete writings of Kierkegaard. His great book, *Either/Or,* should be distributed to every Cuban just as if it were money stolen from them by American gang-sters." He was talking to me.

When my plane landed in Miami, I went to a phone and called Zev. It was almost five AM, but he'd said to phone him the moment I arrived. As soon as he said hello, I told him I'd met Consuela, and I told him about his daughter, Zeva, how she spoke several languages, and how beautifully she danced at the Tropicana, though I'd seen her only as a spangled figure among others, all of them burdened by masses of colorful feathers. "Uncle Zev, why didn't you say the baby was a girl?"

"I couldn't remember."

"Oh, come on."

"When you get older the difference between boys and girls matters little."

I said that Fidel would let Consuela and Zeva go to the States, but with conditions. Either the million dollars is returned to the revolution or the women never leave.

"He spoke to you personally? He told you that?"

"He was talking to someone else, but we were in the same room, and he was looking at me. He knew who I was, and wanted me to hear him. I'm sure of it."

"I believe you, but only Zeva can open the box, and the money is hers, not Fidel's. The key is her thumb. But I got something for him better than money, which is also in her thumb. Wait in Miami. I'll catch a plane this afternoon. Stay with my friend, Sam Halpert. You can get his number from Information. If you're right about Fidel's message, there is reason to be cautious. When you hang up, look around at the people. Then take a walk. Make four or five turns like you don't know the airport. Don't go into a toilet, or anyplace where you might be alone. Stay in plain sight. Then find another phone and call Sam Halpert, and look around again. You'll recognize the one following you, if someone is following you. When Sam answers describe the guy."

"You're scaring me."

"Call Sam and you'll be all right. I'll see you soon."

The phone went dead as I shouted, "Wait." What the hell did he think I was, a person with nothing to do but hang around Miami? I slammed down the receiver and started toward my San Francisco flight, so angry that I forgot to look around at the people, but there were none, anyhow, just a man lying on a bench with a *Miami Herald* covering his face, sleeping. I didn't notice him. I didn't notice his white shoes, either. I was blind with anger, thrusting along the passage-ways where slender tubes of pastel fluorescent light floated, suggesting a chemical blood stream that fed the airport's extremities. My leather shoulder bag slammed against my hip, my breathing was loud. I talked to myself, finishing the conversation with Zev, telling him he was my "favorite uncle"— my only uncle, in fact—and I'd admired him since I was a kid. He'd been good to my mother and me after my father's death. Zev bought me my first car, not only the bicycle and camera. When my high school sweetheart became pregnant, Zev found a doctor in New Jersey and paid for the operation. I owed him a lot, but I was angry.

Philosophers say nothing in the mind is inaccessible to the mind. It's true. I discovered that my mind—not me—had seen white shoes, and taken in the man sleeping under the newspaper, because, minutes after the phone call, as I stood at a coffee counter, tumultuous within, I saw white shoes dangling from legs on either side of a stool and I remembered seeing them before—unconsciously. I remembered what I didn't know that I knew. I also remembered the newspaper, which the man was now reading. I put money on the counter to pay for my coffee, and I went to a phone. I was trying to be efficient, though hurried, and I was shaking all over, but I dialed Information, got Sam Halpert's number, then dialed. Not once did I glance back at White Shoes. I'd seen him and I'd have bet anything that his eyes were set high in his head, and the face had gross texture, pocked and gullied from cheek to neck, as if gouged with a chisel and washed in acid. Somebody picked up the phone. He said, "Can you hear me good?"

"Sam Halpert?"

"Start laughing."

"What?"

"This is a funny phone call. You're being watched."

I laughed, laughed.

"Don't overdo it. What does he look like?"

"Blond. Ha, ha, ha. Maybe six feet. Late twenties. Average white trash." The expression surprised me, flying out of fear, as if to assault the man. "Ha, ha, ha. Blue-and-white floral Hawaiian shirt, white slacks, white shoes with pointed toes. Ha, ha, ha. I'm scared."

"Move your mouth, shake your head, laugh, then hang up and go look for a taxi. Don't run. Don't dawdle. Don't get ideas about calling a cop. Tell the taxi driver to go to Bayside, and drop you at the flags."

"The flags?"

"You'll see like a park, flags at the entrance. An aisle of flags. Walk the aisle of flags. There's shops on both sides. Go straight, go go go till you're on like a ledge facing the bay. Below the ledge you'll see a walkway. Go down to it and walk right. Repeat what I said."

"Taxi to Bayside. Aisle of flags."

"Laugh."

"Ha, ha, ha. Through flags to bay, down to walkway, walk right. Ha, ha, ha, ha, ha. What if you're not there? I'll be alone, Mr. Halpert. Wouldn't it be advisable to wait a few hours until there are people in the streets? Ha, ha."

"Am I here?"

"Yes."

"I'll be there."

"But wouldn't it be advisable ..."

Like Zev, he hung up.

Another outrage. I wasn't living my own life. Walking, talking, laughing, but it wasn't me. There was no trouble getting a cab.

At the flags, I dragged my shoulder bag out of the back seat, paid the driver. He abandoned me in the tremendous black and electrified emptiness of a business center, tall new buildings all about amid older ones alongside the park and Bayside, a mall at the edge of Biscayne Bay. The aisle of flags marked a wide bleak walk into the mall. I heard a car door slam. I turned, saw the blue-and-white shirt getting out of a taxi. I thought to drop my bag and sprint toward the bay, but I wasn't supposed to know I was being followed. The water lay before me, dark, glistening, streaked by running lights of slow moving boats and city lights skimming the surface, defining the shore. Where concrete ended and became a ledge, I saw the walkway, wide enough for two men. A stairway took me down. Water slapped listlessly below, at the wall. There was nobody in sight along the walkway, but then I saw a man up ahead descending a stair. He was taller than the blond, wearing a windbreaker, jeans, and tennis shoes. He stopped to light a cigar. A local yachtsman. He started toward me along the wall, forcing me to the water side. It unnerved me, though there was room to pass. He walked in a loose, loping, athletic way, slightly tipped forward. As we drew close, he looked for my eyes and said, "Good morning, kid" and passed me and then I heard a cry and spun about. I saw the blond in the Hawaiian shirt, kicking and flailing, sailing off the parapet through the air. The tall man still had his arm extended. He'd pushed. He flicked his cigar into the water. The flying blond, having hit with a great splash, thrashed toward the wall, slapping at its slimy face, seeking a fingerhold. There was none. He couldn't drag himself out. Halpert came toward me. "Let's go."

The blond thrashed, white shoes churning, mouth a black O closing, going under, bobbing up, opening to an O again, as if swallowing a pipe, his eyes wild.

"He's drowning," I said.

"Let's go." He began tugging at my arm. I pulled it away.

"That man is drowning, Mr. Halpert. He can't swim."

"Call me Sam."

That instant, a chunk of concrete broke from the wall beside my head—leaving a hole big as a grapefruit—and I heard the gun shot almost the same instant. Much louder than I'd have expected. The blond, going under again, a glint of steel in his hand.

Sam said, "I'll hold your bag, kid. Jump in after him."

I screamed, "Drown, fucker." I took off after Sam.

He drove, sometimes stopping at stop signs, sometimes not. I wasn't concerned. The shot missed my head, but left me proof of my potential for instantaneous nothingness, and the face lingered in memory, mouth and eyes begging life to enter, drowning. We cut through residential areas heavy with the sweetness of flowers and vegetable decay. I lay back against the seat. A dark sensuous weight of air and silence before morning, not real dark, and not yet morning. I noted solemn banyan trees, hulking, elephantine, streaming tendrils, and white houses set back from the road.

"I could go Dixie Highway," said Sam, "but I figured you'd want to look at the neighborhoods. Ever been to Miami?"

"No."

"You'd never guess how little it costs me to live here."

"Probably not."

"Not in the mood to talk, eh kid?"

"What if he drowned?"

"Why the hell do you care? His name, if you're interested, is Wally Blythe."

"The name means nothing, only the face. I keep seeing it go under."

"A face like that should go under. Smell that? Guess what it is."

"I can't guess. What is it?"

"Mango. We're passing an orchard."

"I don't see an orchard."

"Most of the trees were cut down. Beautiful trees. I love mango. Good for the digestion. The death rate in Florida is higher than the birth rate, but the population is growing. Five thousand new residents a week. They need houses. Goodbye mangos. There's money here, to build a lot of houses and big buildings."

"*Drogas?*"

"Ask your uncle, not me."

"I'm dying to sleep, but I'm afraid I'll dream about that guy's face."

"There's my house. You'll sleep and later we'll talk."

"Why does Zev need me?"

"You're family."

"He's got a son."

"Chester is too eager to please. He's a wiseass and a crook. He'll see chances for himself, lose sight of the goal. Between Zev and Chester there is a lack of trust. They can talk, but the air is poisoned for an hour afterwards. Zev doesn't want to owe Chester anything. You're family, and you need money."

"I'm grateful, but I want to go home. I expected to sleep on the flight to San Francisco, and look where I am. Where am I?"

"South Miami, at the edge of Dade County. Hey, do you like mud wrestling? We got mud wrestling in Miami Beach. What do you say? Naked girls in the mud. It'll take your mind off your problems, and make you feel good."

"There must be something wrong with me. I know I should be happy where there's mud wrestling, but I want to get the fuck out of here. Weird, isn't it?"

Sam's house, a stucco box with a flat roof, had a red tile floor in the living room and very little furniture—rattan couch, rattan chairs, a glass topped coffee table and a dining room table with four chairs. No curtains, drapes, or rugs. A bachelor's house. Pages of cartoons, cut from magazines, were

LEONARD MICHAELS

pasted to a wall in the living room, partly hiding cracks in the
sheet rock. There was a tiny kitchen, dining room, and two
bedrooms. He showed me into one of the bedrooms. I dropped
my shoulder bag, undressed, and lay on a thick foam mat on a
plywood base supported by bricks, about two inches off the
floor. I could have slept on the floor. I didn't wash, didn't take
a piss, didn't move. Sprawled beneath a light wool cover, I
shut my eyes and felt a weepy pressure, as if I were about to
grieve, but I was too tired.

SAM'S VOICE returned, saying, "Don't worry, kid, you'll see
Zeva again."

I felt the light through my eyelids, not morning light but
the hot glare of afternoon.

"Was I talking in my sleep?"

He stood beside the bed. Tall with dark, little, close-to-
gether eyes and the sloping shoulders of an athlete, holding a
glass of orange juice in a long hand.

"Did you fuck her?"

I sat up and took the juice from his hand. "I liked her."

"Let's go eat."

He put my bag in his car. Apparently, I wasn't coming
back.

I recognized neighborhoods we'd driven through earlier in
the semi-darkness. Then we were near the center of town and
out of Sam's car, walking through the lobby of a hotel. Somebody was shoving a vacuum cleaner across the rug. It droned,
abdominal and despairing in the shadowy lobby. A buffet had
been set up in the dining room. We took a table in a corner beside a long window, light filtering through gauzy white curtains, bathing us in a smoky glow; like desert light, with holy
intimations. Sam and I ate in silence, soldiers on a mission.
Coffee was served first and last.

Sam looked to see if I were ready to listen. He wanted to
talk, tell me what's what, but I was savoring the luxury of

222

being alive, thinking literally how good it is. He said, "This is about women and power. In Cuba, Fidel is known as The Bull. He told Khrushchev to bomb New York. What a guy."

Sam leaned toward me, glee in his eyes, expecting me to relish the idea of bombing New York. I nodded to show I understood, that's all. He was leaning toward me, grinning, urging me to feel something in myself that wasn't there.

"When Fidel was in the mountains there were no women."

"He was thinking about women?"

"He was thinking about the revolution. Fidel isn't Kennedy. Fidel's a man. Didn't have to prove it. No sex problems. But what about women? What did he do?"

"Nothing."

"Right. Nothing. He isn't Kennedy. He didn't chase bimbos. Women came to him. Every woman wants to fuck a god. But some women were sent."

"Sent by Uncle Zev. Is that your point?"

Sam shook his head and rubbed his eyes. I wasn't listening in the right spirit.

"Gambling, drugs, whores—it makes the world go round. You see in the newspaper a cabinet official is getting off a plane in Berlin with a party of fifteen advisors. They phone Zev. Women are supplied by Cherchez La."

"The modeling agency."

"Even you, a person who knows nothing about nothing, heard of it."

Sam's ears protruded slightly. He dipped his head, as in a tiny, sheepish bow

"When I was a boy, I knew the statistics for every player in the major leagues. I could name the capital of every country. I love facts. Do you know, in the state of Florida, you're never more than sixty miles from water? You feel for Zev's Cuban girl. You want to protect her honor. Maybe you have Latin blood. Maybe you'd die for *La familia*. But this minute you're suffering from culture shock." He stabbed the table top with his fingertip. "You're in America. Miami is America. I'm trying to tell you something. Women were sent by Zev to Fidel, and when they came down from the mountains, Zev put some of them on planes to Zurich, Caracas, Stockholm, and other cities. They live today in distant cities with their sons."

"Sons?"

"Everything is in Zeva's thumb."

"I told her there was money in Zurich."

Sam grinned and raised an eyebrow. "You didn't lie. There is money, and there is information about where to find the women and the sons."

"Can you be sure who is the father?"

"Fidel is prepotent."

"What's prepotent?"

"The mother could be a half-wit midget with a hunchback, but Fidel's baby grows up big, handsome, smart, and looks like him. Six months old it talks and never stops. Six years old, it's kicking ass. Beat it on the head with a baseball bat and it fights harder. The son of a hero. Now Fidel is tired. The revolution no longer feels like his personal expression. He knows about the sons, and he's ready to deal."

"What are you getting at?"

"The sons go to Havana, Consuela and Zeva go to Miami. Zev wants you to find the sons. Fidel gets them, and Zev gets his Zeva. You won't talk to reporters or sell the story, or make deals on the side with the women. You also won't subcontract to other operatives. Zeva comes out in a couple of days and you fly to Zurich with her, go the bank, open the box. You'll find cash, certificates of credit, and the names and addresses of the women. For each one there is an address where money is sent by the bank. The manager will show you the status of the accounts. You go to the women, find the sons, put them on planes to Havana."

"How many sons?"

"Nine."

"They might be anywhere in the world?"

"We think one is in Genoa."

"That's Italy, right? Very convenient. And if Consuela doesn't want to leave Cuba?"

"Who's asking what the hell she wants?"

In Sam's long narrow face and the glint of his small dark eyes, I saw his idea of me. I didn't understand his idea, but figured it was me.

"I can't run around the world. There's stuff I must do. My life, such as it is."

"Like pick up your car at the dealership? The new clutch cost five hundred and seventeen bucks. Your car is sitting outside your place. The landlady said she'll drive it around the block every couple of days. All your bills are paid. Your girl's birthday present ..."

"Oh God."

"You forgot? We bought Nana a pair of earrings at Gump's. Jade. They go with her coloring. In case you're interested, she's involved with one of her professors. He's an important name in gastroenterology. A fat guy."

"My new glasses are waiting for me at Doctor Schletter's office," I said.

"You don't want to see the photo. Here're your new glasses."

He shoved a brown-leather glasses case across the table. I put it in my jacket pocket without looking at the glasses. Sam picked up the check. I followed him to his car, wondering. "What do you mean, photo?" I said.

He plucked an envelope out of his jacket pocket. "You don't want to see it. But since you asked."

The envelope held a black-and-white photo, shot through a window in a laboratory. A woman was on her knees. The man wore a frock coat. Big guy, overweight, in his late fifties, silvery hair, jowly. His left hand, clutching her hair, pulled it away from her neck. I could see Nana's tattoo. The man's pants and underpants lay about his ankles, crumpled, like decorative icing you squeeze out of a tube on a cake. He was facing the camera, obviously conscious of being photographed, and the way he'd pulled Nana's hair back was consciously intended to reveal her tattoo.

"Doctor Hubert Gondolph. Research scientist. Works for the FDA. First we got him on tape tipping off your girlfriend about a drug ten times better than Tagamet. His committee approved it for commercial manufacture. It was a secret. When we played Gondolph the tape, he started to cry. Then he agreed to help us get the photograph. Meanwhile, Zev bought stock in the new drug. The price doubled, and it will double again. We have to thank you, Herman. You'll come out of this whole, with more than a million bucks. We bought for you, too, Herman."

"She was always a flirt."

"No shit? That's terrible."

"I quit my job to follow her."

"Throw the photo away."

"No."

"Well, everybody should have a memento. You could mail a copy to Doctor Gondolph's wife, but why? He was trying to save his career, and didn't do anything to you personally. As for her, if Nana hadn't ate some cock, you'd still be poor. Worse, you'd be insensitive to her truest feelings and deepest needs."

ZEV'S PLANE was a twin-engine jet with two pilots. The first to emerge was a light-skinned black woman. For an instant I thought she was Zeva. The same size as Zeva with her dancer's legs, strict posture, aristocratic neck. She wore a black, one-button jacket with wide lapels, a lavender blouse, and a short tight black skirt. High heels forced emphasis into her calf muscles. The shape of her thighs was evident in the skirt. Standing in the open door of the plane, she looked about the tarmac until she saw Sam's car, and then called back into the plane, telling Zev.

"Zev's pilot?"

"Also driver, bodyguard, business manager," said Sam. "Penelope de Assis. Reminds you of someone?"

"Except for the eyes."

The eyes were mounted on the flared branches of her cheekbones, like wild birds fashioned by a diamond cutter. Fifty feet away, I could see they were blue.

"Where did Zev get her?"

"In Rio, eight years old, dancing in the street, shaking her ass to conga drums. She's been with him for years. Signs his checks, so be polite."

"Zev's surrogate daughter."

"To her mind, nobody else is the daughter. But Zev wants room for the other women, you know what I mean?"

"Not really. There's Zev."

He was coming down the steps from the plane, Penelope at the bottom, attentive, braced to catch him should he lose his balance. He glared at her, despising her concern. Zev's Cossack-yellow hair was still yellow, straight, thick as honey, brushed back flat, the old style of a dancing dandy. When he looked toward us, terrific peasant teeth flashed in the square, heavily structured Russky head, built for hard blows. He wore a white linen suit, pink shirt, gray silk tie. He carried nothing. I hadn't seen him in more than twenty years. He looked much as I remembered.

Sam and I got out of the car. When Zev came to us, I could see the seams in his neck and the increased weight on either side of the wide, heavy mouth. But in his late sixties, he could pass for a younger man, even in the Miami sunlight. The blue-eyed Penelope de Assis stood at his side. He embraced me, shoved me back, and held me at arms' length, his hands squeezing my shoulders.

"You used me, Uncle Zev."

He shook his head ruefully, and released my shoulders. His tone carried the weariness of ancient disappointment, as if I'd let him down many times.

"You did me a favor unknowingly. You feel used?"

"Yes. Now you're asking for a lot more."

"Say 'Uncle Zev, you ask for too much,' and I will walk back to that airplane and there will be no hard feelings." His green and yellow-flecked eyes were fixed strictly on mine as he extended his left hand toward Penelope, palm upward. "You have a reservation, in first class, on the next flight to San Francisco. Sam will drive you to the Miami airport."

Penelope slapped an air ticket envelope into his palm. He held it toward me.

"Use this ticket. Fly first class. Say it—'Uncle Zev. I feel how much this means to you, but I don't live for other people, not even you. My answer is no.' A limo will meet you in San Francisco. From the limo, phone what's-her-name, the girl-friend. Take her to dinner tonight anywhere she likes. It's on me. You've done me a favor. I don't expect more. Say no. I will respect your decision. I will love you no less."

"Uncle Zev, give me a chance to ..."

"Should you say, 'Yes, Uncle Zev,' then know that I have made a reservation in your name at my hotel in Key Biscayne. You have a bay view suite, and a speedboat is at your disposal. It has a thousand horses. Say yes and Penelope will drive you to the hotel. She will buy you decent clothes in the men's shop. Say yes, and an hour from now, you will be dressed like the Prince of Miami."

"This isn't about clothes and speedboats."

"You want to write a screenplay about Captain Cook? It's like digging a ditch. They put in sex, the ditch becomes a sewer. You're soft as a fairy. Maybe digging a ditch could do you good. Herman, I'm not here to waste your time. Yes or no?"

I snatched the ticket out of his hand and ripped it in half.

LOOKING at the epicanthic folds of his tigerish, Genghis Khan eyes, the grainy texture of his heavy skin, and the thick yellow hair, each of the billion strands a wire sprung from his imperious soul, I realized that I worshipped Zev a little and couldn't see him simply as himself, a son of a bitch. Penelope took the torn ticket from me and slipped it into her jacket pocket. Frugal.

"All right," he said. "Settled."

Introduce me to your daughter."

Having said "daughter," I glanced at her. There was no friendliness in her eyes. If they expressed anything, it resembled anger. Zev said, his voice low and harsh, "Penelope de Assis, this is my nephew. Herman Lurie."

She said, "I've looked forward to our meeting. We must talk."

"Yes. Talk. Listen to her," said Zev. "She knows about you. Sam and I will meet you two later for dinner. What do you say?"

"What's the difference?"

"Truer words were never spoken. Buy clothes. Look good. Take a ride in the speedboat. Penelope, explain to my nephew how to live."

Sam handed Penelope the keys to his car.

Penelope concentrated on the road to Key Biscayne, and didn't seem to want to talk. She'd witnessed my confrontation with Zev and decided, maybe, she had nothing to say to me. To be polite, I said, "I hope I haven't caused you trouble. I had no idea of the complications in my Cuba trip. I didn't even know you existed until minutes ago."

She grunted and swung her arm, like a backstroke in tennis, banging my jaw with the heel of her fist. Blindly, reflexively, my hands flew up, catching the next blow on my wrists. The car swerved left and right as she overcorrected, hitting the brake, tearing gravel. We stopped. A fiend with searing cold blue eyes shrieked:

"Why didn't you say no and get the fuck out of here? Don't you know the word? Zev gave you a chance to say no, asshole."

She turned away and stiffened, pressing her back against the seat, and breathing deeply. A hundred cars and trucks passed before she restarted the engine, re-entered traffic. We sped on to Key Biscayne. My jaw was hot and throbbing. I wanted to touch it, but I didn't move and sat like a dummy, though I was alert and febrile. This was Zev's true daughter, blood or not. A wrong word and she might drive us into a palm tree. Her skirt was awry, pulled up to her crotch. She was grinning strangely. Not at all with pleasure, but as if subject to ferocious emotions that she struggled to resist. The grin dissolved slowly.

As we pulled onto the hotel grounds, she said she'd go to the shop, buy clothes, and bring them to me. "You can keep what you like. I'll return the rest."

No talk of styles, colors, materials, sizes, or my taste in clothing.

"Later, we'll go out in the speedboat. You'll want me to go with you," she said matter-of-factly. "Here's the key to your suite."

I could go to my suite, or sit in the bar, or take a walk about the grounds, or look at the trees, flowers, and shore birds. Penelope would bring me clothes, then ride with me in the speedboat. In the middle of Biscayne Bay, far from any help, I'd strangle her. I went to my suite, sprawled on a couch, got right up and looked out the window. Looked, didn't see a thing, went back to the couch, sprawled, shut my eyes, waited, waited ... There was a knock at the door. "It's open," I said, and stood up. Penelope entered with a load of clothing and dropped it all on the couch, then glanced at me with a weird smile, as if anticipating an unusual pleasure.

"Try this on," she said, holding up a jacket. I didn't move. Our eyes met. She said, "You want to hit me? Go ahead."

The slap knocked her backward to the floor, jacket in her hand. I bent and snatched it away from her, as if I weren't ashamed of myself for having hit a woman, and I put on the jacket as I walked to the bedroom, feeling sick with regret. She got up and followed me. Our reflections appeared in the full-length mirror attached to a closet door. Her eyes were wet. She poked the corner of her mouth with her tongue. Then she said, "That jacket looks good. Try on the trousers. I like those shoes, too." She tossed clothes onto the bed, one pile to return, the other to keep. Dressing and undressing, with her watching, I began to sweat and feel irritated with myself, putting on this fashion show. I said, "You're getting a kick out of this."

"Still angry?" she asked, gathering up the clothes to be returned.

"No."

"You're the angry type. The water will make you forget. Meet you at the dock in ten minutes."

She collected the clothes to be returned, hugging the bundle to her chest. The door shut behind her.

I put on bathing trunks and one of the new, colorful shirts and left it unbuttoned. About fifteen minutes later, I walked barefoot along a flagstone path to the dock where a dozen speedboats were moored. Penelope was at the wheel of one, a speedboat with two engines. She was wearing a black bikini and black sunglasses. I cast off the rope that bound the boat to the dock, climbed in, and stood beside her. The engines vibrated, exuded power even before I heard them grumble and felt the motion. Penelope maneuvered the boat away from the dock, turning slowly into the bay, and then the bow reared slightly and the engines thrust us away from land, fast, then faster. The Miami skyline, water, and sky were suspended in the enormous trance of late afternoon as we sped into the heart of space. Minutes later she cut the power. Our choppy, pummeling flight gave way to stillness and silence, towering blue air above vast water, like the sanctified vacancy of a cathedral. Sense surrendered to sensation in the ambient grandeur and I seemed to enter a zone of blood, intensely alert, without thoughts or memories. Looking at her, I could almost understand what comes into being, like another pres-ence, between a man and woman, and could almost feel how they must touch lest neither exists and invincible nothing pre-vails. But I didn't think I wanted to touch her.

An airliner, lifting slowly above the Miami skyline, too far away to hear its engines, seemed to hang nearly motionless, rather like our drifting boat, in the quiet epitome of after-noon. Penelope wasn't concerned to talk. Neither was I. The silence was complete. Gulls wheeling in the distance seemed not quite real, as if they were aspects of light, and might ap-pear or disappear from moment to moment.

Penelope let go of the wheel and then we sat facing each other, our knees pointing at our knees. I gazed slowly up and down along her body, as if it were my privilege. My gaze then lifted to her neck and face. I noticed that she was chewing gum, a motion giving her face a dull, unselfconscious, bovine look, especially since her eyes beneath black sunglasses were invisible. Penelope must have read my expression. She turned away and spit the gum into the water. She then leaned back. On either side of the strip of bikini that passed between her legs, tight black wiry curls revealed themselves. I looked. She didn't move to close her legs. Indifferent to my scrutiny, she said, in a sleepy voice, "You like girls?"

I didn't answer. She shrugged, turned her face away.

Lights went on among faraway buildings, and a twilight moon appeared. Penelope removed her sunglasses, then said, as if conceding to an obligation, "Forgive me for what hap-pened. I mean what I did. I'm sorry."

"I've forgotten about it."

"Good of you to say. Thanks."

"Why did you do it?"

232

"I'm not a nice person. I would do it again. The gesture would be pure, you know what I mean? I never think, so don't fuck with me." She giggled.

"That's no answer."

"I tell myself to be nice, but I forget. What can I say? I don't always understand myself. Maybe I was angry because Sam told you I'm jealous. Didn't he tell you I'm jealous? I'm afraid I'll be shoved out in the cold. You think I'm jealous and afraid? You believe what Sam told you?"

"I don't believe anything. Why did you do it?"

"Sam would as soon shake your hand as push you in front of a truck."

"A simple fellow."

"Also dangerous. But he doesn't know me, or why I have no reason to be jealous. See that one and that one." She pointed toward a cluster of tall buildings. "I own them. I own buildings in New York and Los Angeles, and a ranch in New Mexico and a chain of car washes. Except for my brains and my ass, everything I own comes from Zev Lurie. Zev puts paper in front of me and says, 'Sign.' I sign."

"Why does he give you property?"

"So he won't feel guilty."

"Guilty about what?"

"Wasting my youth, obviously. He doesn't really think about other people, not even people close to him, but he does not want to feel responsible for anything he ever did, or anything he owns. Nobody can sue him, he says, and take his property. Who would sue him? Their kids wouldn't come home from school one day, and the wife would be working in a Bangkok whorehouse. He puts property in my name. He wants to feel young. Irresponsible. Property makes you age. So he's a baby. I'm five hundred years old—I own so much. You know why I'm telling you this?"

"Your heart is broken."

"What's she like?"

"You could be friends."

"What an idea. Why do you think so?"

"She's a nice person, but the thing is ..."

I've said many stupid things in my life. I now said the most stupid thing ever. Penelope's hands whitened gripping the edge of her seat. Tendons stood forth in her neck. Her eyes were huge, the blue shining with pain. I was reminded of how she looked in the car, screaming.

"What do you mean looks like me?"

"The same height, that's all. I exaggerated. I wanted to make you think well of her," I said, trying to mollify her before she became uncontrollable.

"What do you mean, similarity? This face? This neck? These arms and legs? What? She has these breasts?" She tore off the top of her bikini and stood up and pulled down the pants, flung the pieces at her feet, screaming, "This is me. You like to look, right? Go ahead look. This is me, not her."

There wasn't a lot more to see, seeing her naked. She was less modest than a three-year-old. Any erotic desire I'd felt was gone with her nakedness.

"Now I'm sorry," I said, stooping to pick up the bikini pieces at her lovely narrow feet. I slipped the bikini top over her head. She let it hang like a rag necklace. Down on one knee, I held the bottom for her to step into it. She did. I drew it up her legs. We stood face to face. Desire returned in a rush. I groaned as if I'd been stabbed, looked away, looked back instantly, kissed her, and she said, "What's that noise?" her lips against mine, or mine against hers since she did nothing, didn't even tolerate the kiss, but allowed herself to be kissed as if it were merely inevitable.

"What noise?" I let her go and listened, and heard bumping against the side of the boat, dull bumping trailed by a scraping noise along the fiberglass bottom; faint and irregular. We got down on our knees and leaned over the side, peering into the water. "There must be a flashlight in the console," she whispered, as if someone were near enough to hear us. But we didn't need the light. Sliding into view from beneath the boat, bobbing and bumping against the side, came the head and the gaping, glossy, moon-foiled eyes of White Trash, his mouth open as if to inhale the sky. His shirt was rags, and right arm was gone, the stump stringy and glistening red, the white broken bone flashing in the meat.

Penelope groaned, "Sharks." As if she'd invoked it, a smooth gray snout, tiny eyes, and undershot maw burst from below and took White Trash's head with a quick shake and a noise like tearing silk, and then slid back into the depths with its hideous prize. Penelope staggered backward and turned to grasp the wheel. Engines grumbled, propellers took purchase on the bay and we lurched, the stern lifting and gathering speed between white plumes that stood on either side like wings as we raced toward the lights of Key Biscayne. Thrown backward, I sat on the deck yelling against the rage of the engines. "I know him, I know that fuck," I yelled, as if it were a great boast about my social life. Penelope glanced back at me. "His name is Wally Blythe."

"That's right. You knew him? The guy must have been popular. Old Wally wanted to kill me."

I got up, stood beside her, and then she said, "No, he didn't."

I put my hand on hers on the wheel. She was crying. I said, "I make trouble for everybody, don't I?"

Her mood changed instantly. She seemed sweetly bemused, saying through tears, "You've made us late for dinner. Zev will be displeased."

"I don't want dinner, and I'm sorry I kissed you. I couldn't help it."

"Why shouldn't you kiss me? Don't you love me?"

"Should I love you?"

"Wally loved me."

Her voice was ironically mocking. She slowed the boat,

then cut off the power and we drifted. I said, "That's why you hit me?'

"Wally saw you as a big problem, but he wasn't going to kill you. It looked like it, but he wasn't going to do it. The gun was a prop, a thing to scare you away."

"How do you know what happened?"

"Sam phoned the plane. Zev told me. He was laughing at how Sam pushed Wally into the bay, as if he deserved a stupid and degrading death. He couldn't swim."

"Poor fuck. Makes me sad."

"Spare me, Herman. You don't give a damn."

"You're right."

"Say something real. Are you still angry? Are you turned on? What are you going to do to me ... now that we're far from shore ... and I'm so helpless?"

Her eyes were strange diamonds, moon-blue, their authority not to be denied.

The speedboat drifted and sharks feasted in the fateful bay. We lay on the boards slick with our sweat and juices, making love. Clouds were bleached bone white as they crossed the moon. Night fell all about in a soft black swirl, except for stars and moon and the electrical syllables of the Miami skyline singing at the horizon, dividing blackness from blackness. Penelope said, sleepily amused, "I believe you like my body."

"You aren't a monster."

"If I were?"

"It would be a test."

"Zev wants us to get married."

"What are you talking about?"

"Oh, you'll do it. We both go to Zurich with the Cuban. She goes back to Cuba alone. When we're married, I'll give you five percent of one building. Claim depreciation and never pay taxes again. Spend the money on me."

"What about the sons?"

"We'll find them, and I'll know what to do."

"I bet."

In the luxurious sleepy desolation of the moment, I wondered if I loved Penelope. The ogling moon hung upon the question. Zev found her dancing in the street. She reminded him of Zeva. I heard my voice murmuring, "Zev is thinking about his deathbed. He wants his blood daughter."

"She's blood, but not his daughter."

"She isn't?"

"She's Chester's. Zev's granddaughter. He'd care less if she were his own. But she doesn't know, and her mother won't tell her. Zev knew from the beginning, naturally. Consuela was a hooker, already pregnant with Chester's baby, when Zev took up with her."

"Zev took up with her, Consuela, Chester's lover? Took her away from him? And his child, too?"

"Chester was about seventeen years old. He'd spent a week in Cuba having a good time. When he left for the States, he didn't know anything. Consuela then came to Zev and told him she needed money for an abortion. Zev was going to pay her off, but changed his mind, and decided to keep the baby."

"Zeva is my second cousin."

"Sam said you slept with her."

The property was Penelope's dowry, but I figured more was coming to me than five percent of one building. As for Wally Blythe, Penelope cared less than I did. She'd asked him to kill me. That had occurred to me earlier, hastening my orgasm, making it too quick, too intense. Sam was right. Penelope worried about being cut out of Zev's will because of Zeva and me. Chester, the unloved and embittered, had no idea that he was a father.

A white star burned on the water, growing bigger and brighter, racing toward us, shooting daggers of light. Penelope felt the tension in my body, and sat up.

"What is it?"

"I don't know."

She sat up and looked. "It's *El Señor,* Zev's boat. He wants an answer right now."

I made out the high sharp prow and tall masts strung with lights, and then I saw Zev. He was leaning over a rail, looking down at us. *El Señor* was long and high and glacial, shining on the black water. Powerful lights whirled around our speedboat. Penelope stood up and waved. "Isn't Zev wonderful?" she said, like an awestruck little girl, plaintive and adoring. I covered her with my shirt, feeling protective; husbandly. She could have the buildings. She wanted them more than I did. "What should I tell him?" she asked. "Yes? No?"

"I'm considering."

"There's plenty for both of us, but it must be both of us. It says so in Zev's will. I think I forgot to mention the will. There are details you ought to know, like about our marriage. What do you say? I need your help, Herman. I hear one of the sons is in Genoa. There are good restaurants in Genoa and down the coast. You like to eat? I need you, Herman. Please. What do you say?"

"What do you think?"

"I think you're driving me nuts."

I was holding Penelope against my side, waving to Zev with my other arm. He frowned, his expression doubtful, not happy. The expression might have been caused by a number of things, maybe something as banal as stomach trouble, but I attributed it to Zev's understanding truly, for the first time, that he'd lose Penelope. She mattered to him more than he knew. An evil girl. It was remarkable how much I liked her, too. I whispered through my smile, "Tell the old man yes."

—Revised 1999

Also by Leonard Michaels

Going Places *
I Would Have Saved Them If I Could *
The Men's Club
Shuffle
Sylvia
Time Out of Mind
To Feel These Things *
West of the West: Imagining California, *coeditor*
The State of the Language 1990, *coeditor*
The State of the Language 1980, *coeditor*

* Stories from these publications are included in this volume.